The Gingerbread House

The Gingerbread House

Ryan M. Williams

GLITTERING THRONG PRESS • RAINIER

This book (any of my books) wouldn't exist without the support and love of my family. They keep me strong and moving forward. I couldn't do it without you.

CHAPTER 1

I woke before the first officer touched my door buzzer. I smelled them coming, a mixture of sweat, ozone and chemical cleansers that streamed around the door through the tiniest cracks like light from a spotlight. I can see with smells these days. I'm Brock Marsden, a member of the Moreau Society, a private detective, and they had better have a damn good reason to come to my door at four in the morning.

I opened my eyes. I saw the room clearly despite the lack of light. The roses in the vase on the table bled light as their molecules decayed but still smelled sweet. I heard the officers muttering at the door.

I rolled off the couch and grabbed my Lottier 45 loaded with nanoparalyzers for over 150 Rim species. Other than my boxers I didn't have on a stitch of clothing. Who cared? I didn't. I crossed the room in two quick strides, faster than a standard human could manage. I put my back to the wall beside the door. I'd reinforced that section with armored panels. You can't ever be too careful in my line of work as a private detective on Olinda.

The buzzer rang. That triggered the house defenses to come online. Windows shuttered. Recording equipment activated. All sorts of active defenses armed themselves. If anyone broke in while I was gone, they'd be in for a surprise. For a good reason, the Galactics' Moreau Pod in my workshop alone was worth a fortune. A small screen beside the door activated showing officers shielding their eyes from the bright spotlights pointing at them and right in the middle stood a familiar face.

Captain Kynan Brice. His big frame shrouded in a long black coat that matched his short-cropped hair. Very muscled, visibly so even with the coat, and tanned. An excellent swimmer, according to Subha. Four other officers stood with him. He looked up, squinting against the lights.

"Brock Marsden! Come out! We need to talk."

Talk? Captain Brice didn't much like me. I never could decide if it was personal or simply the fact that I'm a Moreau. Even so, we'd managed to work on a few cases. I'd listen. But coming this early didn't put me in the best mood.

I touched an icon on the screen. "Give me a sec."

"Hurry up," Brice grumped.

Right. Like I worked for him. Still, I knew him well enough that this was the last place he wanted to come at this hour. Either it was important, or he wanted to arrest me for some trumped up charge. I grabbed pants and a shirt and dressed quickly. When I got back to the door Captain Brice had a frown on his face. I opened the door and stepped out. The two officers closest to me grabbed my arms.

I reacted. I twisted my hands around and grabbed their arms, stepping back in the same moment into the house, and I spread my arms. They hit the door frame and bounced off as I released them. I spun around the corner, putting the armor at my back. It didn't matter. I could see the men outside with my Euzebian scent-sight. The ones that hit the frame were getting up. The others drew weapons which looked like dark voids that leaked only the faintest wisps of decaying molecules. The men brightened. Angry, hearts pumping harder, sweat glands working harder. Captain Brice held out a hand and waved the others back.

I was a second from ordering the house sealed.

"Brock—"

"What's going on out here?" A woman's voice. My landlord, neighbor, and friend from the other side of the duplex. Sonya.

She entered the range of my scent-sight. She glowed like an angel. Blue-green streamers poured from her mouth when she spoke. I smelled her concern. Her fear shrouded her in sharp orange waves that pulsed off her with each heart-beat.

One of the officers moved in her direction. "Ma'am, stay back. It isn't safe."

"Brock!" Captain Brice stood sideways right outside my door. "Come back out!"

"Why?"

"Damn it, Brock! Just get out here!"

"When your men have weapons aimed at the door? I don't think so."

"Shit!" That from the officer on Brice's right. Scarlet streamers of nervousness bled down from his sweaty palms.

"Make any move, and I shut this door." I tapped the panel. All set to activate siege mode. It'd take a lot more than they had to get in. "Put away the weapons. Send them back to your flitters."

"Brock?" Sonya said. The officer blocked her approach. "Brock? What's going on?"

"Captain? What's it going to be?"

"Brock, damn it, I don't have time for this!"

"Funny. I have all the time in the world."

"Go." Brice waved his hands at the officers. "Back to the flitters! Now, damn it!"

The officers backed away from the door. Weapons still out. They didn't move fast enough for Brice or me. He spun around. "Double-time! Move it!"

They moved. I waited until they reached the edge of my scent-sight and then I eased around the corner. I kept my hands visible. No need to worry them. Captain Brice's brow furrowed as he glared at me.

"Why do you have to make everything so damn hard?"

"Hey, I cooperated until your guys grabbed me."

"They just followed procedure."

"Right. If I was a criminal. What is it, Captain?" He smelled like too much coffee. No doubt the Captain hadn't been getting a lot of sleep lately. "Another Burn operation? More Nosferans coming in?"

"Yes, but I don't need your help for those." Captain Brice ran a hand through his hair.

He didn't say which was true, or both? After the last time, it could be both, and he knew about my status with the Nosferans. Not many people did. I rarely told anyone what I did during the Nosferan-Human war. Most people wouldn't believe I was that old.

Sonya walked down the ramp running along the front of the house and stood beside me. She crossed her arms and stared at the Captain. I didn't need to look at her to know that she felt protective of me.

"We've got a situation. I need you to look at it, give me your opinion, and I need it fast."

"My opinion? Why would you want

that?" I could think of several reasons, and I didn't like any of the answers that came to mind. Not everything I did strictly fit within even Olinda's liberal laws.

Captain Brice put his hands on his hips. "Will you come with me willingly or do I haul you in on an obstruction charge?"

Empty threat. "Tell you what. Pay the agency's usual fee, and I'll be happy to help out the department."

He stared at him. From his scent, I could see the dark green of his anger puffing out of him with each breath. He nodded. "Fine. Fine. Come on."

He didn't wait. He turned his back on me and headed towards the flitters. I looked down at Sonya. "Okay with you if I'm not back in time to milk Dancy and Prancy?"

Milking the goats was one of the things I did around the place to help out. Sonya shrugged, but I smelled her sour worry. "Yes. Be careful. He seems pretty upset."

I looked at the Captain's retreating back. "He's always upset about something. I'd better catch up. I'll see you later."

I slipped back to the door and touched the pad to seal the house. My side anyway.

The place was a duplex, set into the side of the hill. Everything is a hill Olinda. A world of terraces and mountains on the massive equatorial island chain surrounded by the ocean. There are small sub-continents at the poles, but those are mostly locked in ice. Looking out from the doorstep I couldn't see the ocean. Too many miles away with several peaks in between us and the shore. But it was there. Ninety percent of the surface.

I jogged down the biocrete path after Captain Brice. I'm fast. I caught up before he reached the flitter pad at the bottom of the ramp.

Used to be I liked flitters. Not anymore. Since I added the Euzebian DNA to gain their scent-sight, being in a small place like a flitter makes me feel cut off from the world. It was worse in the beginning when I hadn't learned to integrate the scent-sight with my regular vision. For a while there I went around with a blindfold and being enclosed like this with several standard humans would have been overwhelming.

I've learned to close my nostrils since then. It doesn't eliminate the scent-sight, but it damps it down. My visual acuity is much greater a standard human. Sitting in the flitter as we flew above the city and peaks I could make out the people far below. Humans and non-humans of all sorts going about their business. Olinda boasts a very diverse population. It keeps Shanley Walsh, my boss, and owner of the detective agency, very happy. We never lack for cases. I'm sure he'd appreciate that I talked Captain Brice into paying our usual fee.

The flitter flew straight away from the house for several minutes then curved to follow a course parallel to the ocean. Clouds covered the south end of the city which was mostly the docks, warehouses, and fishing vessels. Fishing being Olinda's chief export. We passed over the main commercial district right through the no-fly zone. Being in a police flitter had its advantages. Fifteen minutes after we left my house we descended towards the high mountain outskirts of Olinda. Mostly rice terraces that captured the rainfall when the clouds bunched up against the peaks. Terrace after terrace of biocrete rose up the side of the mountain, alternating bands of white and green. Humans and non-humans alike worked the rice terraces. I watched a quadruped wearing bright scarlet clothing bound up from one terrace to the next. Harvester? I had no idea.

Around the side of the mountain, a structure stuck out of the side of the hill. A collection of a half-dozen biocrete towers growing right out of the sheer rock. Far below a river thundered down along the gorge towards the ocean. The police flitter headed for a landing pad sticking out of the fourth tower. Two other police flitters and an ambulance flitter already occupied the pad. It didn't leave us much room to land. Any room, actually. The pilot kept going for it anyway. Wind buffeted the flitter and knocked us about. I checked my seat belts. Fastened tight.

Captain Brice grinned. "Afraid of flying?"

I shook my head. "No. It's the falling that gets my attention."

I'll give the pilot credit. He brought the flitter right up alongside the landing platform and held it there against the wind. Brice opened the door. The wind howled in with a fury. He wrapped his coat around himself and stepped down from the flitter, dropping down onto the platform. I triggered the release and followed him out, jumping down behind him. The flitter rose off and left us there. I turned and looked over the edge of the platform. Far, far below a rainbow arced across the gorge above the river. I saw Olindan diving bats speeding across the gorge, spiraling and diving through the spray. Native Olindan vegetation grew on the rough slopes. All pale pastel greens and blues. The rice patties on the terraces looked very bright in contrast.

"Stop gawking and come on!"

I looked at the Captain.

He stared back at me. One of these days he's going to come at me. I could see him calculating. How easy would it be to knock me from the landing platform? Not that he'd do that. Captain Brice is an honorable man in his own way. He just sees me as a junkie. If it were up to him, Moreau Pods would be illegal. But Olinda has very permissive laws regarding anything that doesn't directly hurt anyone else, whether that be drugs or modifying DNA.

I left the edge. Time to see what had him all worked up.

He led me through the crowds of police, forensics crew, and the coroner staff. Everyone was standing around doing nothing. A bunch of civilians off to one side behind a barricade looked annoyed and huddled together against the wind. To my Euzebian scent-sight, the whole area was almost like a blizzard. All of the scents being blown around made it almost impossible to see anyone until close to them. I had to tell myself not to close my eyes and instead closed my nostrils. A native Euzebian only had vestigial eyes that picked up light, dark and movement. I'm glad I kept my eyes in the transition.

I followed Brice into the building, and as soon as the sliding doors closed behind us, everything felt much more peaceful. No more howling wind. I could open my nostrils and actually see things normally. The biocrete at my feet glowed very faintly. We were alone, but I could sense more to the scene. I exhaled and relaxed my hold on my neck slits, opening up to the scene. Another Euzebian trait, the neck slits normally look like tattoos on my neck, four on each side. When I open them up, I'm able to take in far more complex scents than I can with just my nostrils. I concentrated and saw ghostly images of people walking through the hallway. Civilians running. All silent but they smelled of spicy urgency.

"What happened here? Why the panic, Brice?"

Brice stopped. "You'll see. I want you to see. How far back can you see?"

"That depends on the conditions." This is why he wanted me. Brice knew about the Euzebian scent-sight. It's more than just seeing what's around me right now. I can concentrate and see what has been in an area. Like watching those people run through the hallway. It's my brain picking up on the scent trails left behind and reinterpreting them visually.

He went on, and I followed him. The wide hallway gave out to a large circular room at the base of the tower. A large relief image of Olinda had been engraved into the biocrete floor. Just enough to define the sphere with the island chain snaking across the face of it like a jagged smile. Several other doorways opened out of the tower, and a glass-enclosed elevator sat waiting on one side of the room. Far above a skylight capped the tower.

Brice went to the elevator. I followed him. In my scent-sight, I saw person after person cross the room and enter the elevator. It felt like stepping into a crowd even though it was only the two of us in the spacious car. Brice flicked the panel indicator for the fourth floor. The car accelerated up rapidly. I watched the floor drop away beneath us. From up here, the engraving stood out more. It felt like we were going into space. In seconds we stopped at the fourth floor, and the door behind us opened. Death poured into the elevator.

The scents oozed along the ground, a brown miasma of putrefaction and shit. A thin mist that spread across the floor and slowly evaporated upwards on the air currents.

"Who died?" I asked.

Brice glanced at me and swept down the curved hallway. His brighter odors mingled and swirled with the scent of death, leaving eddies in his wake. I closed my neck slits. I didn't need to smell that much right now. The images faded and I followed the Captain.

Located a quarter of the way around the tower the room looked like an office. The outside wall nothing but a large window looking out on the gorge and peaks at the heart of the island. Beside the window a long workstation, it looked like imported oak, curved along the wall, and curled out into the room to form a desk. Two leather chairs sat in front of the desk. A couple tasteful paintings of Olindan landscapes hung on the wall, and an Olindan ivy grew up a trellis beside the window. On the desk, a bowl of glitter shells caught the light and sparkled.

I took that all in as soon as I entered the room and then focused on the body. A body sat in the high-backed chair behind the desk. Their hands — such as they were — lay on the desk surface as if they had been working. Everything about the room, the painting choices, the oak desk and the furniture all screamed human, most likely a woman. Except the body behind the desk didn't look human at all. Brice took up a position beside the door. Even with my damped down scent-sight, I could see the faint yellow of his apprehension oozing out of his pores. Something about this one really bothered him and translated into aggression towards me. Why?

The body didn't appear human but was humanoid. Two arms, I assumed legs out of sight, and a head. Long dark hair clung to the wet-looking skin. It looked like the body had been immersed in water. More liquid pooled around the hands on the desktop. The one on the right ended in what looked like a cluster of scarlet tentacles, thinner and longer than fingers. The one on the right had four thick fingers, dark earthy brown in color, with a half-dozen joints each arranged in a circle. The exposed skin on the arms varied in texture from pink flesh to iridescent scales to patches of bristly black spines or fur. Worse of all — the face. As if several different sorts of faces had been melted together. I saw faceted eyes embedded like raisins in oatmeal, half the mouth filled with jutting razor-edged teeth and the other half actually human teeth. A human-looking blue eye stared sightlessly from a pit down beneath an overly large wrinkled black ear. The body was contorted against the chair, twisted partly to the side, the head was thrown back.

An expression of agony was still visible on that face, despite the slackness that came with death.

I realized that I didn't mind missing breakfast so much. Still, I looked over at Brice. "Any chance of some Torlian coffee?"

"Why don't you worry about this?" Brice waved his arm at the body. "Talk to me. Then we can see about your damn coffee!"

"Fine." I walked closer to the desk. I watched where I stepped carefully and considered what I could see.

Her — I'd seen enough to realize it had to be a woman — clothing looked like standard human attire. A bright green blouse with elbow-length sleeves ending in a bit of white lace. A dark stain down the front looked like blood and caught in the folds of the shirt I saw bloodied human teeth. Blood also stained her cleft chin. Despite the deformities, I didn't see any other sign of violence. I didn't like what I was seeing.

"She looks like a Dumpty," I said.

Brice's apprehension increased. Waves of yellow pooled at his feet. "That's what I thought. I cleared the place out immediately."

"So who brought her here? There must be security recordings."

Brice shook his head. "Not up here. Only at the access points. I'll show you."

He pulled out a tablet and tapped the surface. He handed it over. I hit play. Good 3D resolution from the cameras. It looked like I was behind a window looking down on the entrance. A pretty human woman with long dark hair and the same green blouse as on this body walked confidently into the building. She glanced up at the cameras and smiled. She knew the system. It didn't worry her. She walked on out of view.

I dragged the video back and twisted the view around until I was almost at head-height looking straight at her. The same confident walk, smile for the camera and then she walked on past me. I handed the tablet back to the Captain.

"Okay. Who is she?"

"Her name was Montana Haugh. She's chief of research here."

"Studying what?"

"Rice production."

I looked back at what Montana had become. "Really?"

In my scent-sight, I saw Brice take a couple steps closer. "Yes, as far as we can tell."

"So what happened after the video was taken?"

"We don't know. According to the staff, Haugh would have been working here in her office alone. They say there's no Moreau Pods on the premises."

"Are you searching?"

Brice scowled. "Of course. We haven't found anything."

"Well, I doubt she experienced fatal mutations spontaneously." I walked closer to the desk and looked down at the hand with the scarlet tentacles. I'd seen that before. I pointed to it. "This is a hand from the C'lacktal. The cells have a potent sting to them. Semi-aquatic, they use the ability to stun their prey. Stone-age level Rim species cataloged but no official contact. They're supposed to be a quarantined world."

But the other hand. "That one I don't recognize. It is similar to the radial hands of the Balnarians, but I don't think they've got fingers that long." I looked at the rest of her that I could see. "It'd take time to identify all of the species represented here, but it looks like dozens of different species all scrambled together without any plan or purpose."

"But this sort of thing happens all the time. Even when you have a plan."

I walked around the desk still focused on the body. "Not all the time. Sometimes. People make mistakes. Sometimes the new material isn't integrated well. Usually, because someone didn't do enough study to figure out how to integrate the different biochemistries. It isn't like just sowing on a new limb or transplanting an organ."

I focused more on my scent-sight. The body glowed with all sorts of organic activity. Some aggressive decomposition was taking place. Streamers of molecules poured down the body and pooled around on the floor before seeping out into the hallway. Once around the desk, I saw that her legs had also been radically transformed. One had grown by at least six inches, bent backward and had developed a sharp ridged carapace that had split her pants. Pale cream fur and a hoof were visible on the other. In both cases, her black low-heel shoes had come off. More liquid had pooled on her chair and dripped to the floor.

I didn't like this at all. I waved to Brice. "Come over here."

He walked over to stand beside me. "What is it?"

I pointed at her legs. "Tell me that doesn't look like she was sitting here when she changed."

Brice waved his hand at her. "How could that happen? I assumed she was put in a Moreau Pod and then placed here afterward."

"I don't think so. It looks like Ms. Haugh died at her desk."

"So it wasn't a Moreau Pod?"

"No. But something like it. Obviously, Glittering Throng technology is involved here. Do we have any records of who might have seen her last? We need a time-frame for when this happened."

Brice looked at his tablet. "We're working on that already. I'm going to need names and addresses for everyone in your little Moreau Society." Brice looked up, pocketed the tablet and pulled out a set of handcuffs. "Turn around and put your hands behind your back, Brock."

I couldn't help it. I laughed. To my scent-sight, he spiked in reds and oranges. I held my hands out at my sides. "Think about it, Brice. You hired me to look at this crime scene. Why arrest me when I'm being cooperative?"

"Your Moreau Society is the only group I know on the planet that dabbles in this sort of Galactics' tech! You identified at least one of the species DNA used just by looking at the body. And my people just found a matching DNA sample in that refrigerator of yours. Along with dozens of other species. That's enough to hold you. Now. Put your hands behind your back."

I didn't move. "You had people search my place?"

"Yes. After we left, we served your land-lady with a warrant. It's all been seized." Brice took a step closer. "Are you going to make this more difficult?"

I had an idea what he meant. I could disable him. Get past the cops outside, steal one of the flitters and escape. And go where? Get smuggled off world?

"Yes," I said. And then I turned around and put my hands behind my back. "I'm not going to make it easy for you to pin this on the Moreau Society. I'm going to find out who is responsible."

I felt the cool metal of the constrictor cuffs snake around my wrists and tighten. Even with my strength, I wasn't going to be able to break those cuffs. I looked over at Ms. Haugh's body. She had died in agony. Just someone doing her job. I agreed with Brice there. I wanted to find out who did this.

Just as soon as I could convince him to let me go.

Chapter 2

Brice grabbed my shoulder and shoved me towards the door. I stood my ground and didn't budge. His grip tightened. "Move."

I shook my head. "Just a sec, captain. You're passing up an opportunity."

"Yeah? Why should I listen?"

"Come on. You want to catch the person responsible. You don't like me, but it's going to be a waste of your time to take me in. Besides, I might be able to help you with what happened here."

"How?"

"You know I can see the past, sort of."

Brice released my shoulder and stepped around so he could see my face. His eyes narrowed. "How stupid do you think I am? If your group is involved in this, you can make up whatever you want."

"I think you're pretty bright. That's not

it. With my scent-sight, I can see who has been in a room. I could tell you if anyone visited Ms. Haugh and I'd be able to identify them later."

"Your scent-sight?" He chuckled and shook his head. "Sometimes I think you people are just crazy messing around with your DNA. Right now I know you're crazy. Nothing about that would be admissible anyway."

"Then why did you bring me here? You made it sound like you wanted to use my abilities to figure out what happened."

"I needed you out of your house so we could search it." He shoved me again.

I still didn't move. I twisted around. "Give me a chance to see what was going on. Then I'll go. No problem."

"I don't believe a word of this." Brice shook his head. I could see the disbelief spraying off him in lilac wisps. "But what the hell? I'll give you a few minutes if it means I don't have to wrestle you out of here."

"Thanks." I turned around completely and looked at the room. I opened up my neck slits and heard Brice mutter something before taking a step back. The room glowed with light. Different colors and intensities. All of it molecules floating off into the air. Scents that my brain reinterpreted to build up a visual picture of the room. Behind the desk, Ms. Haugh's body burned like a bonfire. At least that's what it looked like. Streamers rose up brightly into the air, spreading out around the body. All that decomposition and gases. Some sank down in a fog across the desk and floor, flowing across the floor towards us at the door where it pooled in a brown miasma around our feet. Despite what I'd told Brice I wasn't sure I could do what I'd said under these conditions.

I concentrated. I tried to see older scents. I don't know how to explain the difference. The older the scent, the staler it smelled. Thanks to the Euzebian modifications I could selectively block out the scents in the room now and focus instead on older scents left behind. Enough in many cases to build up an image of what had happened before.

All of the stuff I saw coming from the body faded away as I dismissed it from my attention. Back. I needed to go further back. An explosion of light came from Ms. Haugh. Sharp blacks of agony, bright blue fear, the scents of pain and panic spread out from the desk. I couldn't hear her, but I saw enough to see her thrashing behind her desk.

Back further.

She sat at the desk. Nothing more than a phantom of herself all in healthy warm tons of gold and light. When I see people this way, they appear like luminous ghosts. It makes me wonder if — on some level — what I see is unique from the Euzebians? Maybe I incorporate more human interpretations into what I see. She worked at her desk, nothing unusual there. Then a beam appeared through the window. Not of light, but of airborne organic molecules transforming and changing. The air molecules danced around, and then the transformations hit Haugh. She lost control of her bowels, I had no trouble seeing that.

I closed my neck slits and allowed my normal vision to take over. Brice stood at my elbow. His dark eyes searched my face for answers.

I nodded at the window. "Whatever it was, it came through the window. A beam of some sort. It hit her and caused the mutations."

"And you smelled this?"

"Yes —"

Brice grabbed my shoulder and shoved me towards the door. I went along with him. For now. I kept trying to work out what I'd seen. A beam that created a Dumpty? That's what we called it when someone made a mistake in a Moreau Pod and scrambled their DNA. The lucky ones didn't survive. Every time a member of the Moreau Society climbed into a pod we knew the risks. But this? It smelled like someone had created a weapon that could act at a distance.

Back down the corridor, back to the elevator. As the glass-enclosed elevator descended towards the engraving of Olinda, I saw several officers and a detective rush into the main downstairs lobby. I recognized the detective. Winifred Booth. Human, near sixty I'd guess with gray hairs and blue eyes. She had plenty of laugh lines around her eyes, but she wasn't laughing when the elevator opened up, and we stepped out. She looked at me then back at Brice.

"Sir, a call came in. He has claimed responsibility for the death and promise more if his demands are not met."

Brice let go of my arm. "Who?"

"A Moreau." Winnie glanced at me again. "Calls himself Kelwyn. He's a snake, sir."

"A snake?" Brice looked at me.

I nodded. "Yes, I know Kelwyn. He used to be part of the Moreau Society, but he left. I expected he'd turn up as a Dumpty before this."

"But you think he's capable of doing what we've seen upstairs?"

"No," I told him. "Not on his own. Kelwyn was impatient and not really smart enough to operate a Moreau Pod on his own. He relied on others to do his research. The last time I saw him, months ago, he showed us a simulation of what he wanted to become and said that someone had made it possible. When we tried to caution him, he left."

"Sir, why do you have Mr. Marsden in cuffs? I thought he was consulting with us?"

"He is a suspect in this homicide," Brice said.

"Still?" Winnie asked. "Based on? Kelwyn's claimed responsibility."

There are reasons I like Winnie.

Brice stepped behind me. My Euzebian scent-sight gives me a full three-sixty view, so

I saw him wave a dark object — had to be a control wand — over the cuffs. The constriction vanished and dropped off into his hand. He pocketed the cuffs. "Our resident expert in Moreaus claims that the victim's mutations show evidence of several species. He also believes that some sort of beam caused the mutations in the first place."

"But we're continuing to search for other explanations?" Winnie asked.

"Yes!" Brice ran his hand through his hair. "Let's take a look at that call, okay? We'll see what detective Moreau here has to say about his old pal."

"He's not my pal."

"Whatever. Come on." Brice headed off towards the flitters parked outside. Winnie and I exchanged sympathetic glances and trailed after him.

As Brice reached the waiting teams of forensics and officers, he waved them on into the building. "Look at everything! Take the windows and see if there's any evidence that some sort of beam passed through them or not. Search the place for any Galactic technology that might be capable of doing this."

The people scattered. Their colors

streamed behind them as they moved into the tower. Winnie and I followed Brice towards a larger flitter. I looked down at Winnie. "What do you think my chances are of getting some Torlian coffee?"

She laughed. "I doubt the captain is going to send out for coffee. But you can ask him."

"I already did."

She shook her head. "Don't look at me, Brock. I'm not going anywhere. Besides, that stuff is going to melt your nervous system one of these days. There's a reason it's a controlled substance on thirteen worlds."

"I should have insisted on making some before I left the house."

"Tough luck."

In the flitter, Brice activated the front displays which projected across the windshield. He glanced over as I got in the other side with Winnie. "Here it is."

The display controls shrank back to the left-hand corner. For a second the display was black, and then it cleared.

Kelwyn sat in front of the camera. Except I wouldn't have recognized him as the same man I'd last seen only a couple months earlier. Then he'd been a pale, thin, sickly man with almost no lips and translucent scales in patches on his arms and face. His tongue had been surgically split. But he had looked more diseased than snake-like. All that had changed.

He looked powerful. Very muscular humanoid shoulders and chest covered in blue-green scales that darkened around towards his back. His neck flared out like a cobra. His head, at the heart of the hood, still looked fairly human but with expressionless black eyes instead of his old watery blue ones. A thin tongue flicked out, tasting the air. I couldn't see him below the waist, but I remembered an image he had shown the group, which had eliminated legs in favor of a long snake body. Kelwyn braced his hands on top of the flat black table top in front of him.

"I am called Kelwyn. I'm sending this message to the Glittering Throng. I know that the Glittering Throng monitors all communications in the Rim worlds, so you'll no doubt already know about the death of Montana Haugh. Her death was required to make sure you take my demand seriously. I only have one demand. Allow me to join the Glittering Throng as a full member as befits the creator of a new species. I offer Ms. Haugh as proof of my qualifications. I possess the ability to modify and improve on Galactic technology. I realize the death of one individual is not of any great importance to you, but she will only be the first. If my demands are not met within one hour, then someone else dies, and each hour after. If my demands have still not been met then by this time tomorrow I shall eradicate all intelligent life on Olinda."

Kelwyn leaned forward on the desk. "This will be the only communication. And for those on Olinda, pray that the Galactics grant my demand!"

Brice reached out and froze the screen with a pinch. He swiveled his chair around and looked at me. "Okay, Marsden. You said you know this guy. Who is he? What's his deal? Why the hell would he think that killing people is going to get any sort of response from the Glittering Throng?"

Winnie said, "Sounds like he's asking for a death sentence to me."

"Maybe," I said. "But I don't think there's only Kelwyn involved here. Sure, it's possible that he increased his mental capacity. But enough to do all of this? I doubt it. And the way he looks now isn't at all the way he looked the last time I saw him." I described how he'd appeared at his last Moreau Society meeting. "Even then he talked about someone helping him. Kelwyn could just be a puppet."

Brice shook his head. "A puppet with a weapon pointed at an entire planet!"

"Where is he?" Winnie asked. "The transmission didn't have an origin tag."

"We'll get the techs on it. Marsden, do you have any ideas?"

I thought about the beam I'd noticed. "Orbit? If he wanted to target the planet that'd make the most sense."

"So we've got a snake-guy up in orbit somewhere with a weapon that can kill by mutation. Am I missing anything?"

Winnie and I both shook our heads.

Brice tapped his fingers on his leg. "Great. Just great. Okay. We've got plenty of people here. We need to get people on this video. Right now we need to get a location on this guy, and we don't have a lot of time. With all of the garbage up in orbit finding him could be harder than finding a particular grain of sand in the ocean. Marsden, I want you to talk to your other Moreau Society contacts. See if you can find out anything that can help us locate and stop this snake."

I crossed my arms. "We've got other business to settle first."

"Damn it, Marsden! There's a lunatic out there threatening the planet!"

"I know. But I want anything disturbed in my workshop restored, and the consultant fee paid to the agency. Without that, I don't work for you."

"I could arrest you for obstruction!"

I could smell his apprehension beneath all the anger. It oozed from his pores in spikes of scarlet. Something about this situation really got to him, and for the first time, I thought that maybe the reason he didn't like me had more to do with a phobia about mutation.

"I can help stop him, Captain. Just stop treating me like the enemy. We both want the same thing."

"No, we don't." Brice grinned. "I want you and those like you kicked off this planet. Look at what it leads to!"

Winnie made a noise but didn't say anything.

"Kelwyn was unbalanced long before he started messing around with his DNA," I said. "Being a Moreau makes me a better detective —"

"You're not better! " Brice leaned forward. "Get out! Get the hell out!"

I opened the door and stepped out. The dark cloud pouring out of Brice's mouth made me feel sick. I closed my nostrils tight against the smell and the images faded. Brice followed me out of the flitter. The wind whipped his coat around him, snapping in the wind.

I stood back to give him his space. Winnie climbed out after him. Brice looked at me, looked away out over the edge of the platform. When he spoke, his voice came out loud and hard.

"They didn't remove anything from your workshop. I'll pull them out. Get me some information I can use! The fee will be deposited as soon as the damn bean counters process the request."

"Thank you."

Brice looked at me then with narrowed

eyes. "Don't thank me, Marsden. Help or get out of my way."

He whistled and waved a hand at an officer. The man ran over to where we stood. Brice grabbed his shoulder and pointed at me. "Take Marsden where he needs to go! Then report back to me!"

"Yes, sir!" The officer was young, human, with short blond hair and emerald green eyes that turned to look at me.

Where I needed to go? If I'd had my choice, I still wouldn't be up yet. If I had to save the world, I needed to get some Torlian coffee first.

CHAPTER 3

Hot white Torlian coffee in hand — thanks to Officer Jasper — I walked into the new Walsh and Marsden Detective agency just after six in the morning. The coffee looked like a bright white blowtorch in my hand as hot molecules rushed up with the steam out the small sipping hole. It almost made me nervous to take a drink. Sometimes the Euzebian scent-sight could be a bit distracting. I tried to ignore it. Scalding thick liquid hit my tongue and set my nerves ablaze. Heaven.

We moved into the new offices last month. I liked the open air design. The offices took up one whole floor of the building. When you stepped out of the elevator, you were greeted by the large open foyer. Straight ahead was the reception area. Massive boulders formed the front of the desk.

The backside of the boulders had been cut, and a top leveled out, but from this side all you saw was a low wall of big black boulders. Eye-catching against the white biocrete floors. Two Olindan vine plants hung down the sides of the desk and added a bit of very pale green to the desk.

Past the reception area was the rest of the floor. All decorated in natural rock and Olindan vines with some sculptures from local artists scattered around the place. Everything arranged to neatly set off different areas of the floor. To the right, behind reception, a floor to ceiling aquarium blocked off the private conference room. I particularly liked that feature.

No one was at reception. I heard voices. It came from the conference room. That's where everyone was. They'd left the doors open and stood in front of the large wall display. A news reporter looked out of the screen with large worried eyes. Or maybe her eyes always looked like that — Lambians are semi-aquatic and have large frog-like eyes.

"—No word yet on how exactly the threat might be carried out but officials have confirmed the death of Montana Haugh, a research scientist working for the Ricers Intergalactic Cooperative."

The whole gang was watching the report. Shanley Walsh, my boss, lean and trim in his fifties with a whole retro sort of looked to him in his neat brown suit. Muriel, my lover, a member of the Moreau Society and fellow detective, beautiful as always wearing a tight white leotard outfit with an exposed midriff, short sleeves, and bare feet. Her brown hair hung in a braid down her back. Frankly breath-taking. The last member of the group stood on all fours, as tall at the shoulder as Muriel, looked like a massive orange and black stripped Halloween monster with thick leathery skin spotted with bristles. Rear legs shorter than his arms. His usual equipment belts crisscrossed his body. Dyami is an Eyotan. Our intern. The Eyota wanted to learn about investigative techniques, so they sent him. He's been useful. Particularly in intimidating information out of people.

I coughed.

They turned away from the display. Shanley waved a hand to dismiss it. I don't know that I've ever seen Shanley look so grim.

Muriel bit her lip and Dyami? I don't know what the expression on his pug-like face meant. In a human seeing that many teeth would mean a smile, but I don't think that was the case. I smelled the apprehension and fear of the humans. Dyami smelled like sunflowers. Hell if I knew what that meant.

Shanley nodded his head at the now-vanished screen. "I suppose you know all about this?"

I grabbed one of the chairs at the conference table and sat down. Shanley and Muriel took chairs. Dyami simply sat at the end of the table and neatly folded his two pumpkin-sized hands on the tabletop.

"I don't know how much the news has yet, but it's Kelwyn."

Muriel bit her lip and gave a little shake of her head.

"That's the snake-fellow you told me about?" Shanley asked.

"Right." I looked at Dyami, but he seemed content to listen right now. Usually, he had some quip about modifying one's life-code. It seemed to offend his Eyotan sensibilities but he tolerated Muriel and I. "Looks like he got what he wanted, he's been changed.

He claims to be responsible for the weapon which murders-by-mutation at a distance. I think from orbit."

"How's that possible?" Muriel asked.

"The woman killed? She looked like a Dumpty. I saw evidence of dozens of species. But when I took a look back at the scent-trail in the room, it showed me her sitting at her desk when it happened. It looked like something came through the window and caused the transformation."

"Weapon needs line-of-sight." Dyami gently thumped the tabletop. For him, anyway, it still shook the whole table. "Inside, away from windows, would be safe."

"Maybe."

"Most of the buildings in the city have large windows and skylights," Shanley said dryly.

"Are they evacuating the city?" Muriel asked.

"It may come to that. But if it does there's going to be widespread panic. Captain Brice wants me to talk to the Moreau Society. I need to find out anything that might help us locate Kelwyn so we can put a stop to this."

"You're going to talk to Subha?"

Muriel smelled concerned. I smiled at her. "I think we can put aside our differences long enough to cooperate on this."

Shanley leaned forward on the table. "What do you need from us, Brock?"

"Try everything else. Dig into records, do the research. I want to know where Kelwyn has been hiding. Maybe we can find something at his former address. Talk to neighbors. We're on a clock here. He's given the Glittering Throng until tomorrow morning to respond to his demand."

"Those in the core do not care," Dyami rumbled. I felt it in my bones. His actual speech is infrasonic, but his translation collar sounds human enough. "They will not grant his demands."

"You're probably right. It doesn't matter. Kelwyn has promised to kill each hour which means someone else has probably already died. We need to stop him before the numbers increase." I got up. "Call me if you get anything."

Muriel rose, her gray eyes — the first thing I had noticed about her — searching my face for something. I managed a smile. "I'll be careful."

She walked around the table to me and took my hands. I looked down at her, and we kissed. A moment, a brush of our lips, and then I stepped away. Muriel was part of my problem with Subha these days. Muriel had been an acolyte in Subha's Moreau-based religion. But even before Muriel left Subha's church my relationship with Subha had been strained. We might have been together except I couldn't buy into her whole creator mythology. If we've learned anything from the Glittering Throng, it is that there are no gods but the ones we make.

I headed for the elevators and the roof. When I looked back out at the offices, I could see them all already busy.

On the roof, I walked across the bright biocrete to my flitter-cycle. Since my last transformation, I preferred the open area design. Not much more than an engine with a seat and some controls attached, the cycle was a slate-blue squashed cylinder. The seat looked melted into place. A transparent windscreen rose up around the front. The cycle floated a few inches above the top of the roof. Yet another piece of miracle technology bestowed on the Rim worlds by the Galactics. No one knew how the whole anti-gravity drive worked, but there was lots of speculation and research.

I climbed on and reclined back in the seat. Coffee went into a sealed holder on the side. Restraints automatically extruded from the seat back and snaked across my chest. I dropped my hands down to the control sticks on either side of the seat. A few fluffy clouds in the blue sky above. I saw other flitters soaring around like birds on other worlds. How could Kelwyn threaten all of this? I had to stop him.

I pressed the accelerator with my foot and pulled back on the control sticks. The flitter-cycle rose smoothly above the roof. I spiraled up and then brought it around and headed for the coast once I'd achieved a safe altitude. The wind blew past the cycle, but the windshield protected me from the worst of it. Beneath me, the world looked peaceful, but that wasn't really the case. People — regardless of species — lied, cheated, stole, abused and killed one another. I think our bad behavior is one reason the Galactics keep us out of the Glittering Throng. Who would want us around?

Why would they give in to Kelwyn's demands? Did he seriously expect that to work?

A bit of shadow fell across my foot. With my scent-sight I saw something above me, a void descending. Another flitter. I twisted the sticks and shoved them forward, turning and diving away from the vehicle above. My foot pressed against the accelerator and I shot out from beneath the flitter. I flicked up rear displays. A large black cargo flitter was right behind me — and accelerating closer.

I shoved the sticks forward and dove down towards the ground and floored the accelerator. Far below was a commercial district with a few taller hotels but most of the buildings were no more than a half-dozen stories tall. On my screens, the pursuing flitter plummeted towards me. I couldn't tell if they'd started shooting or not. Hard to do in these conditions.

I fell towards the ground. Full-out acceleration. My speed increased. The g-forces increased rapidly hitting upwards of nine gees. I was seconds from making a rather large crater in the ground.

I saw people looking up. One yellowish

Torlian looked up from the path. The Torlian's crest cast a shadow like a sundial.

I yanked on the sticks sending the flitter-cycle into a spin and then yanked back hard. I flipped over and shot skyward. The other flitter passed me in a blur. I rolled again and shot away towards the nearest peaks while I watched on my screen what happened.

The crowd below scattered.

I couldn't tell if the flitter tried to pull out. Maybe they didn't see me go past. In any case, the flitter smashed straight into the biocrete road below. No great explosions but the impact pulverized the biocrete and rock beneath for at least a couple meters and sent up a huge plume of dust and shrapnel. I hoped that no one on the ground was injured. Nothing I could do about it now. There wasn't any time. I couldn't afford to get caught up in a police investigation of the crash right now.

I brought the flitter-cycle around in a long curve back towards the shore. The sooner I talked to Subha the better. I didn't believe the crash was accidental. Someone had just tried to kill me. It might not be Kelwyn, but giving the timing, I figured I'd assume it was until I found out otherwise.

§

Subha's house sits right down on the shore and extends out into the ocean, cut right into the black volcanic rocks that jut out into the waves. From the air, it isn't even visible, but I know the place well and the glittering sandy beach and cove beside it. I landed at the edge of the pale yellow seagrass up the shore.

I pulled the Torlian coffee out of the sealed container and took a sip. Still hot. Fire burned along my nerves. Wisps of pale green drifted off the thick yellow stalks of Olindan seagrass. It smelled like thyme.

I left the flitter-cycle and headed across the dry sand towards the cove. To my right, I could see the large windows of Subha's house. Shapes moved inside. Acolytes, most likely. The place also acted as Subha's church. Ahead a family of comber deer nosed through the wet sand, dislodging glitter shells as they foraged for mussels. At first glance, they looked like Terran deer but scaled instead of covered in fur. Their scales glittered in patches against the sandy-colored background. They blended in pretty well with the beach. White salty-smelling light drifted away from them. When they moved for a second, I saw them still where they'd been like ghostly trails left behind. Hearing me the Comber deer jerked up their heads. Long tongues lolled from flat shovel bills. Goofy looking things. They scrambled off across the beach away from me.

I headed straight for the water. Subha always knew when I arrived. I preferred to meet her out here, away from those in the house if possible.

It didn't surprise me when the water ahead parted, and Subha rose up before me. Beautiful, no doubt about that. Her skin is pale blue like a robin's egg and flawless. She's all curves and soft-looking, but that's just the layer of subcutaneous fat. Beneath it I know she's all muscle. All of her adaptations are designed to create a beautiful, functional life in the ocean. She had webbed fingers, longer toes with webbing between them, and gill slits along her ribs. Plus a second transparent eyelid. It could have been monstrous, but she had planned the adaptations so well that everything seemed entirely natural. Seeing her on land, you hardly noticed anything except her beauty. As she rose from the waves, it looked like she had a school of fish swimming around her, but that was just her holographic outfit. It enticed with glimpses of what lay behind the shimmering school as the fish swam in bands around her but never entirely revealed the woman beneath.

"Brock, welcome," she said. Her voice sounded throaty.

I coughed. Facing Subha is always difficult. I could handle how she looks and all, except that she's always wanted to pursue a relationship. In the past, her Church kept us apart. Now there's also Muriel.

"Subha. Sorry to bother you."

"It's never a bother, Brock. I've missed you." She emerged from the water entirely and walked up the beach to where I stood. She stopped a safe distance away. "We've missed you at the Society meetings. And Muriel. You two should come — you can't let our issues take you away from the Society."

"Thank you, but we need to talk about something else more urgent. Have you heard the reports about the murder of Montana Haugh?"

Subha nodded. "Yes, and that poor Vika-lapian a short time ago. They say a terrorist is behind it."

"It's Kelwyn."

Subha gasped. "Really? Kelwyn. I prayed for him. He's been so misguided."

"I know. I didn't believe it when he claimed to have someone helping him. I thought he'd end up as a Dumpty, but it looks like he was telling us the truth. He's changed, just like the images he showed us. I'm guessing whoever is behind his transformation is also behind these murders."

"Why?"

"The weapon Kelwyn claims to have designed murders-by-mutation. It's like someone has taken the Moreau Pod technology and turned it into a long-distance weapon."

"Our Creator will not allow such a perversion of her design to continue."

"Well, we've evidently got two deaths that say otherwise. I need to find where Kelwyn might be. I think he's in orbit, somewhere, but without more to go on it's going to take too long to locate him. Do you know where he was staying in the city?"

Subha looked up at me and pressed her hands together. To my scent-sight, she glowed with a healthy warm yellow-orange glow. She looked radiant. The fish flashed around her giving me glimpses of her breasts. I focused on her face.

"I believe you are the instrument of the Creator's will, Brock. If anyone can stop Kelwyn from causing more deaths, it is you."

"She needs a better instrument then. Right now I don't have a clue, and someone tried to kill me on the way here. You all had better be careful. Even better, go out into the ocean. Just get away from everything. That might be your only hope."

Subha shook her head. "Only some of our members are adapted for an aquatic existence. We can't abandon the others."

"Then tell me where Kelwyn was living. I might find a clue there."

"I'm sorry Brock, I don't know. I had the impression that he lived somewhere in the scab district but I'm not sure if that's even true."

"What about the other members of the Society? It seemed to me that most of them only tolerated Kelwyn's presence at the meetings, but can you think of anyone else that might know where he was living?"

"Calanthe might."

"Calanthe?" *Shit.* Subha didn't need my scent-sight to understand my reaction. "Why would she know?"

"Not what you're thinking. I believe she gave him a ride home once. A kind gesture on her part since he didn't have the fare for a cab. I think she'll help, given the circumstances."

"Not like I have any choice." Before Muriel, I'd been torn between Calanthe and Subha, but it never worked out with either for different reasons. Calanthe took it harder when I started seeing Muriel. "Thank you."

"We all walk the Creator's path. This is yours. Good luck."

"Take care of yourself." I turned and started up the beach. After a couple steps, I heard a faint splash and looked back. She was gone. The beach stood empty. I looked up at the sky. Hansel, one of Olinda's two moons, was visible just above the horizon.

Kelwyn was up there somewhere. I had to find him. I checked the time. Already six thirty. I'd better hurry.

§

Calanthe's apartment is in one of the lower-rent districts on the north side of the city. Not necessarily a bad neighborhood, but more of a transition place. It's got the people moving up and the ones on their way down. Plus some like Calanthe that seem sort of stuck where they're at. It took me about ten minutes to get there on the flitter-cycle, and I wished it'd taken longer. I dreaded seeing her.

I stood outside the building for a minute before I headed in. Calanthe is a member of the Moreau Society, but she's taken the modifications in a whole different direction than most of us.

When Calanthe opened the door, she took my breath away. I was ready for it and managed to set aside the fact that my pulse was suddenly racing. Calanthe just has that effect on people. She's petite and shapely, but it's much more than that. I could see the streamers of pheromones that poured off her in reds and yellows. Teasing, seducing just by being close to her. In addition to the chemical attack, everything that Calanthe has done was designed to make her more attractive and exotic. Her hair is like flames pouring down her back in orange, red and yellow. It looks alive. I knew that — technically speaking — it wasn't hair at all but the hair-like fronds of the Elysians which they used for pheromone communication. That along with modifications to her nervous system allowed to Calanthe to seduce anyone she wanted. Except me. I'd managed to resist. I often wondered if I'd made the right choice.

She gave me an impish grin and smiled slowly. "Brock, you've been avoiding me."

"You know you overwhelm my senses."

"And you've got someone else now." Calanthe's eyebrow arched. "I never expected someone like her would capture you. I always thought if we didn't end up together you'd be with Subha, not one of her acolytes."

"Muriel isn't an acolyte any longer. She's joined the agency. But I didn't come here to talk about that. I need your help."

Calanthe tilted her head to the side. "You only have to ask. What can I do for you, Brock?"

I felt almost dizzy. I closed my nostrils

and neck slits as tight as I could. I had to make this quick because I kept picturing how it'd be to rip the gauzy blue robe she wore from her and carry her inside. She had that effect on everyone. It made her popular as a sensie star.

"Did you see the news?"

She shook her head. "I just woke. I was on set until late last night."

"Turn it on. People have been killed. They look like Dumpties except it didn't happen in a Moreau Pod. Kelwyn claims to have killed them, and he's threatening the whole planet."

Calanthe gasped. Her hands went to her mouth, and for a couple of long seconds, she stared at me. Then she slowly lowered her hands. "Kelwyn? How could he?"

"I don't know. I'm trying to track him down. I think he's in orbit, but I want to find where he was living on the surface. Maybe there'll be a clue there."

"Why is he doing this?"

"He's holding us all hostage in an apparent attempt to force the Galactics to admit him into the Glittering Throng."

"By killing people?"

I started to reach out to her and instead

clenched my fist and shoved it in my pocket. "Please, I need your help. Subha didn't know where he lived but said that you'd helped him home before. Do you remember where he lived?"

Calanthe shook her head. "I don't. But I think I'd recognize the place if I saw it again. It's in the scab district, up in the crags."

Great. That place was a warren of structures and tunnels. And not a particularly safe place to go.

"Tell me as much as you can. I'll find it."

"No! Let's just go together. It'll be a lot easier if I'm there to help you find it." She crossed her arms. "Let's not argue Brock. If Kelwyn's killing people, we don't have time."

She was right we didn't have time. I gestured at her robe. "You can't go there dressed like that."

Calanthe smiled. "Come in, I'll get changed."

I shook my head. "You go ahead. I'll reconfigure the flitter-cycle. Be quick."

She gave a little pout then stepped back. "I will."

I felt like I'd either narrowly escaped or missed out on something. Escaped, I think.

I thought of Muriel as I headed back to the flitter-cycle.

I settled into the flitter-cycle seat and activated the control interface. I tapped the passenger mode. Behind my seat, the rear end of the flitter-cycle elongated and deformed until a second seat formed. As I breathed the cleaner air, my head began to clear. At least in the flitter-cycle, the winds would carry Calanthe's pheromones away. I knew she had control over them to some extent. Hopefully, she'd tone it down given the current situation. While I waited, I pulled up the news reports. Subha was right, an unnamed Vikalapian had been murdered-by-mutation while sunning down on one of the rock beaches favored by the amphibious species. The news didn't show any images of what had happened, but they interviewed several other Vikalapians that had been on the beach at the time. I watched one interview with one sporting a peach-colored carapace.

<*Human world dangerous*>. The words scrolled along the screen. They communicate with flashes of light in bands along their front pincers, a sort of illuminated sign language influenced by body posture and intensity.

Standard translators didn't work for them since you actually had to stand back to see what they were saying.

<Must stop madness ruptured carapace hideous internal skeleton>

I looked up and saw Calanthe coming out of her apartment. I glanced back down at the screen.

<Ending vacation Home bound>

Good idea, I thought. I killed the news feed. Calanthe had changed into black pants and a black leather jacket. She'd even braided her hair and coiled it up on the back of her head. She still looked beautiful, but at a distance, it was easier to simply appreciate the fact without being overwhelmed by it. She slipped on dark glasses as she got close.

"Ready."

"Hop on."

I waited for her to get seated. She tapped me on the shoulder, and I took off. I brought the flitter-cycle up fast and headed across the main landmass towards the scab district.

The scab district is a mass of twisted rock and valleys that tumble down into a rocky bay. Little grew there but scattered about I saw signs of Olindan vegetation taking root. The scab district was the result of more recent eruptions—it is all younger rock and sharp edges.

From the air, it was easy to see why it got called the scab district. Flying towards it I could see lots of shapes flying in the air and diving down into the valleys and bays. Olindan diving bats. The main ground road snaked around the district, often as bridges crossing crevices and the bats loved nothing more than darting right in front of oncoming traffic. It appeared to be some sort of game for them. Most of the time they don't hit the vehicles. Not mammals or birds but uniquely Olindan creatures. Still, physics has led them to be superficially similar to Terran bats. Or Nosferans for that matter, although the diving bats are only about half the size of Nosferans and lack their clever hands and intelligence.

Against the black rock of the district, the biocrete structures stand out like bones. I activated the front and rear displays and speakers.

"Which way?" I asked Calanthe.

A section of my map lit up. "I think it

was around there. I'll be able to tell more when we get closer."

"Okay. Hang on. We're about to get company."

A whole cloud of diving bats had noticed our approach and were flying right at us. I held the flitter-cycle steady trusting their abilities and the strength of the windshield to get us through. In an instant the cloud reached us. I found I tensed for a big impact, but they streamed by all around, breaking away at the last possible fraction of a second. I caught glimpses of their smooth hairless black bodies gleaming like oil around us, plunging us into darkness. Calanthe shrieked behind me. Then in a burst of light, we passed through the cloud. The ground was closer than I'd expected. I slowed the cycle and brought it around to avoid the peak ahead of us, careful with the acceleration since I didn't know how much Calanthe could take.

We flew lower, and the mass of the bats didn't follow. Every now and then one would launch itself from a building or rock face and streak past but most ignored us. We approached the area of the map Calanthe indicated.

"Anything look familiar?"

"Not yet." She sounded a bit out of breath. "Can you fly closer to the road? We were in a ground cab. It might look more familiar."

I could, although it'd break some safety regulations. I didn't think anyone would try to stop us. I brought us over above the road and followed it deeper into the valley. Most ground traffic was pedestrians or bicycles, the occasional ground cab.

"Head left into this next valley," Calanthe said. "I think it was back that way."

I flew up over the bridge supports and down into the valley. The buildings clung to the steep rock faces connected by steep biocrete ramps and bridges. I brought the flitter-cycle down as close as I dared and even then the highest bridges were right beneath us as we flew above them.

"Yes," Calanthe said. "Up ahead on the right there's a cleft with a biocrete bottom. It makes a sort of cul-de-sac — he lives back there."

I wondered if she'd slept with Kelwyn

but didn't ask. Some things I didn't want to know. I saw the cleft. Nothing more than a split in the rock so narrow that the biocrete looked like a river snaking through the fissure. I slowed and made my way up through the split. Wind howled through the space and around us. Three diving bats suddenly flew right past the windshield, each parting in a different direction as they surfed the air currents around the flitter-cycle. Just as Calanthe described the cleft opened up after a little way to form a sort of pocket at the end.

Biocrete buildings clung to the sheer black rock on either side but were stained and malformed. Whoever lived here hadn't been taking care of the biocrete, and it'd grown off-form in several places, making all sorts of odd protrusions and branches. Olindan diving bats clung to the buildings and to the rock walls around. I heard their strange chuffing cries as the flitter-cycle entered the pocket. Several diving bats flew at the cycle and sped past but as they did their sharp-toothed mouths shot downward at me. Behind me, Calanthe gasped.

"I guess they don't like visitors." I shoved

the sticks forward and put the flitter-cycle in a dive towards the ground.

Diving bat attacks are rare. But they will defend their nesting areas. From the looks of things, a colony had settled here, maybe when the buildings were abandoned. The bats have a tooth-ringed mouth they use to seize aquatic prey, but they could just as easily use those teeth on us. More bats started chuffing and took to the air as we dived.

"Stay down! Here they come!"

I couldn't really do anything at the moment. The bats flew towards us, grazing the flitter-cycle. Their mouths stabbed downward. One grazed the side of my head. I ignored it. The sooner we got down, the safer we'd be. The bats flew past, and we were clear with the ground right there. I pulled back and brought the flitter-cycle to a gut-wrenching stop right before we hit the biocrete. I edged it forward until we coasted right up next to one of the building entrances. Behind me, Calanthe groaned. I looked up but although there were bats flying anxiously above they didn't appear to see us as much of a threat on the ground. I killed the drive and released my restraints. Jumping down I turned to check on Calanthe.

She'd been hurt. Blood trickled down her face from a cut on her temple. She gently touched it with her fingers and stared at the blood. "Ouch."

To my scent-sight, the blood not only trickled down her face, but it rose off her face, and from the cut in misty red streamers. I reached past her waist and keyed her restraints off. I took her hand and glanced up at the circling bats.

"We should get you inside, there might be first aid supplies."

She reached for me, and I helped steady her as she got down from the flitter-cycle. I almost expected her to stumble, fall into my arms or something but as soon as she got down, she stepped away with a chuckle.

"Wow, some ride, Brock. I'm okay."

"We still need to get that cut cleaned up."

Calanthe turned and crossed her arms looking up at the structure. "I don't know. The place looks like it has been abandoned for a while. Kelwyn hasn't been around."

"There still might be some clue to where

he's gone." I pointed to the closed doors. "Let's see if we can get those open."

The door was a reinforced alloy of some sort, dull black in color with almost a sandpaper texture to it. I didn't recognize the material. I also didn't see any signs of a control panel or locking mechanism.

"It just opened for him when I was here," Calanthe said. "He could barely walk and was pretty much out of it, but it opened up."

"Did it swing open or slide back?"

"It slid to the left."

I ran my hands over the biocrete around the opening. I didn't see anything, but then a molecular sensor keyed to Kelwyn wouldn't have to be that visible. The biocrete gave off an unhealthy yellowish-green of decay. I didn't want to try to look for any fainter scents with Calanthe right here. She'd overwhelm my scent-sight. I put my hands flat against the door and gave it a test push. Nothing. I braced my feet again and tried to push the door, but it held fast. I stopped before I tore the skin from my palms.

"I don't think we're going to get in this way. Let's split up and look around for any other openings. There might be some other way in. Watch out for the bats!"

"Sure." Calanthe headed to the right.

I went left. The structure made a 'U' shape around the end of the crevice with three to four floors rising above. There were windows. I stopped at the first, but the inside of the place was dark. I couldn't see anything. I hit the glass with my knuckle. It felt very strong. I doubted I could break it easily. For the moment I kept going. Other than trying to crash the flitter-cycle through a window I didn't see any good options yet for getting inside. A little further on I saw something white and dried up stretched out on the biocrete. It gave off little scent — a sort of faint spicy smelled that floated lightly away. When I reached it, I realized after a second what I was looking at. A skin. About as long as my leg, tapered at one end and ragged at the other. A snakeskin. I crouched down and gently picked it up. As big as this was it didn't look nearly large enough for Kelwyn as I'd seen him in the transmission. And this was here, where wind and weather would have washed it away before long. It crinkled in my fingers. I dropped it.

We weren't alone. Someone or something else was here. Above me the bats continued to fly about, still agitated over the flitter-cycle, their chuffing noises floating down to me. I stood.

I opened up my neck slits and inhaled deeply. The world around me pulsed with light and became more alive. I could see the healthy sections of biocrete and those that needed care. The skin at my feet glowed in a pool of white light. I wanted to see how it got here. I concentrated on its smell.

There.

It touched the wall above in a few places. I saw it falling down between the two sections of the house, touching one side than the other. Above. It came from up higher. Maybe I'd have a better chance of getting in on the upper floors. I considered going back for the flitter-cycle, but that'd attract more attention from the bats. Besides, there were other ways to do this.

I backed away from the wall out into the courtyard. Far off to my left Calanthe blazed in reds and yellows like a living flame.

"Brock?"

I ran at the wall. At the last moment, I

jumped towards the section on the right. My left foot hit, and I jumped off towards the opposite section. Jumped again, reached up, and caught the top of the wall. I pulled myself up onto that section of the roof. In my scent-sight, I saw two bats dive towards me in reckless rage. I tucked and rolled out of their path. White light exploded around me, and I smelled that same faint spicy smell. Skins crinkled beneath me. The bats flew past.

I stood up. Skins covered this upper deck. *Dozens of them.*

CHAPTER 4

I stood on top of the first level of Kelwyn's home on a sort of biocrete stone garden complete with benches and a few potted Olindan plants. A pair of glass doors at the back beneath a sort of porch. Dozens of dried white snake skins lay scattered around on the black rocks as if sunning themselves. Each skin at least as large as my leg. But unlike the skin I'd found down below, some of these showed arms and heads. And none looked to be as large as Kelwyn.

"Brock?"

More bats dove at me. I threw myself down into a roll to get away from them.

"Brock?"

I got to my feet and looked down. Calanthe stood below. I waved towards the front door. "Go wait by the door! I'll try to get in up here."

"Okay."

She left. I saw bats spiraling around above. More were joining those in the air. Time for me to get inside. I skirted around the pile of skins and ran towards the doors. I heard the wings of the bats as they swooped toward me like flags snapping in the wind. I ran faster. The doors didn't have any visible handles. The bats came within range of my scent-sight, still blurry but I could just see them flickering in and out of sight. Skins crunched beneath my feet like so many dried leaves. I dodged around the largest rocks, jumped over the smaller ones and passed beneath the porch. I didn't even try to stop. I crashed right into the center of the doors.

Metal screamed and popped. My shoulder felt like it'd been hit with a sledgehammer. The door flew open, and I staggered inside, across a hallway and crashed into the wall. In my scent-sight, I saw the diving bats flying past the doors. I turned around. One crashed into the door frame and screeched. It flopped on the ground just outside. I pushed away from the wall and walked over as the last of the bats flew away. The injured one lay on its back. Black and yellow eyes closed. It shuddered and lay still. The left wing had been torn almost clean off. Dark red blood poured from the wound, and in my scent-sight the molecules blazed upward and out, spreading away across the deck and creeping into the house.

I pushed the doors closed, although they didn't latch anymore.

So much for a quiet entrance. Whatever was here must have heard all that racket. My shoulder throbbed, but I didn't think I'd hurt it too badly. I reached beneath my coat and pulled out my Lottier 45. Although technically a non-lethal weapon, the needles used to deliver the nanoparalyzers could be deadly at close range. There'd been times I'd had to take advantage of that feature.

I looked both ways down the hall. Hard to say which would be best. I opened up my neck slits again and breathed in deeply. The biocrete hallway glowed faintly. I concentrated on the white, spicy, dry smell I'd gotten from the skins. A ghostly shape appeared on my left and slithered away down the hall. Kelwyn or something else? I turned and followed the scent apparition into the house.

Down the hallway past dusty-smelling

rooms. At first, I couldn't see much of the apparition. A vague, misty white shape moving ahead of me. As I went deeper, the smell became stronger and I could see a bit more of it. A long tail slithering against the stone. I couldn't make out any details above that yet. Obviously, something shaped like Kelwyn but I couldn't tell if what I was smelling was him or another snake. The scent led me down a flight of stairs to the first floor and then turned to lead deeper into the house. Away from the front door. I hesitated and thought of going back to let Calanthe in. But if I did that her pheromones might overwhelm my sense of smell, and I'd have more trouble following this apparition. And I'd have to watch out for her. She might be able to take care of herself, but that wouldn't stop me from worrying about her.

So I followed the apparition instead. I'd apologize later.

Deeper in, the house must have been cut into the rock itself, but the interior had been finished with biocrete so you couldn't tell where the biocrete walls ended and the rock began. So far the whole place looked mostly empty. The only furniture I'd seen were some biocrete benches. No paintings. No decorations of any sort. Maybe it had all been packed up and moved away. If the place was empty, this might not turn out to be of any use. I'd been sure that Kelwyn would have left behind something, some clue as to his plans. It was beginning to look like I hadn't given him credit enough. He had evidently cleared out of here, and it didn't look like he had planned to come back.

I still wanted to see where this scent-trail led me, so I kept following it with my Lottier 45 held ready. The place was a bigger warren on the inside than I would have thought, but it was cut deeply into the rock. I followed the apparition deeper past empty rooms and all the while the smell grew stronger. The shape of the thing clearly matched Kelwyn's appearance on his message, but I couldn't see enough detail to tell if it was him or not. I reached a ramp that spiraled down and descended. The corridor was wide and tall enough to drive a cab through. It took a long wide spiral as it descended and I started to smell the ocean.

The ramp led out into a large natural cavern far beneath the house. I could see, but only with my scent-sight. The whole thing glowed in greens and blacks. A cavern bigger than my house. With the sound of water dripping and falling, each looking like a faint star as they dropped down. Small waves lapped at the stone in a pool in front of me. There must be underwater caves connecting this chamber to the ocean. Muriel would love this place. Private ocean access. I could see why Kelwyn would have found that useful too. He could have moved supplies in and out of the cavern without anyone on the surface seeing anything. And he had the Olindan diving bat colony living upstairs to drive off any but the most determined.

What had he been doing here? Obviously, he had backers who could afford this, he never would have been able to before. Heck, most of the residents in the scab district didn't live like this.

My apparition stood beside me as if waiting. I inhaled and followed the trail. I actually expected the scent-trail to lead down into the water, but it turned instead and went left around the pool towards the back of the cavern and an opening there which glowed redly in my normal vision. As I got closer, I could see again. Something back there was giving off light. And heat. I felt warmer air pouring from the mouth which lit everything up even more with a rich yellow sulfurous egg smell. My stomach grumbled, reminding me that I'd had nothing to eat this morning and only one Torlian coffee. Not my usual routine at all.

I held the Lottier 45 ready and followed the apparition into this new tunnel. It got warmer and after about four meters opened up into another chamber. The heat ramped up, and I could, at last, see what was giving off the light. The rocks glowed red at the back of the cave. Steam poured out of vents making it hard to see what the cave contained. Obviously, the builders must have used geothermal energy to heat the rocks. The floor had been cut smooth, same as the tunnel and the cave outside. The apparition had taken on solid form, lying right in front of the glowing red rocks. No clothes from what I saw.

"Hold it right there," I told the guy. "Don't move."

He hissed and snapped around, rising up in front of me, but stood — is stood really the right word? — chest-high. Like Kelwyn this one had a cobra sort of hood and a muscular human-like torso, but thin. And small. The snake-like face looked somehow boyish to me. His scales looked blue, tinged red by the light from the rocks. His odor gave off the same white sort of smell that I'd followed down here. This was definitely the apparition I'd been following.

"Who are you?" I asked.

Black eyes watched me without expression, but his hands came up as if to shield himself from me. "Don't hurt me! I didn't do anything wrong!"

"Who are you?"

"Blaine. Blaine!"

"Okay, good Blaine. My name is Brock. You live here?"

"Yes." Blaine lowered his hands a bit. "You're not going to hurt me, are you?"

I shook my head. "I'm not planning to hurt you. Answer my questions, and I'll leave you alone."

"No!"

I snapped up the Lottier 45, ready to fire.

Blaine cringed away, hood deflating around his head, hands out as if they could stop the needles. He peeked out at me. "Sorry, sorry. I just, well, I don't want to be alone!"

Oh. Shit. Blaine sounded scared—and young. I lowered the weapon but was still ready in case this was all some sort of ruse. "Okay. I'm not going to hurt you. Why are you here if you don't want to be alone?"

"I didn't know where else to go? I came back, and he was gone."

"Kelwyn?"

Blaine looked at me. Gave a little nod. He lowered his arms and turned to face me. "Yes. He left without me. I didn't know what to do."

"How long ago was this?"

Blaine thought for a minute. "Three weeks? I'm not sure. It's my fault. He warned me to stay close. He said that he wouldn't be able to wait. But I didn't listen. I went for a swim. Stayed out too long. And when I came back, he'd left."

"And you've been alone since?"

"Yes."

I thought about the empty house upstairs. "What have you been eating?"

Blaine flicked his hand at the tunnel.

"Fish, other things I like in the water. I'm a fast swimmer."

"Blaine, I need to know. Do you know where Kelwyn went? Where he was going?"

"I'm not sure. Space, I think. He mentioned them."

"Them?"

"The Glittering Throng. He talked about them a lot." Blaine slid forward a few centimeters. "Oh, and he said something about his ship. It was going to be ready soon. I helped."

"Okay." I put away the Lottier 45. I spread my hands. "Now, Blaine. This might be a hard question. How did you end up here? With Kelwyn?"

"He saved me." Blaine looked down at his hands and back up at me. "He said I'd been hurt and he saved me, made me strong like him." Blaine paused, then said bitterly, "But then he left me."

I couldn't take Calanthe and Blaine on the flitter-cycle. It could be reconfigured to carry just about any species, but it couldn't carry all three of us. We'd have to go up and get a cab. "Do you think that you could show me where he kept his ship?"

"If I do, will you take me with you?"

"Yes. I'll take you."

Blaine smiled. It looked really awful on him with his lipless mouth. His tongue flicked out and tasted the air.

"Come on." I headed back out towards the ramp leading to the surface. I hadn't gone more than a few steps out into the larger cavern when I heard a noise ahead. A scuff of a foot against the biocrete floor. I flattened up against the wall and motioned Blaine back as well. He pressed himself up against the rock. I drew my weapon and inhaled deeply. I could see the cavern ahead with my scent-sight. The far edges faded in and out of reality but I still got enough from everything to have a sense of it. And there were three new scents coming from large sources around the corner from where I stood. Someone moving carefully through the dark, not using any light but hugging the wall. That told me two things. One, they already knew the layout of the place, and two, that they couldn't see in the dark.

I ran out into the cavern as silently as I could. I heard a startled gasp from one of the men. I turned as I ran and pointed the

Lottier 45 at them. And fired. A sharp puff from the shot. Then a man — human — who looked blue-green and smelled of salt collapsed as the needle hit him. I fired again and hit the second man. He growled, took a step and dropped as well.

By then the third man opened up with his weapon. Automatic shots rang out across the cavern. The rapid-fire stitched across the darkness towards me. I only had one option. I dove into the water. Bullets plunked into the water behind me. I couldn't see anything. My scent-sight doesn't work unless I'm breathing and I was blind in the cavern. I hugged the bottom and waited. None of the bullets found me. They stopped hitting the water. Then a light appeared in the cavern. It flashed across the pool and then away. Back. Away again.

I rose up from the water, saw the light swinging back my way and fired. I threw myself to the side. A brief burst of automatic gunfire scored the biocrete. Then the shooter collapsed. I climbed to my feet and walked carefully towards the fallen men.

Closer up I could see them better by both the light and smell. All mostly human, but with the beginnings of snake-like features. Scales across their brows and snake-like eyes. But they all still had their legs. I kept the Lottier 45 trained on them just in case the nanoparalyzers weren't as effective against their modified DNA.

"Blaine?"

His head appeared around the corner first, and then he slithered out into view. "Are they dead?"

"No. You can see them okay?"

"Infrared," Blaine said. "I see everything. You are very bright."

And in my view, Blaine glowed with a white light as molecules drifted from his body. "You too. Listen, do you recognize them? It looks like they are also Moreaus."

Blaine lowered his torso closer to the unconscious men. "I don't think so. I haven't seen them before. They aren't dead?"

"No." I thought of Calanthe waiting up above, hurt. "Let's get out of here before they wake up."

I hurried towards the ramp. In my scent-sight, I saw Blaine following behind me. It looked a bit unnerving, a ghostly white snake-figure following me. My apparition made real. I didn't exactly trust the kid yet, but he sounded sincere about helping. Then he stopped.

I turned around. "What's the problem?"

"I'm afraid to go upstairs."

"Why?" Calanthe was upstairs.

"That's where the others are."

I tried to stay patient. "Others? I thought you were alone?"

"I am! The others don't like me. They pick on me. So I stayed downstairs on the warm rocks or went swimming in the tunnels and the ocean."

"The place looked empty when I came in. Maybe Kelwyn took the others with him."

Blaine hissed. "No! They've been there since he left. Getting meaner all the time. We need to stay away from them."

I still had the Lottier 45 in my hands. I lifted it up. "That's fine by me. Let's just get out of here. Okay?"

"Okay." Blaine didn't sound convinced.

I just hoped we'd get out without attracting any more attention. I should have known that it wouldn't be that easy. We hadn't gone that far up the ramp when I heard sounds of a struggle above — a woman's voice raised in anger. *Calanthe.* I took off running up the ramp. I saw that Blaine didn't follow me. I'd find him later. Right then all I cared about was finding Calanthe.

At the top of the ramp, I burst out into the long room there and smelled a dry peppery smell on my right. Too late. I spun around, but a head lunged forward at my extended arm. I caught a glimpse of a snake mouth with two long fangs in an instant before they pierced my arm. A quick strike in and then out. I swung at the snake-man, but he dodged away.

In my scent-sight, I could see several more slithering in a rush across the floor towards me.

I couldn't catch a scent of Calanthe. I thumbed the Lottier 45 to auto, ignoring the burning in my arm, and sprayed needles at the snake-men. I turned in a circle as I did casting needles all around me.

As quick as they were, they couldn't dodge all of the needles. The snake-men — and two snake-women — collapsed limply to the floor. I stood in the circle and took a deep breath in. My scent-sight picked up a trace of something scarlet and smelling of roses that could be Calanthe right at the edge of my range towards the right. Back towards the front door.

My right arm throbbed painfully. It felt hot. I switched the Lottier 45 to my left hand and ignored the pain. I might be poisoned, but first I had to find Calanthe. And Blaine, so that I could track down Kelwyn. And at this rate I'd need another Torlian coffee before long.

I walked past the sleeping bodies, stepping carefully over them. Captain Brice would be so happy to have suspects to question. "Blaine?"

I heard rustling from the archway leading to the ramp. Blaine came out. He stared for a long time at his fallen kin.

"Blaine! My friend is up here. We need to find her."

Blaine flicked around, and his lidless eyes fixed on me. "They're sleeping?"

"Right. Come on, they can't hurt you now and won't wake up for a while." I headed down the corridor. Calanthe's scent increased. It was her. I recognized the complex flavor of her scent. As we got closer, I saw her running. The white apparitions of the snake-people chased her. Their scents intermingling. Then, there, just ahead in a doorway I saw her lying on the floor. I ran ahead through the insubstantial scent images to her side. I put away the Lottier 45 and crouched down beside her.

Two punctures on her arm, just below the elbow leaked blood, and angry red lines radiated out from the injury. With my scent-sight, I saw two more dark red points of mist rising from her inner thigh. I looked closer and saw the blood there, almost hidden by her black pants. Blaine slithered up behind me.

I turned to face him. I felt sweat on my forehead. "What's this poison? Can you help?"

"I don't know," Blaine said. "Are you going to die? Is she?"

"Not if I can do anything about it." I reached into my pocket and brought out my tablet. I called Captain Brice.

"Brock! You'd better have —"

"Captain, I've found someone that can help. Get here." I gave him the location. "We've been poisoned. I need medical help."

"Don't go anywhere," he warned.

Like I planned to. I pocketed the tablet. I looked up at Blaine. He was much smaller than the others. Now that I'd seen them I had a sinking feeling. "How old are you, Blaine?"

"Ten."

A young kid. Kelwyn had transformed a kid.

"How did Kelwyn find you?"

"I was on a Cautarian passenger liner. My mother got sick. She died. They said that I needed to work off her medical debt. I came down to the surface with the cook looking for supplies, but I ran away. I hid out. I wanted to get on a ship that would take me home, but then I got sick. Kelwyn found me and brought me here." Blaine looked down at his hands. "He changed me."

My arm burned. I grimaced, and the dizziness increased. I sank to the floor. Blaine wavered above me. "Don't go anywhere. The police will be here to help."

Blaine's hood flared out. "Kelwyn said to stay away from the police. They'd give me back to the Cautarians."

"He lied. Don't worry about that just tell them you want to stay with me." My vision blurred. I felt very tired even though I could tell my heart was racing. "Stay."

Chapter 5

Captain Brice blocked my way from the hospital room. "You're not going anywhere, Brock. You're done! Off the case."

I'd woken up here after having been treated for the poisoning. Behind the Captain, Blaine crossed his arms and tried to look away. I'd been told that he supplied the venom necessary to produce the anti-venom that saved our lives. I owed the kid.

"Fine. You still can't keep me here." I couldn't very well shove him out of the way. That'd just give him an excuse to lock me up again.

"Look, I only came here so you could talk to the kid and tell him to cooperate with us."

"I'm not his boss," I said.

"He says he'll only talk to you!" Captain Brice took a step closer. He smelled of sweat and frustration. It poured down from his forehead like a veil. "Tell him."

I smiled. "I've got a better idea. I'll talk to Blaine and continue my own investigation. If I find out anything that can help you, I'll pass it on."

"I've got four more deaths," Brice said. "Four people murdered by this mutation ray. The last happened right out in the open on the street. A man walking his dog started screaming. Witnesses said it looked like he was being turned inside out. The dog was far enough away that it wasn't affected."

"And the more time we stand here arguing the longer it's going to be to find Kelwyn and shut him down. Let me work, Captain!"

I almost thought I had him, but right then Doctor Reaba showed up. She's Centaurian, human but a bit different. Descended from the first interstellar human colonies around Alpha Centauri, her people adapted to life underground and a communal style of living. Short, hairless, albino, and blind. She smelled like a fresh-baked lemon meringue pie. She uttered a series of clicks as she entered the room and stopped.

"What is this? Patients should be in bed."

"Sorry Doc, we've got a guy holding the planet hostage. I've got to stop him."

"You risk cardiac damage if you do not stay in bed!"

That made me hesitate. "I thought you treated me for the poison?"

Dr. Reaba pressed her small hands together in front of her chest. "I did. However, poison continues to circulate in your system. It takes time for the antivenin to bind and flush your system."

"Thanks, Doc. I appreciate that, but I can't stay here." I looked at the Captain. "And yet again someone has tried to kill me. I'm not going stay here and risk someone coming after me in my bed."

Dr. Reaba's lips pressed together. Then she uttered a string of clicks. "Fine. I'll discharge you, but I will note it was over my protests. Don't come here if you have a heart attack."

"I'll be fine," I assured her. "Captain?"

"Damn it, Brock. *Fine.* Get some answers out of the kid. Call me before you do anything else stupid."

The Captain spun around and stormed from the room leaving behind a slowly fading scent-trail. Doctor Reaba didn't say anything else as she left the room too. I looked at Blaine.

"How're you doing?"

His arms dropped to his side. That sour-milk smell seemed like fear. "You nearly died. They said Kelwyn's threatening to kill everyone on the planet. Is it true?"

"'Fraid so. That's why it's important that we find him. We need to get over to the spaceport. If we identify his ship, then we can trace where it went when it left the surface. But we don't have much time. He's killing people every hour until his demand is met."

"He wants to join the Glittering Throng," Blaine said.

"He told you about that?"

"Yes. Kelwyn said he was as smart as any of them. That we were his first children, the first members of a new species. We'd all be welcome among the Galactics once they learned what he could do."

"Well, I think he's going to be disappointed. The Galactics aren't going to allow him to join the Glittering Throng."

"Couldn't they stop him?"

"Yes, if they wanted to, but I doubt that

they even care what happens here. They don't interfere."

Doctor Reaba reappeared in the doorway holding a tablet. She uttered another series of click and then orientated her position towards us. "Mr. Marsden? I have your discharge forms here."

"Thank you." I took the tablet. Standard legalize. I signed the form agreeing that I had left the hospital over the advice of my doctor. I gave it back. "You know what, Doc? You smell fantastic."

A small smile flickered on her lips. "Flattering me won't help you. Be careful."

"I will. Blaine, let's go." I was partway down the hallway before I thought about how we'd be getting to the spaceport. "Did anyone bring my flitter-cycle to the hospital?"

"I don't know," Blaine said. "I rode with the police. You and the lady were in an ambulance."

Calanthe. In my rush to get out, I hadn't even thought about her. I stopped and looked back down the hallway. I should go back. Check on her, but I knew she'd been treated as well. Going back would just use time we didn't have.

"We'll call a cab. I can have someone from the office go retrieve the flitter-cycle."

I called the cab company first. As we entered the elevator to the roof, I called the office. Muriel answered.

"Brock. Where are you?"

"Leaving the hospital now."

"Hospital?" I could hear the tension in her voice.

"Yeah. Look, my flitter-cycle got left at Kelwyn's old place." I sent her the address. "Do you think you can have Dyami get it and bring it over to the spaceport? I'll meet him there. Tell him to watch out for aggressive diving bats."

"Of course." Silence for a moment. "He's on his way. What did you find at Kelwyn's?"

"Help and trouble. But it's okay. The bad guys are in custody. I've got a young man here, Blaine, that knows something about Kelwyn's plans. We're going to try to track how he left the planet."

"I might be ahead of you there. Shanley uncovered the name of a shuttle registered to Kelwyn. The *Ouroboros*, classified as a standard cargo shuttle. It'd only get him up to orbit or to the moons. Nothing more than that."

"Great. Tell Shanley I owe him."

"Do you want me to come with Dyami?"

"No," I said that too quickly, thinking of the attempts on my life already. "Keep digging. See what else you can uncover about Kelwyn. Let me know if there's anything useful."

"I will. Brock, be careful, will you?"

"Always," I said lightly. "Love you."

"You too," she whispered.

The call disconnected as we reached the roof. I checked the time. Just after 9:00 AM now. This whole business only started five hours ago. And I'd been out for about an hour of that time.

The elevator doors opened, and I led the way outside. Blaine stuck beside me, saying nothing. A flitter-cab sat straight ahead in the designated landing zone. I hurried towards it. As I got closer, I saw the driver turn sideways and his hand came up holding something. A weapon. I heard the first shot and moved quickly to the side. Another shot whizzed through the air past me.

I kept moving but glanced back. Blaine

lay flat on the roof. He didn't move. I didn't smell blood, and there wasn't any sign of it to my scent-sight. I smelled something pungent and tart, his fear oozing out across the roof in a thin, sickly yellow color against his usual white odor.

A biocrete bench provided meager shelter from the shooter, but I took it. Best I'd get at the moment. I peeked up and took a look. The cab hadn't moved. In fact, the shooter had opened the door and was behind it, using it as a shield.

Wind blew across the roof-top. The Lottier 45 wouldn't be the best weapon in these conditions. With the wind and distance, the needles wouldn't reach the shooter. I needed to be a lot closer.

Best way to do that? Do the unexpected. I rose and rolled over the bench. More shots missed. I sprinted across the rooftop towards the cab. I didn't dodge. I ran full speed right at him. The gun steadied. Aimed right at me. I twisted to the side, and the first shot flew past me, missing only by an inch or so. I took the next stride wide and twisted the other way. Another shot missed.

I was close enough that I could smell

something from the man. Faint, being carried away by the wind, but a rough alcohol smell seeped from his pores. Not a profession killer. Most likely just a cabby with a gun. Hired to kill me.

Close enough.

I brought up the Lottier 45 and fired. The needle hit him in the throat. He coughed and slumped behind the door. I ran right up to the door with my weapon ready and eased around.

The man lay unconscious on the landing pad with his pistol beside him. A nasty-looking piece, all sharp angles. Small, though. Sort of thing that would be easy to hide. I picked it up and slipped it into my coat pocket. Then I went back to Blaine.

He stirred as I approached and pushed himself up. His tongue tasted the air. He still smelled scared.

"It's fine," I told him. "He's unconscious, but we need to go."

"How did he know to find us here?"

"I don't know. Kelwyn might be monitoring communications on some level. We need to get moving before Kelwyn targets us with his Dumpty ray." I felt an itch between my shoulder blades like someone was behind me. Watching.

Nothing happened when we got into the cab. I left the cabby lying unconscious on the hospital roof. I'd really rather have my flitter-cycle than the cab. I couldn't even open the windows on the cab. It made me feel very closed in. Blaine settled into the back and lay down.

Poor kid was probably exhausted. It bothered me that several times now Kelwyn had sent someone to kill me. At least I still assumed it was Kelwyn. Other people might want me dead, but the timing made it more likely that Kelwyn knew I was on the case and wanted to stop me. So far his attacks with the Dumpty ray appeared to be random people with no connection to Kelwyn. I didn't want to hold still long enough for him to target me.

The hospital I'd been in was located in the scab district. It was going to take time to get across the city and then out to Spaceport Island. It's off the coast of the largest island in the Olindan chain. It's also a somewhat artificial island. What started as a maze of sand islands just under or just above the water had been transformed into a large irregular circular island of biocrete slowly expanding outwards. While we flew, I turned on the news.

Wide-spread panic and riots had started across the city as news of the threat leaked out. Two Shey fishermen had been attacked evidently because of their somewhat reptilian appearance. Idiots. The Shey were harmless, simple people. Pacifists. And not really snake-like at all. Scaled, sure, but humanoid with wide webbed feet and hands. Big eyes and wide mouths. I probably had met the Shey attacked. I'd gone with Subha before to ask for DNA samples — which they happily provided. Subha used elements of their DNA in some of her own modifications. Angry now, I turned off the news.

From up here, I couldn't see most of the problems, but I did see two police flitters dive towards the city with flashing lights. Kelwyn would have a lot to answer for when I finally caught up to him.

Eventually, I left the main island and flew out over the ocean. Other than a scattering of islands and the ice at the poles the ocean continues on in all directions covering ninety percent of Olinda. In the 700 years since the first colonists visited the planet much of the world hasn't been explored. The area around the main island chain but little beyond that. Even species adapted to live in the ocean, or Subha and her people, haven't ventured far.

The ocean is big, people don't realize how big. There are some relatively shallow 'seas' — areas that perhaps could be considered continents if the sea level decreased. I know scientists speculate that historically much more ice would have been locked up in the poles and on those continents but the planet is only now slowly coming out of a green-house phase. As it cools perhaps more surface will be revealed.

Right now all I cared about was ahead of me, on the horizon. The spaceport. Olinda's gateway to the universe and where I hoped we'd get our first break in tracking down Kelwyn.

CHAPTER 6

My first order of business at the space-port? Torlian coffee. Fresh. Made right there by fourth generation Torlians. The cafe was busy today when I walked in, followed by Blaine. Behind the counter stood two larger Torlians. Yellow to my eyes, well over seven-feet tall with long bony crests rising from the back of their heads. Big hard black beaks on their faces. Their arms are small but nimble, and somehow they manage to keep from knocking everything over with their long balancing tails. Purplish mist dripped from their skin. That came from the oily secretions that kept them looking shiny. I stood in the line to wait. The whole place was alive with colors from the various beverages. I loved coming into places like this. I inhaled deeply and could see the whole place around me. It was beautiful. Too bad I couldn't just kick back and rest.

"Shouldn't we be going to find out about the ship?" Blaine asked.

"Aren't you hungry? It's still early, and I don't know about you, but I haven't eaten all day."

"Yes, but—"

"Good. We'll grab something here to go." I hesitated. "What do you eat?"

Blaine wavered back and forth as he studied the menu. "Fish is fine. Uncooked, if they have it."

"They probably do." When our turn came, the Torlian at the counter clacked her beak at me and brought her head down to eye-level.

"Brock, Brock! What's Brock doing out here?" Esbeth sounds human-enough. Given the number of humans on the planet, Esbeth learned to speak to them without a translator. Mostly.

"Tracking someone, Esbeth. Have you seen a man in here, looks somewhat like this young guy but bigger?"

Esbeth swung her head around to study Blaine. Torlians are nearsighted. Her crest waggled back and forth. "Yes, Brock. You saw a being like this one many other times. This being the man Brock tracks?"

"That's right. When did you last see him?"

"You last saw this being three weeks ago and you didn't like him."

Did I mention she still has a few issues with pronouns? "Why didn't you like him?"

Esbeth blinked big dark eyes. In my scent-sight, I could see the pair of women behind us were getting impatient. "You thought he was rude."

"Okay, thank you. Can we get a Torlian coffee, a sausage breakfast muffin, and a raw fish if you have any?"

"Of course, Brock!" Esbeth clacked something away in Torlian to the others working. "You are glad to see Brock."

"Me too."

The food and coffee came up quickly. I thanked Esbeth, and we headed back out into the bright sunny day. The cafe opened onto the outside of the main terminal building as well as the interior to serve people on both sides. I walked over to a nearby bio-crete bench and sat down. Blaine slithered up beside me. I took my muffin from the bag and handed the bag with the fish over to him. He took it and peered inside, his tongue flicking out.

"Great! I love these."

I sipped my coffee. Scalding hot. Perfect. "Glad to hear it."

I would've looked away when he ate the fish but with my scent-sight that wasn't really possible. One of the drawbacks. I see all around me, all the time. Full-field vision. It has advantages, but it also meant I could see him unhinge his jaw and swallow the raw fish whole. I tried not to think about it and bit into my spicy breakfast muffin instead. Hot grease rushed across my tongue. Wonderful.

"Okay. So you came out here with Kelwyn, right?"

Blaine held up his hand. The visible lump in his throat moved a bit further down. "Ah, yes."

"Okay. We're going to go check out his hangar for anything that he might have left behind. I'll also want to talk to the flight controller about any flight plans he filed. And keep an eye out for a big Eyotan with orange and black stripes. He should have my flitter-cycle."

"Sure, okay."

I finished off the muffin and stood up. "Ready?"

"Yesss."

The spaceport is a high-security area. No unauthorized intrusions were allowed into the airspace. Perimeter defenses made sure of that. Only one safe approach and anyone wanting to access the port needed to go through the main terminal security. I declared the weapons I carried as I entered. The Lottier 45 and the gun the cabby used went into a security box and then off to port security for storage. If I decided to book a flight the box would be sent to the appropriate flight. I hated to be without it. Assuming Kelwyn was in orbit that might be my next step if I could narrow down his location.

The terminal itself looked like many other terminals with wide corridors and art from a number of diverse worlds. The Olinda Spaceport handles a great deal of traffic, so the place bustled with travelers. Some human, many not, all Rim species as far as I saw. I kept my Euzebian neck slits tightly closed to damp down the odors as much as possible. The concourse provided a wide range of shopping opportunities, but the only one with blatant advertising was Chatha Toys, one of the few chains on Olinda. He used a variety of archaic — but effective methods — to attract business. I found him disturbing. He always wore a clown suit with baggy yellow pants, a red and white striped shirt with one blue sleeve and one green sleeve. For hair, he had an enormous three-lobed pile of purple curls. The finishing touch? A white smiling humanoid mask with a red nose. But none of it hid the fact that Chatha looked like a deep-space mummified monster. And I knew for a fact that he preyed on emotions. I couldn't wait to get away from the waving holographic version in front of the store. Too creepy.

Past the main shopping area, the terminal divided off into passenger wings and commercial wings. I slowed. "Which way?"

Blaine pointed down the commercial concourse. "That way, I think."

As we went, the concourse became more utilitarian and generic. Bureaucratic in that dry efficiency-driven approach revealed in the sorts of vendors on display. Shipping and transport. Various professional services. Financial institutions including the ever-present Galactic Bank — not that the bank actually had anything to do with the Glittering Throng. These days the word galactic tended to be associated with all sorts of businesses wanting to imply their superiority. Kids even use galactic as a slang word, as in, that was a galactic catch. Annoying, but I've handled a case before from the Galactic Bank, and I was paid well and on time.

A robotic tender glided down the other side of the concourse spraying down the biocrete. A faint blue mist smelling slightly of the ocean rose around the big hemispherical device. Travelers moved aside as the robot passed.

"Please mind your step," the robot said. "The floors may be slippery."

Right. Blaine eventually led me to a berth access hatch. He pointed at the closed doorway. "I think his hanger was through there."

I walked up to the big double doors. Clearly secured. No information about what might be on the other side, if anything. I took a slow sip of my Torlian coffee, savoring the taste as it burned along my nerves while I considered our problem. We needed to get out, to the other side of those doors. But with security being what it was, I wasn't sure I had what might be needed.

Sometimes, the easiest problems are the ones that I don't have to solve myself.

I took out my com and called Captain Brice. He picked up immediately. "Brock? What?"

"I'm at the spaceport standing in front of the doors that lead to a hangar rented by Kelwyn. According to my pal Blaine, this is where he kept a shuttle. Muriel found records indicating that Kelwyn owned a shuttle call Ouroboros."

"Don't touch anything! I'll be there with a warrant in thirty minutes. Park it somewhere. Drink some of that shit you like so much."

I raised my cup. "Doing that already."

Brice killed the connection. I gestured towards some of the seats lined up along the concourse. "We wait."

I took a seat facing the doors next to a biocrete pillar. Blaine slithered up onto the seats and stretched out, taking three of them for himself. He propped himself up on his elbows.

"So you're like a private detective?"

"That's right."

"Why don't you work for the police?"

"I do, sometimes. They hire me as a private consultant. Mostly it's about being your own boss. My partners and I work well together. We decide what cases we take, and we get paid a decent amount for the work. The police have a lot of different roles, they don't get to focus on investigating like we do. They also enforce the laws. That's very different."

Blaine nodded. "Back home the police made up the laws. That's partly why my mother booked the passage with the Cautarians. She wanted to go someplace better. But then she got sick."

"I'm sorry."

Blaine's hood spread out and collapsed. "The Cautarians didn't like me much. They bit me when I didn't do things fast enough. I couldn't wait to get away."

I knew of the Cautarians. Small, about Blaine's size, with short, dense yellowish fur and a mouth full of sharp pin-head sized teeth. Six eyes, if I remember correctly, that let them see a full three-hundred and sixty degrees. Not really bipedal but they tended to sit up to free their hands for work. Pack-mentality and notorious for their short tempers.

"I understand that." I studied the door. I didn't see any signs of weakness. It didn't matter. Once Captain Brice showed up, he'd have a warrant, and the door would open as if by magic.

Blaine sighed.

"What's wrong?"

"Nothing." His tone suggested otherwise.

"Blaine, what is it? Are we on the wrong track?"

"No." Again the hesitation, but then he continued. "It's just, well, Kelwyn helped me. He got me away from the Cautarians. He made me stronger and made sure that they wouldn't recognize me."

"I can see that. Do you have any family we could contact? Let them know you're okay?"

"No. My father was executed when I was a baby for talking out about the government. There's no one left since my mother died." Blaine shook, but his eyes remained dry.

It didn't matter. I could smell the sadness pouring off him like a pale gray mist that smelled of tears. He might not have tear ducts, but he was crying. I sipped my coffee and let him have his moment.

Captain Brice and a whole gaggle of police stormed into the concourse a half-hour later. The Captain's face looked tight and angry. A thin stick-like humanoid alien with limbs that looked like nothing but bones scrambled to stay in front of the Captain. The alien wore a blue tunic and a badge showing it to be a spaceport employee. The only thing animated about the alien was the wide face and large pale eyes. It smelled like lavender, but I couldn't put that in any sort of emotional context. Going on body language I'd say it was scared, but there was no way to really know. Interesting, mainly because I didn't recognize the species. With all the Rim worlds out there that was hardly a surprise.

I stood as Brice got close. Blaine slithered off the chairs and took up position behind me. "Captain, glad you could make it." I tipped my coffee cup at the doors. "No one's gone through the doors since we've been here."

"Good." Brice scowled at the alien and shook a tablet at it. "Go on! You've seen the warrant. Open it up!"

The bony-looking alien looked my way. Nervous? I still couldn't tell. Then it barred rather pointy teeth at me in a look that made me want to reach for my Lottier 45. I wasn't used to being without it. No telling what the alien was doing, maybe it meant for that to be a smile. Prudence paid off. The alien walked with its disjointed gait over to the door. It touched the locking panel and quickly entered a code using both hands. The big doors swung slowly inward.

"Go! Go see! Empty, as I said!" The alien spat the words out. "Left weeks ago!"

I was at the doors as Brice went through — ignored his scowl — and we walked through together with the police officers behind us. Bright sunshine poured down from above. The doors opened into a large round hangar with a roll-back roof currently retracted. But the hangar wasn't empty. Retracted gantries and a large control booth sat against the far wall. Along another wall floated several empty cargo pallet cars. Everything that a trading shuttle needed to ship cargo to or from orbit. The only thing missing was the Ouroboros herself. I didn't smell any chalky biocrete dust. The whole area looked healthy to my scent-sight. One area near the middle looked a bit brighter. An oblong sort of shape, narrower at one end and rounded at the other. Blaine slithered up beside me. The police officers fanned out across the hangar to secure everything.

I headed for the control booth and wasn't surprised at all that the Captain stayed right with me. At least he hadn't kicked me out. Yet. A couple officers accompanied us.

Closer to the middle of the hangar I realized that the difference in the biocrete was because that section was more active. It must be recovering from being shadowed by the Ouroboros.

"The shuttle was here for quite a while before it launched," I said.

Brice glanced at me but didn't slow his pace. "Why do you say that?"

I explained the color difference.

"Fascinating," Brice said. "And what does shit look like to you?"

"Depends on the species."

He shook his head and almost — *almost!* — laughed.

One of the officers with us, a mature woman with a tanned leather face and deep laugh lines around her eyes suddenly stopped. "Captain—"

I smelled it first. An electrical sort of smell in the air, coming from what looked like a sunbeam in the midst of the bright sunny day. A spotlight with the officer right at the center. Her mouth opened and she flared with scents. Black fear shot from her pores and bright red scents of agony crawled across her skin. Her whole body went rigid, and then her head snapped back mouth open. Her scream brought the other officers running. They drew weapons, but they couldn't shoot this. Captain Brice started to reach for her.

"No! Get back! Get under cover!"

Blaine took off across the hangar towards the control deck. A couple of the police listened and headed back towards the terminal, but more continued to come closer. The Captain clenched his fists.

The woman's bent over, and then there was a sound of cloth ripping and a burst of dark blood and blood-stained bone spikes grew out of her back. I pulled off my coat.

"Brice!" I snapped the end of the coat at him. He caught it, and I saw him understand. We ran towards her, the coat held out between us, like a rope so that we didn't enter the beam. The coat hit her and dragged her out of the beam. She collapsed at our feet still crying and sobbing.

The electrical smell grew more intense, stinging my nose. I looked back over my shoulder. The beam was widening. I grabbed the woman's arm and looked at Brice. "It's getting wider, we've got to go!"

Brice nodded. He grabbed her other side, and we hauled her up.

"Clear out!" Brice bellowed as we started to run for the control booth. "Get under cover!"

We carried the officer between us as we ran towards the control booth. Behind me, I could see the beam widening. Officers scattered but one cutting across the hanger ran right into the path of the beam that he couldn't see. He screamed and fell to the ground. Then we had gone far enough that I couldn't pick up any scent of him and he faded away into the fog that obscured everything at a distance. With my eyes, I focused on the control booth and ran.

We made it to the door which slid open

automatically. We carried her inside. There was a couch on one side of the room. We put her on the couch, on her side with the bony spines sticking out. I covered her with my coat, for all the good it did.

"Blaine? Are you here?"

I smelled him before I saw him, that dry snake-like smell. Blaine rose up from beneath the control panels. He slithered out into the aisle. "What happened to her?"

"Kelwyn did this, with his beam. We need to get these windows covered. Help me."

I left Brice with her and went to the windows of the control booth. I couldn't tell where the beam was now, but I could see the other officer down on the ground. He was motionless and had gained extra limbs. The control booth windows had blinds which I started closing. Blaine started at the other end. I didn't know if the blinds would help or not, but it seemed like the best thing I could do quickly.

Captain Brice rose as I came back. Blaine curled up at the far end of the booth and watched us.

"How is she?" I asked.

Brice was breathing heavily. He rubbed

his nose. I understood. She smelled of fish and shit and blood. He took a few steps further away from her. I backed up to give him room. He shook his head.

"I don't know. Hell, look at her back! But she's still breathing. Unconscious. That's something."

I turned and looked at the control boards. "Something here must close that roof. Let's get that done, and we can help your man out there."

The Captain nodded. Together we studied the boards. Brice found the controls. "Here we are. It's labeled on the menus."

He tapped the screen. A graphic of the hanger came up. Brice dragged the roof closed. Outside I heard the sound of machinery as the roof moved into position. The light dimmed. Interior lights came on automatically. I eased past Brice and went to stand over the fallen officer. The bleeding had stopped. I knelt and looked at her back. The skin was growing up around and between the spines. Before long it looked like she'd have a sail along her back. Some species used sails like that for heat regulation or displays. I checked her pulse, fast but steady. Her body was busy with the changes, so that wasn't much of a surprise. She looked brighter than most people with lots of molecules floating off. Her right hand had changed, fingers fusing together into a three-fingered hand with thick nails. Amazing that so much could be changed in that instant of exposure. I went back to Brice.

"She seems stable at the moment. Hard to say what other changes there might be, particularly internal changes, but if I had to guess I'd say she's going to survive."

"Like that? What sort of life is that?"

"Better than none at all."

He shook his head.

"Besides," I added. "With a Moreau pod, it's possible that the changes could be reversed."

"You think she should risk exposure to that sort of thing again?" Brice shook his head. "You're almost as crazy as that snake up there!"

"No, but if she wants to look fully human again that might be her only chance. After enough study to pin down exactly how much has been changed."

Blaine stirred and slid forward. His

tongue flicked rapidly at the air. "Could you change me back? Make me human again?"

What could I say? I told him the truth. "Without the records of what was done, probably not."

"But why, if you could help her?"

"Because her changes aren't that extensive, at least from what I can tell just looking at her. Most of her DNA should be intact. It'd be possible to identify what had been changed and undo those changes. But you? Kelwyn changed everything about you. I'm not sure it would be possible unless we had the Moreau pod used to change you."

Blaine slumped. "Oh."

"If we find Kelwyn maybe we can get the Moreau pod too, and figure out a solution."

Blaine didn't say anything. The Captain's com squawked at him. He pulled it out and spoke. Kelwyn had made another call. My hearing is acute. I could hear Winnie on the other end.

"—demanding that Brock be staked out in the open at the center of the hangar and the roof retracted. If we do, then he says that he'll hold off on killing anyone else for the next six hours. Otherwise, he's going to start

killing people at random every fifteen minutes until Brock is given up or the Galactics
give in and respond to his original demand."

Captain Brice glanced at me and turned
away. "No. We're not bargaining with him.
I'm not giving him anyone. And if he carries
out this threat, we'll take him apart. You hear
that? We'll take him apart!"

I dragged the roof control back open.
From the hangar, I could hear the sound of
the roof retracting.

Brice looked away from his com. Blaine
rose up and slid forward.

"What are you doing, Marsden?"

"If I go out there it saves lives. Buys us
six hours. Sounds like a fair trade to me."

CHAPTER 7

I had never imagined that I'd die someplace beautiful. I didn't lead the sort of life that ended in a bed surrounded by flowers and loved ones. Years ago I had figured out that when I went, it would probably be in some back alley, some normal, unremarkable place that I wouldn't recognize as the place I was going to die until too late. The hangar outside about fit the bill.

"Just—"

"No!" Brice shook the com at me. "No. We're not giving him an inch."

"— scrape me up afterward and get me to my Moreau Pod. Call Muriel. She'll know what to do."

I saw the hesitation in the captain's eyes. "We don't have a lot of time Kynan, trust me. I don't plan to die out there if I can help it. He must be watching the hangar. He's going to see the roof opening. I have to go. Contact Muriel. Tell her what's happened. Subha or the others can help your officer."

I moved to brush past Brice and noticed Blaine coming up behind me. I held out my hand for him to stop. "Stay with the captain. He'll take care of you from now on. Okay?"

"Yesss."

Brice grabbed my arm. "You don't have to do this."

"We both know that's not the case. And hey, if it doesn't work out, at least I tried."

I walked out into the hangar. Ambulance crews had already removed the officer that had fallen at the center of the hangar, but I could see the blood and other fluids still on the biocrete. Given time the biocrete would absorb it all. More nutrients as far as the bio-crete was concerned. Soon the little buggers would get a taste of me as well. Maybe I'd make them sick.

As I walked out, I unbuttoned my shirt. The beam could come down at any moment, but I didn't want to ruin my clothes if I didn't need to. I still hoped I'd come out of this able to wear them again. I was a quarter of the way across the hanger when a big orange and black shape burst through the terminal doors. Police scattered. Dyami ran on all fours out into the hanger.

"Get back!" I shouted. "It isn't safe!"

Dyami didn't hesitate. He kept running towards me. Most of the places I saw him in he just looked big and out of place but here I could see his power. His massive muscles bunched and flowed beneath his bristles. Let the big guy out in the open like this and I could picture a whole pack of Eyotan running through a forest. We met at the center of the hangar, Dyami sliding to a stop, and I didn't believe for a minute that Kelwyn would mind one bit about killing Dyami too.

"You have to go — Kelwyn is going to use his beam. It alters the life-code!" Dyami has never accepted DNA manipulation. It seems to be an instinctual phobia.

He shuddered. "I won't leave."

"You must. Get back. After it's over take my remains to Muriel, okay? She'll get me straightened out."

Dyami's big head hung low. "Much sadness."

I pushed his shoulder. "Go! You have to get out of here before he pulls the trigger!"

Dyami swung away. He moved too slowly. "Go!"

His whole body picked up speed. I smelled something in the air. The beam hit. I saw Dyami was out of the path of the beam, heading back towards the door at full speed. Then pain blossomed in my chest.

I threw the shirt and coat away and bent over holding my chest. Beneath my hand, I felt the tissues there boil and move. The pain grew more intense, and liquid poured out across my fingers. Did the Moreau Pods hurt like this? I didn't know, I'm unconscious in the Pod.

It ripped into me. Tore me apart. I grew. And blacked out.

§

I woke in the Moreau Pod. A golden light filled the pod, and I was the source of that light. It pulsed gently with my breath. I smelled of sweat mostly. Not offensively so, but like I'd woken after sleeping on a hot, humid night. That pretty much described the pods.

They'd done it, actually gotten me back

to my pod and Muriel. She knew about the program that I'd been working on. A safety measure that always seemed lacking in the Moreau Pods. I'd designed what was essentially a backup system. That way if a transformation when wrong it would be easier to roll back your modifications to an earlier scan. But I hadn't had the opportunity to test it yet.

My Euzebian scent-sight still worked fine. I raised my left hand and watched the fine stream of molecules rising from my fingers. Except the last time I looked, I didn't have a hand that was a cluster of scarlet tentacles, each longer and thinner than fingers. That was the hand of the C'lacktal just like we'd seen with Kelwyn's first victim, Montana Haugh. The tentacles curled inward at my thought and then straightened out. I could reach out with just one of them or move several at once. Okay, so obviously the backup program hadn't quite worked as planned. My right hand still looked and felt normal. I hit the release. The lid of the Moreau Pod slid back out of the way, and the light from my body spread out. I finally opened my eyes and blinked against the bright overhead lights. When I could see that over-powered the scent-sight around me.

Muriel stood beside the pod. Her lips pressed tight together and she reached out towards me. "Brock —"

She'd seen my left hand. I pushed myself up. "Don't worry about it. I can deal with that."

I looked at my hand, and the tentacles braided themselves into four fingers and a thumb. It looked a bit weird but not too bad otherwise. I flexed the 'fingers' experimentally. "That'll do for now. I'm not noticing any extra eyes or anything, how does the rest look?"

Muriel wasn't alone. Dyami crowded the back of the workshop. Subha stood on the other side of the pod. Detective Winifred Burke and Sonya stood nearby. Muriel leaned on the edge of the pod.

"Good, Brock. You look good. I don't know why the hand didn't get reverted along with everything else."

"I was a mess, wasn't I?"

"You very nearly died," Subha said. "Dyami grabbed your body and used your flitter-cycle to get here as fast as possible. I think he might have broken a few aviation laws in the process."

"No one is going to press charges," Winnie said.

They all smelled a bit tense and sour. "What's wrong? What's happened?"

"With everything going on Blaine disappeared," Muriel said. "He must have left when they were retrieving you."

"Probably scared out of his wits. He thought I'd protect him and he didn't trust the police." I smiled at Winnie. "No offense."

She shook her head. "I get it. I'm glad you're okay, Brock, we need you on this. I've got to get going, I just wanted to make sure you'd pull through."

As she headed to the door, I swung my legs out of the pod. "If someone could get me my clothes?"

Muriel blushed and picked up neatly folded clothes from beside the pod.

Sonya laughed. "We've all seen it, but I'll get out of your hair. I'm glad you're okay Brock. I'll tell the girls."

She meant her goats, Dancy and Prancy. "Thanks, Sonya."

She left. Subha lingered a moment. "I'm

happy you are doing well, Brock. We should talk about this backup program of yours. When you have time."

"Of course."

She left. Dyami came to the edge of the pod. He shook his big head. "Very bad. I thought you became a Dumpty."

I reached out and thumped his shoulder. "This time all the king's horses and men were able to put me back together again." I lifted my scarlet hand with the braided fingers. The ends of the tentacles twitched. "Mostly, that is. Still, this might be useful."

Muriel shook her head. "We're changing that first chance we get."

"Thank you, Dyami," I said.

He bared enough teeth to make most people faint and then gingerly picked his way out of the workshop. I'd get a bigger place, but that'd mean leaving Sonya and right now I couldn't see doing that.

I slid out and started to dress. Muriel crossed her arms and talked while I dressed.

"Shanley wanted to make it, but he's following up leads. Same with the Captain. We did manage to get a flight plan from the hangar systems. Looks like Kelwyn went up to Hansel."

Hansel. One of Olinda's two moons. The other being Gretel, of course. Hansel was also the major space-based trading outpost for the planet. From there all sorts of ships would be heading out to the hundreds of space stations, asteroid colonies, and other outposts. But Kelwyn's shuttle couldn't go much further than that, so he probably went there for transportation to somewhere else.

"Any word on him from Hansel?"

Muriel shook her head. "They aren't saying anything. The police forces on the moon are too bogged down as it is. They haven't even confirmed if his shuttle remains docked there. We'll have to go up and ask around ourselves."

"We?" I pulled on my coat. My new hand felt tingly like I'd stuck it in an electric outlet or something. The tentacles unbraided themselves, and it felt much better, just like any limb that has fallen asleep. I stuffed the hand in my pocket.

"I'm going with you," Muriel said. "Dyami too. He's out right now getting transportation back to the spaceport."

I could see that they weren't going to listen to any arguments. And it'd be nice to have help. "What about Kelwyn? Has he kept his word about not killing anyone else? How long has it been?"

"It's about one o'clock now. And yes, so far we haven't heard any reports that anyone else has been killed. No word at all from Kelwyn. It seems like he got what he wanted."

"He always did have an issue with me."

"That's because you weren't crazy." Muriel stepped up close. Her stunning gray eyes studied my face. She reached up and ran her fingers through my hair. "You still look the same. Are you okay?"

I lowered my head, and we kissed. I could drown in her kiss, our lips pressed together forever. Except for the mad snake up in orbit somewhere murdering people by mutation. I pulled away.

"I'm good. Let's go."

Dyami had brought the flitter around to the garage. A good move as it let me get in without ever going outside. If Kelwyn was still watching to see if I survived he wouldn't find out just yet. He had to suspect something with Dyami bringing my body here, but I figured he probably felt it was too unlikely that anyone could survive his ray.

I reached into my pocket using my left hand without even thinking. But when I felt the tentacles slide around the smooth tablet casing, I got a sharp chemical taste in my mouth. As soon as I let go the taste faded.

"Swell." I used my other hand to get out the tablet.

"What?" Muriel asked.

"Evidently my new hand has taste buds."

Across the aisle where the front seats had melted down into the floor, Dyami shook himself. "Tasting with fingers? Do not say these things."

"Sorry, big guy." I called Captain Brice. He picked up immediately. "Brice."

"Reports of my death have been exaggerated but let's keep that to ourselves, okay?"

"Sure," Brice said dryly. "How'd you do it so quick?"

"Benefits of spending a lot of time in the pod. I'll explain later if you're interested. Right now we're heading up to Hansel."

"Don't expect much support," Brice said. "The locals like to keep business to themselves. Law enforcement is minimal and costs."

"We'll keep that in mind. If anyone asks about me just say that they tried to save my life and failed."

"Gee, thanks. I couldn't have come up with that on my own. We're going to be busy. The council is talking evacuation."

"That'd be chaos. Your day is going to suck."

Brice laughed. "Right. Why don't you see if you can help out with that?"

He hung up. I put the tablet away. "You heard him. We're on our own after this. Let's get up there, figure out where Kelwyn is and stop him."

"With much anticipation," Dyami's translator said. The whole flitter vibrated with the sound of his voice. For added emphasis, he thumped the floor with two massive hands.

"Don't do that," I said. "You might make us crash."

Dyami's mouth hung open in his version of laughter even though it looked to me like he thought we'd be good to eat. Who knew? Maybe he did?

The flitter brought us into the spaceport

and merged with traffic. I waited until it reached the overhang before calling for it to stop and let us out. Dyami went first, scattering the crowds out in front of the terminal. A pack of a half-dozen toddler-sized aliens hopped away making a noise like sticks breaking with each hop. A wince-causing noise if I ever heard it. I kept my Euzebian scent-sight damped down as much as possible. Everyone still had a faint aura of their natural odors and perfumes, but it didn't become overwhelming. I headed directly for the Torlian cafe. Muriel and Dyami knew better than to try and stop me. I also felt ravenously hungry, a side-effect of coming out of the pod. My metabolism would remain geared up for several days at least. I ordered a couple fish and chips meals to take along with us.

Back into the terminal but this time we headed to ticketing. The agent was a pale green egg-shaped standing on a tripod of dark green legs with lighter rings. The pastel coloration made it a good match for the Olindan ferns in the terminal. Three bony-looking arms midway up and a small cluster of sensory organs around the closed opening at the top. It smelled faintly of wet sand.

"Hi, we need transport to Hansel." I stuffed several fries into my mouth.

Muriel smiled. "And we need to get there as soon as possible."

The opening at the top opened with three fleshy lips. "Nope. Can't do it. Nothing available."

I coughed and sipped hot coffee to try and clear my throat.

"Listen," Muriel said. "It's very important we get up there. We're working with the police to stop the man behind the recent murders."

"Then you'd better talk to them about getting to orbit. Every sentient on the planet decided to leave about two hours ago. There's nothing available."

I managed to clear my throat. "Surely there's some private shuttle that can be booked?"

"Nothing."

"No executive ships?"

"Nope."

"Cargo —"

"Nope. Nothing. 'Fraid not!" The alien sounded so cheerful about it.

I started to say something else when I realized that the woman at the next ticketing booth was having the same conversation. Same at the next. Nothing available. Can't leave.

I tapped the counter. "Thanks. Have a good day."

I walked away. Muriel and Dyami came with me.

"We have to get up there," Muriel said.

"Agreed," Dyami said.

I headed for one of the private booths along the side of the terminal. "Let me make a call. I can think of one way we might get transportation."

Stepping into the booth sealed out all the noise and bustle of the terminal. The field blurred everything outside the booth when it came up and shut out all the noise. Peaceful. I touched the com panel on the wall and entered the contact information.

The screen cleared on a dark warehouse. A large limb moved in front of the screen. I could see a couple other legs tapping away at other screens. Nothing more than that. The

Tretan, owner of Galactic DNA Suppliers. Once the Tretans belonged to the Glittering Throng, but they had been expelled to mingle among the Rim species. I'd heard all sorts of rumors about what had happened. Genocide being the chief reason cited. I had no idea. What I did know was that this Tretan supplied rare and difficult to obtain DNA to Moreaus as well as the associated supplies and equipment. I thought it might help now.

"Marsden." The Tretan's voice sounded like rocks being ground together.

"Are you interested in the technology that Kelwyn is using to commit these murders?" I knew the Tretan would be up on all of the news. It didn't miss anything.

"That information could be of interest. What price do you have in mind?"

"I want to pay off my Neridian debt." My most expensive samples. Neridians went extinct when the humans still fought wars with swords. Wiped out by the Galactics supposedly because the Neridians dominated the Rim worlds. A rare case of interference. Outside of the Galactics, the Neridians were considered perhaps the most intelligent species to develop in the Rim and even then they had been rejected by the Glittering Throng.

"That would be an acceptable trade," the Tretan said.

"I also need expenses covered and transportation for myself and two associates. All standard commercial transport is booked."

"I have a vessel. If you fail, the costs will be substantial."

"Fair enough. We need to get to Hansel first, but there may be other destinations."

"My ship and pilot will be at your disposal. Do not get them destroyed, Marsden." A leg shifted into view. "I am sending you the appropriate authorizations."

My tablet buzzed in my pocket. The transmission ended.

I took the tablet out. Sure enough. Authorization to enter the Tretan's secure hanger as well as a flight plan already filed to Hansel. The Tretan must have had that ready before I called. How had he known? Or had it just been a prudent precaution? I had no idea how many moves ahead of me the Tretan played.

I left the booth. Muriel and Dyami were

waiting right outside. "I've arranged transport. Come on."

§

I didn't know how long I'd have before Kelwyn figured out I was alive but at least no one tried to kill us on the way to the ship. We got there without running into any trouble. I didn't get a whiff of danger from anyone. My touch — with my right hand — let us through the checkpoints to reach the Tretan's hangar. Heavy security.

The hangar itself looked a lot like the one that Kelwyn had used only about four times larger and full nearly to the ceiling with cargo containers. The place was about three-quarters full of them. The rest of it was taken up by the ship. Not a standard shuttle. It looked like two big eggs melted together as it floated a meter off the hangar floor. No visible openings or instruments marred the featureless black skin. It showed no reflections from the lights above. If anything, the ship looked like a void in the air. It was hard to get a good look at something that is featureless, and at least in the visual spectrum appeared to absorb any light that fell on it. It defined itself as an absence rather than a substance.

"Am I the only one confused?" Dyami asked. "Is that a vessel?"

Muriel walked ahead towards the ship. "I've never seen anything like it."

"The Tretans supposedly were part of the Glittering Throng. It makes sense that they might have a few tricks up their sleeves."

She spun around. "The Tretan? That's who you talked to?"

"Yes."

Muriel held up her hands. "We can't do this. We can't use his ship."

"Why not?"

"Why not?" She laughed. She turned to Dyami, but the big guy hung his head in response. She looked back at me. "What could you have offered him?"

I didn't want to tell her about the deal. What other choice did I have? I couldn't hide it from her. I'd probably need her help. "I offered him Kelwyn's technology."

Muriel shook her head. "You can't be serious. Really? You're going to trust him with that technology. The ability to induce mutations at a distance?"

"Yes. Actually, I am. The Tretan has done okay by us so far, hasn't he?"

"I don't know. If the Tretan hadn't brought the Moreau Pods here we wouldn't be in this mess now, would we?"

She had a point. "No, but none of that matters. Kelwyn's in orbit. We've got to get up there to do this. He's got the resources we need. So let's just go stop Kelwyn. Okay?"

I didn't wait for an answer. I walked past her to the ship and spread my arms. "We're here? Pilot?"

A bright white dot appeared on the skin of the ship and rapidly spread out in a starburst pattern. The lights rotated and an opening had formed in the side of the ship. Warm daylight poured out through the gap. Standing right in the gap was a metallic version of the Tretan, crouched on six silvery legs. Bright glowing blue eyes regarded us from the head. To my scent-sight, it smelled like ozone and fried eggs. The head glowed in a way that looked almost organic.

"I am your Pilot. Please, enter."

"It's a robot," Muriel said.

"In actuality, I am a cybernetic mnemonic clone," Pilot said.

"Okay." I looked back at my friends. "Let's get going."

CHAPTER 8

Once upon a time, people used chemical reactions to hurl themselves, in fragile ships, into space. Thanks to the Galactics we've come a long way, but the Tretan's ship made even our current spaceships look like antiques. The Tretan's ship seemed perfectly designed for the three of us. Nice comfortable seating for Muriel and I, and what looked like a long flat log on the other end of the cabin that had Dyami thrumming happily as he stretched out on it. Pilot went forward through a hatch without saying much of anything else. As soon as we entered the ship the hatch to the outside vanished.

"Would you like a view?" Pilot's voice asked.

"Yes, please," Muriel answered.

The front end of the compartment turned transparent. That's what it looked like. Some sort of holographic display made it seem as if the front half of the ship no longer existed. It lacked any glare or other artifacts to suggest a window or a screen. As far as I could tell even with my eyes, the ship was now open to the air. It couldn't fool my scent-sight, though. Thanks to that I could still see, in a way, the wall on the other side of the view. It still made for a compelling display.

"Departing now," Pilot announced.

The cargo containers fell away as the ship rose up, just clearing the partially open roof. As we continued to rise straight up, I saw the roof sliding shut below. Slowly the view rotated. It looked like the ship turned but it could just as well be that the picture turned. I certainly couldn't feel any sensation of movement. People used to use rockets to leave worlds. Now, thanks to the Galactics, we simply float away from a world like seeds in the wind. As far as I know, no one in the Rim worlds really understands how the drives work. Does any sub-atomic particle actually have a fixed location? The guesswork says that the drive somehow modifies the coordinates of all of the sub-atomic particles that make up a ship and its occupants.

Referred to as the Space-Time Coordinate drive — although even that is just a guess — it is manufactured by the Galactics and installed by Galactics, who only work with Rim species they feel have potential. Humans aren't counted in that number.

Regardless the ship rose up from the surface of the planet. I watched Olinda shrink away beneath me until all I could see were clouds and then the curve of the horizon against the black of space. It had been a long time since I had seen this view. Not since I first came to Olinda. It was very different from Seabrook, Mars, or Nosfer. I didn't have any desire to reminisce about the past.

I looked at my companions. Muriel, smart and resourceful. Beautiful. New to the detective agency but clever with all sorts of technology. I still didn't know a lot about her past, but I trusted her to back me up. Dyami. The massive Eyotan could intimidate anyone, but he actually seemed like a very gentle creature. He came to us as an intern, wanting to study investigative methods that he could take back to his people. So far he didn't show any inclination of leaving. Not exactly the most subtle guy but plenty of times I needed a show of force.

"When we get to Hansel our first priority is establishing where Kelwyn is now. We'll talk to anyone that had dealings with him at Hansel. The faster we track him down, the more lives we save."

"He could be on Hansel," Muriel suggested.

"I don't think so. If he were conducting this from Hansel someone would have turned him over already. He's probably got some secret station or outpost out here."

"That could be a problem," Muriel said. "He wouldn't want to file a flight plan to his hideout. He's probably gone off plan to make this happen."

"Supplies," Dyami said. "He might receive supplies."

"Good point. Even if Kelwyn didn't get supplies delivered right to his hideout, he still might be visiting someplace nearby to gain supplies. Any possible contact he has made we'll have to follow up on."

"That's going to mean visiting some other habitats and stations," Muriel said. "Is the

Tretan willing to give us the use of his ship that long?"

I ignored the tension in her voice. "He is."

"Ever wonder why he's so agreeable?"

"Not really, no. He knows that I keep my word. We have a good business relationship."

Muriel shook her head. "He wants that technology. He has some motivation for it, or he wouldn't bother. What if he turns around and uses the weapon himself?"

"Then we'll cross that bridge later. Right we'll catch Kelwyn. Who knows? Maybe we'll get lucky."

It didn't take long until the view rotated and the ship flew along, apparently upside down relative to the planet. All I saw were clouds with a gap now and then. Only the ocean below us as the planet slowly turned. The ship flew right up to Hansel, no need to catch up with the moon until velocities matched. Such a direct approach would have been impossible back in the days of rockets.

Even at this distance, I could see the activity around Hansel. It looked like a cloud of fireflies swarmed around the moon. A small moon, but large enough to have a rounded shape, Hansel and its twin Gretel enjoy a dance in the sky. When both moons rise, it is light enough to read by outside. Colonization has permanently altered the faces of both moons. I could see parallel lines of the mining operations curving around the moon's face. Automated scrapers slowly circled the moon gradually peeling off one layer after another. The raw ore is broken down in fusion torches into the component elements which then could be used in manufacturing. The same process by which smaller asteroids were sometimes ground up entirely. Given enough time that might happen if Hansel had remained unpopulated, but there was a growing movement now to retain more of the moon. Both for the sake of the planet below and for the inhabitants.

One of the cities came into view as a cluster of structures and lights across the dark surface. Wellington. First colony on Hansel and the stated destination on Kelwyn's flight plan. It wouldn't be long before we landed. Then we'd track him down and find out where he went next.

Pilot managed the landing as smooth as anyone could wish. The ship came down in a large hangar. Just like back on the planet only without quite so much stored cargo containers. At last the ship halted.

A door appeared in the viewscreen hologram and Pilot emerged from the forward compartment. "Mr. Marsden, are you planning to disembark?"

"That was the idea."

"Very well. I will await your return here. If you have need of me just call. Your tablet has the necessary contact information."

I touched my pocket. "Thanks, I guess. Stay out of trouble yourself."

"I do not seek out trouble," Pilot said. "I will be quite content to remain so."

Muriel grinned. "Let's go see what we can find."

The door in the side of the ship opened revealing a transparent tube leading down into the surface of the moon. The tunnel made a smooth spiral cut into the actual rock and heat-sealed so that the surface looked like glass. The air smelled of machinery and hot, moist bodies. Even Muriel raised a hand to her nose.

"Ugh, remind me why I wanted to come?"

To my scent-sight, the air looked foggy. Thick with mingled odors and water vapor.

Nothing about it suggested anything immediately harmful, but the air wasn't at all what we were used to down on the surface.

Dyami sneezed like a rock splitting.

"I can go on my own," I offered. "You two can wait here in the ship."

Muriel shook her head.

"No. I must accompany you," Dyami said. He thumped a big fist against the deck of the ship. It hardly made any sound. He peered at the floor suspiciously. Dyami's big head came up. "Smells bad."

"Okay. Let's go. Sooner we find what we need the better."

The tunnel led us down into a short corridor before we reached a security door. I palmed the panel with my still-human hand, and the door opened. That let us into a wide corridor with an arched ceiling. All sorts of pipes and conduits ran along the roof of the corridor while lights ran along the walls just above head-height. The whole place looked dim but was even foggier to my scent-sight. With so much in the air I could smell Muriel and Dyami clearly, but beyond that, the effectiveness dropped off dramatically. None of that stopped me from seeing that someone was coming. I held out an arm.

"We've got a problem."

Muriel had already turned to put her back to mine. "Yep, and I see them coming."

I saw more shapes down the other way moving towards us. Not all human, but they had spread across the corridor to block any chance of escape. Dyami growled, and I felt the sound through the soles of my feet.

"The Tretan," Muriel said. "He set us up!"

Maybe. "Not our immediate problem. Options?"

"Crush them all," Dyami said.

"Simple, but effective. Watch each other's backs." We didn't have time for much more than that. One of the figures ahead of me yelled, and then they charged.

I shook out my arms and found my footing. My altered hand squirmed. Eager? I wasn't sure. The tips of the tentacles glistened. Footfalls echoed in the corridor along with hoof beats. One of the beings charging had hooves instead of feet, and I could make out a long tail. Biped but not exactly humanoid. Then they were close enough to see clearly. Thugs. None of them remarkable.

Three humans ahead of me along with the rather toothy hoofed alien. A glance behind and I counted two more humans and a pair of stout aliens covered in short black fur. They ran on powerful short legs with thick claws. I'd have thought them animals except both wore matching pink outfits and right as they got close stood up on their hind legs to plunge into the fray.

Eight against three. Not the best odds. But two Moreaus and a gigantic fanged Eyotan. Not the worst odds either.

I went for the alien first figuring they wouldn't expect that. A massive wedge-shaped head snapped at me, but I slipped around the bite and gave it a sharp right hook. Its head snapped around after my fingers. It smelled like seaweed. This close in I could see the other three humans circling around me. They smelled of sharp excitement as the adrenaline rush made them brighten to my scent-sight.

The alien's tail swung at me. I jumped back out of reach toward one of the humans. I spun around and grabbed his hand with my left, with the C'lacktal tentacles. I felt the ends bite into his skin and something pushed through the tentacles. The man convulsed and fell to the deck.

That could be useful.

No time to worry about it. Two other humans closing in and the hoofed alien lunged my way with an open mouth.

Muriel held her own against one of the other humans on that side while Dyami enjoyed the attention of the remaining human and the two aliens.

Dyami's punch sent that human sprawling down the tunnel.

I ducked blows from the two humans attacking me. Snatched at one with the C'lacktal hand but he managed to keep out of reach.

Muriel grunted as a blow caught her in the gut. She dropped to one knee. I could smell her bluff. She wasn't hurt nearly as bad as she made it seem.

I couldn't help but grin when she landed an uppercut in the guy's balls.

She followed it up with a sharp blow to his head when he dropped.

A blow hit me on the back. I saw it coming and had braced. I turned around and enjoyed the shocked look on the man's face right before I grabbed his head with the C'lacktal tentacles. He dropped convulsing and foaming at the mouth as he screamed.

It sounded painful.

The alien screeched a high-pitched cry and jumped at me. I dropped and rolled out of the way but kicked out, sweeping its legs as it landed. The alien tumbled and rolled across the tunnel.

Muriel had left her man groaning on the floor and was boxing with my remaining human. I went after the alien. Behind me, Dyami fended off the snarling aliens.

The alien got up and paced warily in front of me. I held out my hands. "Doesn't look like this went too well. Who sent you?"

The alien hissed at me. If it wore a translator the hiss didn't register.

Muriel dropped the last human, but he bounced back up.

Dyami managed to land a kick that sent one of the aliens tumbling. When it got up, it dragged its back leg but still launched itself back at Dyami.

The hoofed alien charged at me. I charged right back at it. I roared as we closed the distance. At the last second, I jumped and did a flying kick at its midsection. The blow hit, and we both crashed to the floor.

It thrashed as I rolled and reached for its leg. I grabbed it with both hands. The C'lacktal tentacles burrowed into its skin. The alien screeched and went into convulsions which threw me off.

Muriel's human dropped to the floor from a round-house kick to the head.

Dyami, roaring, picked up both aliens and smashed them together. He dropped them. One started crawling slowly away.

I got up and looked at Muriel, then Dyami. "You're both uninjured?"

"I'm fine."

Dyami did his big show of teeth.

"Great. Let's see if we can get some answers." I walked over to one of the men lying on the floor groaning lay clutching his balls. I shoved him over and planted a knee on his chest. I held my left hand above his face. The C'lacktal tentacles reached for his face. He struggled to get away. "Who sent you?"

"I don't know!"

"Come on. You were waiting for us. Someone told you we'd be here. Who?" I lowered my hand slightly and glanced over at one of the others that I'd stung. He was still foaming at the mouth. "You know, this is all new to me. Honestly, I'm not sure if these are causing permanent injury or not? It's always so hard to tell with something like this."

His eyes widened as the tentacles danced right above his face.

"Please, no. I don't know. Really!"

I looked at Muriel. "You think one of the other men might be more talkative?"

She shrugged. "Can't hurt to try."

"Okay." I lowered the hand so that the tentacles just touched his skin. As light as a feather. He screamed.

"Wait! Okay!" He sobbed. I lifted my hand slightly. He caught his breath. "Okay. His name is Crombie. Crombie the zombie. Warren Six. He hired us."

I didn't know the name. Crombie the zombie. Sounded charming. "Why? What were you supposed to do?"

The man sobbed. "Please, don't. It's not my fault. I didn't have a choice."

"Hired to do what? Kill us?"

He nodded miserably.

"Okay. Thanks. I appreciate that." I stood up wishing I had my Lottier 45 but as far as I knew it was still back in storage at the spaceport along with the cabby's gun. Hansel security didn't allow firearms anyway, most stations didn't in order to protect vital systems. That worked to our favor with this lot.

Lacking the Lottier 45, I didn't have a lot of other options. I reached down and grabbed his arm with my left hand and stung him. He went into convulsions. I can't say I worried too much about whether they recovered or not.

"Come on. Let's find Crombie. I want to know why he hired these thugs."

"Okay," Muriel said.

We followed the tunnel and up ahead around a bend came on our first checkpoint. I slid my left hand into my pocket. Two human guards, one male, the other female stood on our side of the checkpoint. The woman glanced over at the man nervously.

I stopped in front of them with Dyami and Muriel at my back. "Greetings. We've just arrived from the surface. We'd like to check in."

I could smell the sour tension pouring

off the man, sharper and more acidic than the woman. It looked lime green to my scent-sight. His sweat caught the light and made him glisten. Obviously, these two find up-standing guards had accepted bribes to let the thugs through and keep everyone else out. Nice to know. I smiled.

"Is there a problem?"

"No," the woman snapped. "Let me see your identification."

I pulled mine out of a pocket with my right hand and handed it over. She scanned it, handed it back and motioned to the scan arch. "Do you have any weapons? Metal objects or hazardous chemicals?"

I shook my head and stepped forward. The arch pulsed green.

"Clear," said the other guard. "Welcome to Hansel. We hope you enjoy your stay."

Muriel went next. No problems. Then Dyami.

"Only the translator," Dyami said.

"That's fine," the woman said. "Go through."

Dyami barely fit in the arch. It still glowed green.

"Clear. Welcome to Hansel —"

We'd already walked away. One more short tunnel and we entered the first large chamber we'd seen since arriving. A massive cavern beneath the surface. Buildings filled most of the cavern like so many crystal growths. Some rose from the floor to the ceiling above, but others came out of the walls and connected to vertical buildings or to the other walls. The whole place hummed with activity like being in a beehive. Lots of pedestrian traffic from all sorts of species. I recognized many including a group of three Nosferans flying by overhead. I wondered if they saw me and recognized me. If they did, they didn't stop their flight. My scent-sight wasn't able to extend very far here either. Too much stuff trapped in this closed air system. I closed my sense of smell down as much as possible and went ahead anyway.

Just beyond the opening of the tunnel was a large holographic map display showing the inside of Hansel. I remembered much of the layout. From this central hub, eight primary lines radiated outwards to eight new hubs. From there additional lines would radiate out and eventually link up in an ever-expanding web until the entire moon was surrounded in a habitable layer. At that point, the long-range planners intended to work deeper into the moon making layer after layer. Population estimates suggested that the moon could ultimately house a billion sentients.

I pointed to the map. "According to our friend Crombie is in Warren six. We can catch the train there and start asking around. I doubt he'll be that hard to find."

"Maybe we should ask around here first, get more information about him before we just plunge in," Muriel said.

"Dyami?"

Dyami thrummed. "Go now. Tired of waiting."

"I agree. Let's get on with it."

Muriel shook her head. "One of these days that impulsiveness is going to land you in trouble. Oh, wait, like that hasn't ever happened?"

I slipped an arm around her waist. "Maybe once or twice. But we're still here."

Dyami led the way through the crowds. It's like having an ice-breaker. He cleared out everything and made the walk much easier. The air in the place was starting to give me a headache. It can't be healthy. The sooner we got out of Hansel, the better.

The train turned out to be nothing more than maglev platforms with railings. Thanks to Dyami we had one car almost to ourselves. Two human girls, teenagers in feathered tops with black leather pants, stood leaning against the far rail as if chained there. Both of them looked at us and looked away, bored. I guess we just aren't all that interesting. The car beeped, the rails pulsed with yellow light and then the car accelerated smoothly down the line. The rails switched to a red light as the car moved.

Riding through the tunnel to Warren Six gave me a few minutes to rest. The bad thing about my scent-sight? Even when I close my eyes, I can still see. That was the only good thing about the air in Hansel. When I closed my eyes most of the world disappeared into a fog. I could make out Muriel and Dyami and to a lesser extent the two girls standing at the far rail but not much else. I'd mostly gotten used to always seeing things, but it'd be nice if I could turn that sense off entirely.

"What did you do to those men back

there?" Muriel asked quietly, leaning against my right arm.

I took my left hand out of my pocket. The C'lacktal tentacles squirmed about. I concentrated, and they braided themselves into five clumsy fingers and a thumb. I flexed the 'fingers.'

"As far as I remember the C'lacktal use their tentacles to stun their prey. But they're also excellent manipulators. Kelwyn must have a DNA sample that he has used in his weapon."

"They didn't look stunned."

"I know. I didn't research this. I don't know what the effects of C'lacktal venom are on humans or any other species. Maybe their prey animals have a tolerance for the toxin."

"We need to find out."

"I'd like to figure out why this change didn't get reverted along with the rest. The backup program should have restored me to my last scan."

"I saved all the logs. But the changes were extensive. Maybe it was too much to unravel."

"It was that bad?"

Muriel nodded against my shoulder.

When she spoke, her voice was very soft. "You were unrecognizable. We almost couldn't fit you in the pod, there were so many appendages and mutations."

I felt her shudder and hugged her close. "You did good. You saved me. If I'm going to be stuck with this hand for a while, that's a small price to pay."

The train entered Warren Six. The light was dimmer. The buildings looked more worn than the main hub. Graffiti, visible damage to structures and black-leaved plants grew over many of the structures. The atmosphere here smelled more like a swamp but was oddly cleaner than the hub. Fewer pedestrians out walking around and those that were waiting to board the train looked tired and subdued.

"Different crowd," I remarked as we got down.

"Talking about a different crowd." Muriel nodded her head at an approaching group.

Police. Black uniforms with silver stripes. A tall woman led the group. At least twelve centimeters taller than me and powerfully built with short-cropped blond hair. Three other officers with her all in heavier assault armor carrying glue rifles. Two humanoid, human or not I couldn't tell through the armor and helmets. The third looked like a heavily armored centipede, and it held four glue rifles all on its own. A Grenalian. Not a species I'd like to tackle with even without the armor and weapons.

The police officers stopped at a safe distance from us. All of the rifles snapped up and aimed at us. The woman smiled.

"Brock Marsden. Muriel Reinhard. Dyami of Eyota. I am placing you all under arrest for attempted murder, murder, and aggravated assault. Your rights are hereby suspended pending trial. You will be fined for life-support costs during the duration of this investigation as well as all associated legal costs."

"Rights suspended?" Dyami asked. "Means what?"

I kept my C'lacktal hand in my pocket and patted Dyami's shoulder with my other hand. Avoiding the stiff bristles. "Don't worry about it. I'll handle this."

"Officer, if you'll check with Captain Kynan Brice on Olinda he'll confirm that we're working to stop the terrorist currently holding the planet hostage. The beings that we fought ambushed us in the tunnel after we left our ship."

She pressed her hands together. "Perhaps I didn't make myself clear. I don't care about your defense. That's not my problem. The only thing I need to worry about is bringing you in according to the arrest warrant. It's up to the lawyers and judges to determine whether or not your story is true."

Muriel spoke up. "Who issued that warrant? What if it is the same person that sent those men to kill us?"

"Still not my issue. I want you all on the floor now. Cooperate, and this will be a much easier experience for you."

"Right." I glanced at Muriel and Dyami. "I guess that we don't have any choice, then, do we?"

Not when the lives of so many on the planet were still at risk. But this was going to complicate things a great deal.

I'm fast. Faster than a normal human. Enhanced reflexes. I didn't expect the police to be too much trouble for us even if I hated fighting them. I usually gave cops their space. The only one in the group I expected to be a problem was the Grenalian and even that I thought we could handle. I went for the woman first.

Big mistake.

I didn't think she would even have a chance to react. Not only that but she slipped away and jumped over my head. I tracked her movement and spun around to catch her with a kick, but she had already turned to the side, and my kick missed. She caught my leg and held it.

"Oh. Shit."

She hung on to my leg and swung me up into the air as if I weighed nothing. She brought me down hard onto the ground. I heard the glue rifles firing and saw Muriel dive forward in a somersault to avoid being hit.

The officer still had my leg. She twisted and spun me over. I braced myself and kicked back with my other leg. She released me, and my kick hit nothing but air. But her kick hit my ribs with bone-cracking force.

"You shouldn't resist," she said.

I rolled away and came up in a crouch facing her. "Can't help it. Planet at stake and all."

"Not my problem." She snarled and leaped forward at me.

I growled and launched myself at her as well. Her first blow caught my shoulder and felt like Dyami had punched me. I managed to catch her in the side. She grunted and came back at me hard. I deflected what blows I could. Took those I couldn't and sought my own openings.

Muriel had one of the officers down and fired the glue rifle at the other. Dyami had a panel evidently ripped from a wall and was using it as a shield against the armored Grenalian.

A right hook to my jaw staggered me and reminded me to pay attention. I managed to deflect the next blow. I was pissed now. I knocked aside a swing and got in two solid blows to her gut. She grinned at me and came on. I blocked and then got my chance. I grabbed onto her arm with the C'lacktal hand. I felt the tips dig in and that push as the venom injected. She hit me in the face. Once. Twice.

I staggered away. Stumbled and nearly went down. I tasted blood in my mouth, and more blood trickled into my eye. She rubbed at the red marks on her hand and came on.

I shook it off and came up. Tried to block her blows but each hit with bruising force. I couldn't keep it up. Muriel spun around and fell with a glue web spreading across her arms. She cried out.

The Grenalian tore the panel from Dyami's grasp and threw it away. The two of them crashed together, wrestling for control. Dyami might have more mass, but the Grenalian had dozens of limbs and was nearly as big.

I ran at the officer. Lunged for her. She danced away, and for a second we were back to back. But I can see behind me. I bent and kicked back as hard as I could. The blow caught her between the shoulder blades. She stumbled forward and dropped to her knees. I continued down into a roll and grabbed an abandoned glue rifle. I didn't bother turning, just brought it around my left side and fired right at her back. The glue web struck and immediately spread around her back to immobilize her arms. She crashed forward onto her face. I brought the gun around and shot two more rounds at the other officer sending him staggering back until the glue web immobilized him and sent him crashing to the deck.

I stood up and shot the woman again to make sure she couldn't pull free. Then I aimed for the Grenalian. "Throw him!"

Dyami roared, which I felt in the roots of my teeth, and shoved the Grenalian up and away. Three shots and the Grenalian lay anchored to the floor by the glue web. I dropped the rifle and went over to the nearest officer. I found the solvent spray and quickly cleared Muriel. She got up wincing.

"Are you okay?"

She nodded. "I'll be fine."

I ached too, but I went over to the woman still struggling against the glue web holding her fast to the floor. I crouched down. She looked up at me glaring with green eyes.

"Who sent you?" I asked. "You're not exactly police are you?"

"It doesn't matter! The local police will be here soon enough."

"And you can explain to them why you are impersonating their officers. You're not exactly human, are you?"

"Neither are you," she said.

I nodded and stood. "True enough." I waved to the others. "Let's get out of here."

The fight had drawn a few curious onlookers but now that it was over everyone scattered away from us. Muriel slid her arm around my waist as we walked. "So what's the plan?"

"We look for Crombie. Either he sent the fake cops or Kelwyn did. And Crombie is probably working for Kelwyn. We just need to find out where Kelwyn went from here."

Muriel stepped away and looked at Dyami. "Dyami? Do you think you could head back to the central hub? Maybe talk to workers there, see if any of them loaded supplies for the Ouroboros?"

Dyami's big head bobbed. "I can do that."

"Watch your back," I warned. "There could be others out there looking for us. And you don't exactly blend in."

"I will try." Dyami turned away and loped off towards a nearby tram station.

Muriel and I continued on together looking for Crombie the Zombie.

CHAPTER 9

My stomach growled, and I eyed a noodle place up on the right. I looked down at Muriel. "You hungry at all? We haven't exactly had a chance to eat much today."

She looked at me and smiled. A heart-stopping smile. I remembered when I first saw her, covered in the acolyte robes that Subha had them wear. At the time I couldn't see much but her gray eyes that drew me in, and later when we actually got together, I realized how lovely she really was. Not exotic like Calanthe or Subha. Muriel might be a Moreau, but her changes had been internal. Strength and lung capacity mostly. She still passed as human, unlike some of us. Right at that moment, I wished we were just on vacation together taking in the sights instead of trying to track down a crazed Moreau.

"We have to eat," I added as we reached the noodle place. "We might not get another chance."

She laughed. "Fine. Let's eat."

I reached out and pulled the door open. I didn't even think about that I was using my C'lacktal hand until Muriel walked past and glanced down at the tentacles holding the door. I followed her in.

Rich hot spicy smells drifted through the air in multi-colored currents of light. I sniffed one golden stream, and my stomach growled. I passed through another more orange that smelled hot enough to make my eyes water. The place itself was a standard prefab room with metal walls, metal tables, and metal chairs. The one resource Hansel had plenty of in its crust. The place looked clean. Only two other customers, both humans, were in the front part of the place. One sat at the long bar at the back. The other at a table for two along one side.

Muriel and I walked through the tables to the counter. A long-whiskered walrus-looking fellow came up to the counter. He tossed a stained once-white dish towel over a shoulder. "What can I get for you?"

"I'd like the curried rice noodle stir-fry," I said.

Muriel studied the menu displayed on the counter surface. She dragged up a dish with an unpronounceable name, some sort of alien seafood pudding. "I'll have this."

"Right up. Take a seat, I'll bring it out. Drinks?"

"Do you have Torlian coffee?" I asked.

"I'll send the boy over a couple blocks for one if you like?"

I nodded. "Thanks."

"Water," Muriel said.

The man beamed. "Right away."

After he left Muriel leaned forward with her elbows on the table and her head in her hands. "I'm so tired."

"Tell me about it." I stretched my arms up and felt the bruises from the fights. Too many fights. "We can rest tomorrow. By then it should be over one way or the other."

Muriel shook her head. "It won't be over until we get Kelwyn."

"We'll get him."

The gentleman who took our order was back at the counter. "Just a sec."

I walked up and dropped onto one of the

empty stools. The other man eating, young with dark hair, glanced over at me then back at his soup. He smelled as tired as I felt. The walrus-looking fellow behind the counter beamed at me.

"Your coffee will be right over. The boy is fast. Is there something else I can get for you?"

"Information?"

His mustache drooped. "It isn't a good business to be in around here. Noodles are much better. Much safer."

"I just need directions. Any places we should avoid while we're here?"

He pursed his lips and leaned on the counter. "The tourism board wouldn't like me saying it, but the area around the Warren Seven junction is perhaps not too safe. Otherwise, enjoy everything that Hansel has to offer!"

I rapped my knuckles — or attempted to, but my tentacles just squirmed across the surface of the counter. I pulled my hand back and stuffed it in my pocket. "Thanks."

As I returned to the table, Muriel raised her eyebrow. "What was that about?"

"I think I know where we might find Crombie."

"How'd you manage that?"

I shrugged. "Just depends on how you ask folks."

The 'boy' came in with my coffee. Hardly looked like a boy, standing nearly as tall as me. Six limbs, he walked on four, covered in short brown fur with a bright scarlet sort of cloth wrapped around and between the rear set of legs like a diaper. A matching scarlet ribbon encircled his head, neck and then split and wrapped down around his arms until ending in gloves. His hands had five fingers and a long thumb. His face was the only hairless part of him and looked rather ape-like in structure but his head extended back in a long melon shape. The walrus-looking man gestured at our table. The boy stopped and bowed as he extended the Torlian coffee cup.

I took it. "Thank you very much."

I offered him a gratuity which disappeared into his folded diaper-like cloth before he scurried on into the back. A minute later he returned with Muriel's water and our food. The smells rose from my plate and Muriel's bowl in a multicolored vortex.

"Will there be anything else?"

I shook my head. "Smells wonderful."

"Thank you," Muriel said.

He disappeared again into the back. We both dug into our food with gusto. The rice noodles were perfect. Hot, spicy and tender without being soggy. The stir-fried vegetables tasted wonderful. Hansel obviously didn't have any problem getting quality supplies. We ate in silence, enjoying the chance to rest for a few minutes and enjoy our food. All too soon it was gone.

I accessed the bill from the table screen and paid. I stood up. "Ready?"

Muriel groaned but stood up. "Let's go. I hope this Crombie guy isn't hard to find. I'm getting grumpy."

We left the noodle place, and I led the way towards Warren Seven. I noticed less pedestrian traffic and more closed up shops. People tended to avoid our gaze when we did approach anyone.

"These people are scared of something," Muriel said.

I noticed something different in the perpetual haze. A dark redness and a smell not unlike blood. I couldn't pin down any particular source. It seemed to penetrate everywhere. I recognized the scent. Burn. I touched Muriel's arm and studied the doorways around us.

"There's burn in the air."

She stiffened beneath my hand. Most drugs are legal on Olinda so long as the user isn't hurting anyone else. Saves a lot on law enforcement. Burn is one of the exceptions. In humans, it accelerates metabolic activity, increases aggression, suppresses pain receptors and even provides increased regenerative capabilities. Side-effects, aside from the aggression are thirst, red eyes from bleeding, and a tendency to spontaneously combust when exposed to sunlight. Burrowed in beneath the surface of Hansel this could provide the ideal environment to manufacture burn.

I studied the traces. "I don't think there's enough here to cause any lasting harm, just traces saturating the air."

"Great. If my eyes start turning red, you let me know, okay?"

"Will do."

We went on into the neighborhood around the junction. Finally, I saw our first barrier. A crude gate cutting off the corridor ahead. A couple of humans in environment suits, without helmets, stood outside it with metal bars in their hands, sharpened and pounded flat at one end. Primitive spears and space suits. Great.

I kept my hands out of sight in my pockets. Let them worry about what I might be concealing. I stopped a good three meters back from them and studied them both. Older men, both with short-cropped graying hair. Their eyes were red just like Muriel worried about. No doubt they were jacked up on burn. They must be habitual users to be facing us with such apparent calm.

"We're here to see Crombie," I said. "We're not looking for trouble, just a few questions answered."

The one on my left bared his teeth and then looked at Muriel with a look more like a man faced with a good meal than a beautiful woman. At least a normal man. The other one shook his head.

"You've left a trail of bodies," he said in a raspy voice. He paused and took a sip from the neck collar of his suit. "Crombie doesn't want your questions."

Muriel smiled warmly at them. "What if we promise to be nice?"

"We don't."

People stepped out of the buildings around us, doors opening and they all smelled like Burn, and to my scent-sight, they all looked like they were already on fire. Bright, with streamers of reddish haze flying off them to join the haze filling the air. That's why the whole place was so saturated. It came from the users. And a bonfire had just surrounded us. More than a dozen armed burn users. No matter how good we are, they'd tear us apart.

"At least Dyami isn't here." I reached out and touched the small of Muriel's back. "Run!"

She looked up at me. Our eyes met, and I could have drowned in that gray expanse. It was like being out on a calm ocean that went on forever. In my scent-sight, the human torches charged. Distantly I heard them yelling at us, but it didn't matter. I wanted to be with her forever. Lost in the depths of her. Feel her breath against my skin.

I tore myself away from her. My own shout rang out in answer. I spun and charged towards the only possible way out. The two burn users in front of the gate. I ran at them as fast as I inhumanly could move. Muriel ran after me but not nearly as fast. The gap between us widened, and it hurt. It was the only way she was going to get out of here.

The two burners reacted quickly. Their spears pointed at me. No stopping. I closed the distance. I twisted as their spears thrust at me. I grabbed one of the shafts as I turned. The other grazed my side leaving a line of fire. I meant to wrench the spear from the burner's grasp, but he hung on. The burn gave him the strength to match mine. He snarled at me and lunged forward to bite. The other burner was turning, a torch in my scent-sight towards the cooler shape rushing towards us. Muriel. I wrenched the burner around, throwing him into the other's path even as I held onto the spear.

I locked eyes with Muriel. "Jump."

I gave the burners a shove and turned, cupping my hands. I saw everything. Muriel's lips tighten. The bright sparks of tears form-ing in her eyes. The mass of burners right behind her. In my scent-sight, the other two untangling and turning their spears in my direction. And several more coming out of the buildings around us. Beyond the gate, the way still looked clear. It might not be any better, but it was a chance at life. The chance I could give her.

Muriel took it. She kept running. Her foot planted in my hands and I rose, yelling, and hurled her high into the air. She cleared the gate and landed neatly on the other side. She took off as quick as she could. Who knew? Maybe she'd get help in time.

The first spear hit my arm. I twisted away from the main thrust, but it still cut through my coat and the arm beneath. The second went through my shirt and cut along my back.

I lunged through the gap between the two burners, knocking them aside. I shed the coat. Blood seeped from the cuts. The other burners reached us. I was in a corner between the building on one side, the gate on the other and a mob around me.

I wasn't going to make it easy. I grabbed the closest one's face with my C'lacktal hand and injected him full of venom. He screamed and dropped to the ground. And then a thin blue fire swept over him from head to toe.

He screamed and screamed and convulsed on the ground as he spontaneous combusted.

Interesting. I raised my scarlet hand of tentacles in front of me. "Come on, then. Who's next?"

A woman with long dark hair screeched and charged. Not alone. Several others came at me as well. They jumped across the burning body. The ones with spears thrust the deadly points at me.

I avoided the spears and grabbed one. This time I slid my C'lacktal hand down the shaft to the burner's hand and stung him. He jerked away releasing the spear. He clenched his teeth and screamed before he fell and blue flame spread from his hand up his arm.

I used the spear to block the next spear thrust. Kicked the woman in the gut. Took a blow that knocked me back against the wall.

Hands tore at my shirt. A burner on the ground grabbed my leg and tried to bite me. I hit him in the head with the shaft of the spear. It knocked him back for a moment but more grabbed at me. Blows hit me.

I thrust the spear into the chest of another woman. Her red eyes bulged, and she coughed blood out in my face. I twisted around and kicked her off at the others. For a second a space cleared.

Barely blocked another spear thrust. Dodged the next.

Then they closed, and the punches rained down on me. Burners grabbed at my legs.

Hands wrestled for control of the spear. I stung one, but even as that burner fell away, others took his place.

My feet were pulled out from under me. I fell to the ground. A kick caught my side, and I heard the snap of a rib. The pain flared up. I flailed the spear at my attackers and left a long bloody gash in a thigh. Moved my head just in time to avoid a boot heel.

I felt calm.

I couldn't win this fight. Too out-numbered. But I wasn't going to give up and just take it either.

I roared and rolled into the mass of burners. I thrust the spear up into the groin of the other spear-wielding burner. I grabbed the face of another that tried to bite my throat at the same moment. Both fell.

I caught the spear from the burner, wrapping my tentacles firmly around the shaft and I swept both sharp ends around me. Cutting. Hitting burners.

And they fell back slightly.

Enough for me to get up on my feet. I hurt in multiple places, but nearly a half-dozen burners lay on the ground dead or dying.

No time to gloat. The calm remained. I spun and cut two throats with the spears. Burners dropped gasping and holding their throats as blood spurted through their fingers.

I kicked one over onto one of the burning bodies. And thrust the spear into the chest of the other. A slit throat might regenerate but not a spear in the heart. I wrenched it free along with a torrent of blood.

Burners came back at me trying to get the spears away. Driving me back towards the gate. I fended them off. Blocking blows and cracking limbs with the spears. They kept up the assault. If they got the spears, I'd be done.

I thrust a spear into the chest of a tall burner with short buzz-cut hair. I left it there for a second and stung another nearby burner. I spun, driving the other spear into yet another even as I wrenched the second spear out of the chest of buzz-cut.

Three more down.

Two petite burners with long hair and narrow red eyes jumped on me before I could block them. The clung to me, and one bit my already cut shoulder. They chomped onto my chest.

More grabbed the spears. I let go of the spears.

I used my legs to drive back at the gate at the same time I reached up and stung the burner clinging to my chest. Her mouth came off me as she screamed. I crashed into the gate with the burner on my back taking the brunt of the impact.

The one on my chest burst into flames, but she wouldn't let go. The flames seared my chest and neck. Burners lunged at me with the spears. I twisted around, and the spears pierced the burner on my back. I stuck my human hand into the flames and shoved the other free. She fell away convulsing and burning.

I staggered and caught my balance. Bodies littered the corridor. The stench of burning flesh filled the air. Only five burners left. Two held the spears.

I laughed and spread my hands. "Come on, then. Let's finish this."

They roared and charged. So predictable. With their hyped up aggression they couldn't do anything else.

I ran right at them. At the last moment, I jumped. Gravity on Hansel is less than standard. I rose up and flipped over, landing behind the spear bearers right in the midst of the group. I grabbed the necks of the two with the spears and brought their heads crashing together even as I stung the one in my left hand. I dropped them as the flames spread across the one I stung and plucked their spears from their hands as easily as a diving bat snatched fish from the water.

I could see the others charging behind me. I roared, flipped the spears and thrust them behind me spearing two through the chest. I let go of the spears and spun around, reaching out for the last burner.

I grabbed his face and stung him. He dropped to his knees before I released him. I yanked my tentacles away as he burned.

The flames spread quickly and jumped to the others.

I staggered. Fell to my knees and sank back on my heels. My head dropped. My arms felt like lead. Each breath hurt my broken rib. I didn't know if I could ever move again.

Until I thought of Muriel.

That brought my head up. She'd gone over the gate. I crawled up onto my hands and knees and shakily stood. Blood trickled down beneath and over my shirt making the fabric cling to my skin. I walked over to one of the impaled burners and yanked the spear free. Flaming bits dripped from the end.

All around me nothing but death and thick, sticky smoke. What had I become that I could do this?

I grabbed my coat and gingerly put it on before I left the scene. I broke the lock on the gate with the spear and walked with it at my side. Now and then I leaned on it until my head stopped spinning.

Crombie couldn't be far.

I felt better when I saw the double-doors on the building just ahead. That looked like just the sort of place where someone like

Crombie might be hiding. Ordinarily, I'd expect to see some guards out front, but I had a feeling that most of his guards were still smoking behind me.

The doors refused to open when I reached them. Locked. The panel on the wall didn't respond. Fine. I forced the spear between the doors and pushed. For several seconds the doors held then something snapped, and they slid open. I walked inside.

One the first things I noticed as I entered was how much cleaner the air was in the building than out. The doors slid shut behind me, and I breathed in deeply. Cleaned and filtered air. It kept out all the filth outside. I felt like a blindfold had been lifted. I could see all around me clearly again. Rich navy blue carpet covered the floor. A reception desk with a polished stone top curved in front of me. Everything had been done in dark colors, blues, and blacks, with bluish-white lighting softly glowing from panels overhead. A hologram came to life at the reception desk. She looked human enough. Blond, with waves of hair falling around her shoulder. She smiled at me with deep ruby lips.

"Greetings. How may I help you today?"

No mention of my torn and bloody body and clothes. That was nice. "I'm looking for Crombie."

"Mr. Crombie isn't seeing anyone right now. If you'd like to leave a message?"

I couldn't help but laugh. "No thanks. I'll just go see him anyway."

"Sir, I'm really sorry, but Mr. Crombie isn't seeing anyone right now."

"Oh? You mean he's not seeing anyone right now?"

The hologram's smile widened. She nodded happily. "Yes, sir. That's right."

"Okay." I leaned on the counter and gave her my best smile. "I guess I'll have to come back or make an appointment. Maybe you can help me with something?"

"If I'm able I would be happy to help."

"I can't seem to remember. When Mr. Crombie does see people, which floor is that on?"

"Mr. Crombie's offices are on the sixth floor."

I pushed off the desk and tipped my bloodied spear to her. "Thanks a bunch."

And I walked past the desk and on into

the building lobby. I headed towards the elevators which were clearly signed. The floors were polished rock. Cut right into Hansel. Actually very nice-looking.

"Sir, you can't go up there!"

I didn't listen. I walked past the elevators to the stairs and opened that door. Many of these holographic receptionist types have control over automatic building systems like elevators. I didn't want to get in one and get trapped. I climbed the stairs, glad that I was doing this on Hansel. As tired as I was I needed the lower gravity.

At the sixth floor, the door opened, and I walked out into a corridor with no lights. Not that it mattered to my scent-sight. I could still see my surroundings fine. Obviously, Crombie knew I was coming, but he didn't have all the information about me. Too bad for him. The corridor led back towards the front of the building. I walked past the elevators and into another open reception area. A hologram identical to the one below stood at the reception desk, the only source of illumination. She glowed with her own inner light.

"Sir, you really must leave at once. Police

services have been notified. If you do not leave, they will arrest you."

"I doubt that's true, but thanks for the warning. I'll just look around a bit."

"Sir, please, you can't do that!"

I walked away from the desk. There were some rooms around the reception area but I could see a larger space further down the corridor. I went that way. I opened up my neck slits and breathed deeply. Ghosts of people moved through the corridors. Burners, mostly. Given how faded they were I'd say most of the ones I saw had already run out of here to go confront me. The front half of the building had an open layout and that's where I found Crombie.

I'd been wondering why he hadn't left. Now I knew. The man hung suspended from the ceiling. Alive, if you want to call it that. A medical suit covered his entire body. He hung in the center of the room with a square of light panels still dimly illuminating him as I walked in. Tubes ran to and from his suit into an array of equipment around him. I recognized the setup. It was a full immersion rig. With that gear, Crombie could spend all of his time in sensies. A normal sensie rig is a non-invasive band worn on the head that activated the centers of the brain responsible for dreaming, using the brain's own power to create entirely real, full-sensory environments.

But this was much more than that. Crombie need never disconnect. The immersion rig would maintain his physical health while letting him live entirely in his own dream-addled reality. No wonder they referred to him as the zombie.

"Crombie, we really need to chat."

"Mr. Marsden." His voice came from all around, hidden speakers, rather than the body I saw hanging in front of me. "I really need someone like you working for me. All my lovely children slaughtered and here you stand. What are you?"

"Just a private detective."

"Ah, such modesty. You're much more than that. Look at what you did!"

The corridor where I fought the burners reappeared around me. A hologram, but a good one, at least for the visually inclined. I could see every detail of their blackened skulls and the blood congealing on the ground. But the smell was lacking. None of the remembered crisp, smoky smell of burnt meat. To my scent-sight none of it existed which made the whole scene look very unreal. Funny, I'd obviously adapted to smelling everything. No matter how convincing the hologram it wouldn't fool me.

"It didn't have to be like that. You could have just answered my questions."

"I wasn't paid to answer your questions, Mr. Marsden. I was paid to see you killed."

I was surprised that he so readily admitted that, what else would he tell me? "Why is Kelwyn so determined to see me dead?"

"I suppose there's no point in making useless denials, but as for his motivations, that's not something he shared with me. We're not confidants or lovers. I'm only an independent contractor. He paid for a job done and for once I'm surprised to find that I've failed in my task."

"Too bad. Where is he?"

"I don't know, Mr. Marsden."

I walked towards Crombie, ignoring the hologram. "I doubt someone like you took a job without knowing more about who hired you than that."

"Ordinarily you'd be right, but he did pay a substantial sum."

I tapped the spear on one of the medical units monitoring Crombie's body. "Maybe you need a dose of reality, Crombie? That might wake you up to your situation."

He laughed nervously. "Mr. Marsden. Really? You think I'm like this because I choose to be? Because I'm so addicted to sensie pleasures that I can't stand to be unplugged? I'm afraid not. A construction accident many years ago left me deaf, blind and paralyzed. Entirely cut off from the world. Fortunately, doctors could tell that my brain remained active. Sensie technology provided me with a way to communicate and preserve my life. This immersion suit sustains that life. Shut it down, and I die. Worse, for you, I can't communicate without it. So if you simply want to kill me — go ahead!"

I didn't have time to figure out if he was telling the truth or not. I couldn't get a good sense of him through the suit. I looked at the displays. I could see displays monitoring his vitals, but those would be there in any case. Nothing that told me one way or the other if he was telling the truth.

"Mr. Marsden? What are you going to do?"

I looked up at that faceless suit. I couldn't kill a helpless man. Not like this. And it didn't sound like I had any leverage to use against him. "Nothing. You're right. Threats don't mean anything. I've had enough killing today. But Kelwyn, he's threatening an entire planet. That's an entire market he's going to sweep away for his agenda. Are you ready to see that happen?"

He chuckled. "Ah, that does get to the heart of it, doesn't it? And truthfully, you're right. Killing everyone on the planet hardly helps a businessman like myself. But sometimes I have to accept my losses. This whole business has cost me a great deal. Perhaps it is time to relocate. Yes, I think that might be best. You can take that as a free tip."

"Relocate? To where?"

"That's up to you. I'll give you something else Mr. Marsden. Kelwyn, he did pay a substantial sum. And you're right. I normally look carefully at my business partners. What I found suggested that Kelwyn didn't come by that sum on his own. He had help. There are things with this that I don't dare touch."

Interesting. Kelwyn had talked about someone who was going to help him become what he dreamed of being, the powerful snake-man. And that had happened. Who was backing him?

"Okay, Crombie. I think relocating sounds great. It'd be best if I don't hear of you being back in Olindan space again."

"I'm sure," Crombie said dryly. "Are we finished, Mr. Marsden? There's a great deal of work to be done."

"We're finished." I threw the spear down on the floor. "I'll show myself out."

CHAPTER 10

Crombie the zombie hung in his immersion suit surrounded by the hologram of the burners I had killed, and he laughed. A dry, coughing laugh, as if I had said something amusing. I hesitated, knowing I shouldn't care, but I asked anyway.

"What's so funny?"

"You are, Mr. Marsden. You left a trail of bodies on your way here. I doubt that the Hansel authorities are going to let you walk away."

"We'll see." I left him hanging there and headed back towards the stairs with his laughter dogging my heels.

Trouble was, Crombie was right. After everyone that Crombie sent to stop us ended up either dead, glued to the floor, or poisoned, the local police probably figured I was a bigger threat. And ordinarily I might stick around and at least attempt an explanation, but it is hard to build a self-defense case. Worse, it takes time. Time I didn't have if I was going to stop Kelwyn. I still didn't know where Kelwyn went next. Only vague confirmation that he had powerful backers. It made me think that Kelwyn was nothing more than a front man. But why have a frontman demand admittance to the Glittering Throng?

I reached the stairs and started down. And heard voices below. Cop voices. I knew cops. Knew how they sounded. I pressed up against the wall. Crombie. That's why he laughed. Not just the thought of my capture, but he must have known they had already arrived. The receptionist hologram did warn me that they had been called. I hadn't worried too much figuring that Crombie wouldn't want to risk exposure. If he really did have the police called that meant he had an escape plan for himself.

I ran back up the stairs, but when I reached the door for the sixth floor, it wouldn't open. Locked tight with no visible locking mechanism. Nothing I could do about the door. Lights flashed up the stairwell. I needed to move on up when all I wanted to do was take a long nap and nurse my wounds. Or better yet, have Muriel nurse my wounds. That wouldn't happen in lock-up.

Three more flights of stairs up and every door I tried was locked. The structures in Hansel didn't need a roof. From what I'd seen they connected one level to the next. The only level above this was the surface. This building might not even have access at the top. I could climb up all the way to the top and still find myself trapped. But going down would only lead me right into the police. I spread out my new tentacles. Somehow I didn't think poisoning the police would help my case.

More flights. Eighteen in all before the stairs ended in a square room with one secured door. And one other thing. An air vent. It might be a tight fit — if I got the cover off. Now I wished I had kept that spear. It was high on the wall above my head too. The cover didn't look particularly strong. Then horizontal slats across the opening tilted to direct air downwards. The breeze blew past me, clean and cool. That explained why the air in this building was so much better than the air out in the main Warren. The air must be filtered by the circulation system. I went to the railing and looked down.

Far below lights flickered from flashlights as the cops conducted their search. Probably moving floor-by-floor to flush me out. I looked back at the vent cover. I might as well give it a shot.

Two quick strides and I jumped up and grabbed the slats. Several bent beneath my weight. I hung on and planted my feet on the wall. Then I did a lifting motion, using my legs just like I've been told. Several things happened. Metal screamed and tore. The cover flew back over my head when it came free, and I lost my grip on it. And I fell to the floor flat on my back. My rib screamed at me. I winced from the sound of the vent cover bouncing from one side to the other on its way down to the cops.

I groaned and got up. Excited shouts rose up the shaft behind me, and I heard the sound of rapid footsteps on the stairs. I jumped up, grabbed the open vent and pulled myself up inside. Except it didn't work. I didn't fit. No matter how I twisted I couldn't get my shoulders in, and I could hear the cops coming up the stairs. I growled and dropped down. Scratch that plan.

I couldn't let the cops arrest me. Too much was at stake. Even assuming I ended up judged as acting in my own self-defense it wouldn't happen in the next twelve hours which was about all we had left according to Kelwyn's demands.

Only one option left. One I really hated. I climbed up on the stairwell railing, and I jumped towards the flight below. My coat flapped around me. I landed lightly on my feet, turned and jumped down to the next. Turn and jump down again. Three flights down, only twenty-one to go!

Eight flights down the police saw me. I heard swearing from several and lights flashed up the stairwell. Time for more drastic steps.

"Stop right —"

I jumped. This time I altered my angle slightly so that I skipped the next level and instead fell to the one below. I landed much harder. Lower gravity or not, I have the same mass on Hansel. Cops grabbed for me, but I turned and jumped before they could grab me. Misjudged the jump. Two steep an angle this time.

One flight. Two. Not good.

Hit the third flight hard enough to knock my wind out, but it also put me past the police. I heard shouts and yells above me. No time, I turned around and jumped down two more flights just as glue webs smacked the spot I'd been standing on. I landed better and even managed to take a breath. I swung my legs over the railing and ran down the stairs. At the bottom lobby, I stopped and walked out as casually as I could manage. I kept my hands at my side with the C'lacktal tentacles braided into fingers. I smelled the nervous scent of the police before I ever opened the door. I heard shouts and rapid footsteps above from the cops coming back down. I licked my lips and tasted blood, whose I didn't know. I opened my neck slits and inhaled deeply as I walked out into the lobby to face the cops waiting.

I saw them all. The officers taking cover behind the holographic receptionist's desk. The others in two lines in front of the doors, three crouching and three standing above them with weapons ready. Not glue guns. Evidently, they had authorization for deadly force.

"Freeze!" The cry rang out from a silver-haired woman standing at the center of the armed row. A detective or captain, given her plain clothes. A cybernetic eye put a bright red laser dot on the center of my chest. She had other enhancements, not immediately visible but I smelled the sharp nickel taste of them. The eye, cochlear implants to enhance hearing, and the left side of her face looked younger than the right. Some sort of accident.

I stumbled and dropped to a knee. I reached out. "Please, you've got to help me. He's crazy!"

Confusion, always a good weapon. Cops exchanged glances, but the cyborg captain didn't flinch.

"Hands on your head. Now. Don't resist."

"I need help! He attacked me, sent those monsters after me. I need medical attention."

She still held the weapon trained on me. "You'll get treatment after you are processed."

She nodded to one of the men. He holstered his gun and pulled out cuffs. He walked around the line but stayed to my side so that he didn't get in the line of fire.

Well-trained. He hesitated when I didn't put my hands on my head.

"Hands on your head!" She barked the command.

I lifted them slowly towards my head. "It's Crombie you want! Not me. I'm working for the Olindan police, call Captain Kynan Brice."

"After we process you we will consider all options. You must comply first!"

My hands approached my head, and the officer walked closer. I had to try one more time to convince her. I didn't like the way this might go otherwise. "You must know about the threat to Olinda? I'm here tracking the man that made that threat. He came through Hansel. He hired Crombie to try and kill me."

"Obviously he didn't pay enough. I've got over twenty dead or injured sentients today!"

"I didn't have a choice."

She shook her head. "I don't believe that."

"I still don't have a choice." The officer grabbed my C'lacktal arm to slap on the cuff. I unbraided the tentacles which bent back and bit into his hand. I rose, pulling him around in front of me at the same time, bending his arm up behind his back. The cuffs clattered to the floor.

"Release him!" The Captain barked.

"I can't do that. Move your men back. Let me go."

She shook her head. "That's not happening."

"It is unless you want more bodies on the ground and millions dead on Olinda. You have to let me go, Captain."

She held firm. "Release him. Someone else can stop Kelwyn."

I wish that were true. I couldn't take the chance. I moved fast, knocking the officer to his knees as I released him. He caught himself as I'd anticipated and I used his back to jump off over the officers in my way. I heard one of them swear. I landed and ran out the doors. I turned immediately and ran away from the opening. I dodged down the next corridor and focused on my breath.

The thick air closed in around me. My scent-sight became almost useless. I heard pursuit behind me and kept going. I needed to find Muriel and Dyami and get back to the ship. I pulled out my comm as I ran and slipped it onto my ear.

"Conference Muriel and Dyami."

The comm buzzed.

"Brock?" Muriel came on sounding concerned.

"Hello?" Dyami asked.

I looked ahead and saw a tram cruising towards the main hub. I picked up speed and sprinted after the cars. "Get back to the ship. We've got trouble with the local authorities."

"It looks like Kelwyn headed on from here to Gretel."

"Gretel? Are you sure?" It didn't make any sense. "What's for him on Gretel?"

"He took many supplies," Dyami said. "The Ouroboros was loaded to capacity."

I reached the cars as I heard shouts behind me. I ran faster, ignoring the pain from my wounds. People on the car moved back to the other side. I jumped and caught the railing. My left foot slipped off the side, and I almost fell. My foot banged against the ground, and that didn't feel very good. I managed to pull myself back up and I swung over the railing onto the car as it whizzed along towards the main hub.

The cops would be waiting. I tried to

catch my breath. I'd have to get off early. That wouldn't be much fun.

"I'll see you there," I told Muriel and Dyami.

My companions on the car included two human women and an alien, male, I thought. The three of them looked like they were together. The alien was a big guy, several centimeters taller than me with a chest as big as a couple men, with enough arms for a couple men too. Thick, stocky legs and a long tail that curled around the railing behind it. The head was long and flat shaped with two widely-spaced eyes. He wore a black and white suit that looked suspiciously like a tuxedo redesigned for his physique. Must just be a coincidence.

"Sorry to drop in," I said to everyone. "I can't be late for my flight."

One of the women curled her lip in a look of disgust. "You're dripping on the car."

She was right. Blood had dripped down onto the floor. I couldn't decide which of the several cuts it came from. I seemed to have a lot of blood on me. Much of it wasn't mine.

"Yeah, can't help it."

The alien shrank back as if fearing contamination.

I leaned against the railing. I'd already used up most of my rest time. It only took a few minutes for the maglev to reach the central hub. The tunnel walls blurred past me. Even more so to my scent-sight. The alien smelled oddly of roses. The humans were a whole mix of scents including fear. Of me. The wind blew most of that away.

Now that I wasn't moving every part of my body started to speak up and cry out in pain. Even the tentacles ached, but then I had been using them a lot. Useful as they'd been I still thought I might want to trade back up for actual fingers at some point. I ran the tips together, one end against the other. They felt slick and slipped smoothly against one another. It felt pretty good. I stopped when I realized that it was having an effect elsewhere. I hadn't known that the C'lacktal's tentacles could also be an erogenous zone.

My time was up. I could see the end of the corridor coming up. I needed to be off the train before it came to a stop, but not so far back that they could stop me from getting to the ship. I trusted Muriel and

Dyami to get there on their own and just hoped I could make it before the police cut it off. I hoped that they hadn't identified which ship we used yet.

The maglev slid smoothly into the main hub, and I pushed off the railing. I took two quick strides across the car to the other side. The humans all shrank away from me like I had a contagious disease or something. The alien blinked at me with his big yellow eyes and didn't budge from his position. I guess he didn't worry that I'd mess up his suit.

I jumped the railing and landed in a roll. Well, I meant to. I really sort of hit the ground and tumbled much less gracefully than I'd imagined. I thanked Hansel for the lower gravity and peeled myself up off the ground. Time to run again.

I ignored the thick air as best I could, but I looked forward to being on the ship. Give me a planet any day of the week, or at least a decent atmosphere recycling system. Hansel seriously needed a retrofit.

It looked like it would be easy to get out without running into the police again. I walked along between the buildings trying to look as inconspicuous as I could being raggedy and bloody around the edges. But I do think that some of the good citizens called in their concerns to the police because I hadn't even made it halfway to the docking tunnel before I heard rapid footsteps coming towards me.

Why couldn't they just let me leave? I called Muriel again.

"Where are you?"

"We're on the ship."

Thank the Galactics. I thought I might actually get out of this only a little less intact.

"Great. Get started on departure. I'm going to need an evac."

"We can't disengage. Hansel Space Authority has locked down the ship."

"Don't tell me Pilot can't get you out of that? I doubt the Tretan would ever allow a colony to seize the ship."

I turned into the nearest building. It was full of Pluffs. Dozens of them scattered about on cushions with sensie bands around their rather seal-like heads. Their long arms waved about as they did whatever Pluffs did.

"Don't get up," I muttered as I wove my way around them. I went to the nearest elevator and slipped inside as the door opened. I studied the panel.

Muriel came back on. "Pilot agrees, under protest. What are you doing Brock?"

I found what I wanted. "Evacuating. Leave dock. Look for an escape pod."

"Another refrigerator?" I heard her sigh.

"Only when you're around to pull me out," I said. It's a long story about how we met. Really met, for the first time.

The elevator rose swiftly to the floor I had selected about mid-way up the building. Centrally located to give all the poor Pluffs the equal opportunity to stuff themselves into an escape pod if a catastrophe ever struck.

As soon as the doors opened, I ran out and went to the nearest hatch. It opened automatically when I pulled the lever set about my knee height. I reached inside and pulled myself up in. Cramped but I got my legs inside before the door slid shut. A white light pulse one slow pulse. Then another. And another. Faster. Some sort of countdown. No controls that I could see. There had to be some sort of communications or piloting controls, but all I saw was a smooth egg-shaped chamber that pulsed with light. The air must circulate right through the material of the seat. I could at least breathe easier than out in the main hub. The light stopped flashing and stayed on.

Had I launched? A stabilization field would kill all sense of motion. Without any external access, how could I tell what was going on?

Well, either I had launched, or I was just hiding in an escape pod waiting for the police to come and open the hatch.

CHAPTER 11

Nothing about the egg-shape escape pod chamber suggested any sort of compartment or hatch or controls. I couldn't even see a release to let me back out of the escape pod. I didn't know if I had launched or if I was still just sitting in the Pluff building waiting for the police to come and drag me out. The flashing lights suggested that some sort of countdown had taken place.

I pressed on the pod surface around me. Nothing changed. It continued to glow with the same white light. Air circulated through the seat beneath me. I could see the molecules from my own body, the bright fountains from my bleeding wounds, the slow leakage from the burns, and just my normal body odor being drawn off into the seat while fresh air came up around the outer edges. It created currents that swirled all the red and yellows and blacks around in interesting patterns.

Sometimes I really hated seeing what I smelled.

If the escape pod was moving, I couldn't tell. Who designed an escape pod to have no outside connection—

Pluffs. Damn Pluffs!

The whole damn Pluff species used sensies for everything. Actually quite intelligent, even charming people, but you couldn't get a Pluff to move unless it involved sex, eating or in rare cases, saving their own thick hide. It must have made perfect sense to the Pluffs to push all of the controls off into an immersion interface. After all, who would get into one of their escape pods without a sensie band?

Only me, clearly.

I resisted the urge to hit the pod. I didn't want to damage anything. I took a deep breath instead. Let it out and took another.

It'd be fine. I had told Muriel that I would be launching in an escape pod. Pilot would track the pod, and they'd pick me up. Then we could get on to Gretel and figure out where Kelwyn went next. And hopefully, stop him before he used his warped Moreau technology to commit murder on a massive scale.

If I could only straighten out my legs, I might actually be able to get comfortable in the pod and catch a little rest.

I couldn't stop yawning. I tried turning on my side and found a position that didn't press on too many wounds. I wish I had access to the controls if I had really launched I could have turned off the stabilization field and just gone weightless. That would have been nice.

Even so, I managed to doze off.

I woke up when the light in the escape pod flashed twice and turned off. If it'd been anyone but me, they would have been sitting in darkness. Well, any species that saw in the visible light spectrum. As it was, with my scent-sight, I could still see clearly.

The hatch opened.

I swung my relieved legs out of the pod. Police or Muriel, it didn't matter, at that point, I just wanted out.

I ducked and slid out pretty much coming to a sitting position in front of the pod. First thing I noticed was the smell. Lots of methane and a grassy sort of odor. And it came from the sentient standing a meter or so in front of me. A tall sort with shaggy black fur with a white strip down his front. Skinny legs and two skinny long, multiple-jointed arms. The face was long and pointed with big flexible looking lips. Two ears stuck straight up from the top of his head. I didn't see any clothes, but he did hold a tablet.

And he wasn't alone. Four others, variations in coloration ranging from black and white to tan and white, to a mixture of all three, stood around me on a deck covered in a blue grill. A rank odor billowed up from beneath the grill, and I heard a sound of water and machinery.

The fellow in front of me tapped on his tablet and turned to the others. They spoke to one another. The language sounded like they were having a cross between a sneezing fit and a yodeling contest. I don't know what they decided, but the one holding the tablet turned his muzzle back to me. There was more of the sneezing and yodeling.

"What are you doing?" the tablet asked with a sort of breathless, off-world accent.

"What am I doing?" I started to get up.

The other sentients started sneezing and yodeling all at once. Their fur fluffed out like someone had plugged them into a live current. I held out my human-looking hand and sank back down to the deck.

"No problem. I can stay here. Thanks for getting me out of the pod there."

The tablet did some of its own sneezing and yodeling, which was new to me. I don't think I've ever heard a tablet do either. The fellow holding it replied with his own assortment of noises.

"Why were you in the escape pod?"

That made a whole lot more sense. "I missed my ship. I thought I could catch up with them if I ejected in the pod. They were supposed to pick me up."

The whole group started talking at once in their own peculiar language. It didn't stop until the tablet holder let out three sharp yips then everyone fell silent, but several fellows' hair still stood on end.

The tablet translated the next barrage. "A ship approached the pod. We claimed salvage rights. They lost the dispute."

I leaned forward and looked up at the sentient who suddenly didn't look all that cute no matter how furry he was. "Lost the dispute? What do you mean?"

"We destroyed them," the tablet translated.

My vision narrowed. I came off the desk and went for his throat with the C'lacktal tentacles. I wanted to see him convulsing at my feet. I wanted to tear apart the entire ship.

I got a kick to the head instead that sent me skidding across the floor. I tried to rise, and everything got all fuzzy. Then I went elsewhere.

§

When I woke the first thing I noticed was a splitting headache like my skull had just been depressurized. My eyes didn't seem to be able to focus either. That didn't seem good. By smell alone, I could pick up some sort of vegetation, but it had a sweet smell to it like sugar. I closed my eyes and just looked with my scent-sight, and that worked a lot better.

I was in a room about three meters on each side with dried plant stalks and leaves covering the floor. The vegetation gave off a faint brown mist of molecules, but slow. Each time I crushed one as I moved it released a bright cloud and the sweet smell intensified. I heard a water burbling, and through the plant stalks, I could see indigo streamers rising up from below. I brushed aside the plants and was rewarded by a sour fount of indigo coming up from the water beneath a grill floor like that I'd seen when I came out of the pod. It stunk like a sewer, and I'd begun to get the idea that it was exactly what it smelled like. From the look of things, this species designed their ship so that they could void themselves where and when they felt like it.

It probably made sense for a grazing species.

I closed down my Euzebian neck slits to damp down how much of the stuff I had to smell. I got enough anyway to see the room around me. Watching the streamers rise up I discovered vents in the ceiling to circulate the air. Bad design as far as I was concerned. I'd have been happier if the air system pulled the air down and across the water below so that any odors were drawn away.

Obviously, they liked the smell of their own sewage.

I opened my eyes again, and this time I could see a bit better. I reached up to rub them and nearly stuck myself in the eye with my tentacles. I switched to my regular hand and managed to rub a bit of the gunk out of my eyes. That helped. I blinked a bit, and that helped more.

My eyes burned a little. Something in the air but I could see again. The light came from a single round ball on the ceiling above. Bluer than Olinda's sunlight. The stalks and leaves on the floor looked greenish, but I think under the light I'm used to they would have been more yellow.

There was what looked like some sort of door in one of the walls, but it was divided into four sections. Some sort of accordion door that folded away instead of swinging or sliding?

I got up and felt a bit dizzy and sick to my stomach. I leaned on my knees for a minute and tried to catch my breath. I think the only part of my body that didn't hurt was my left earlobe. The rest of me? I could go to bed and sleep for a week.

Destroyed.

I wasn't going to think about what the

damned furry shit-breather's tablet said. It could have been a translation problem. Substituted destroyed for disabled. I didn't know, and until I actually had evidence to the contrary, I was going to believe that Muriel and Dyami were fine.

Besides, the Tretan had been part of the Glittering Throng at one time. Somehow I found it hard to believe that these guys could have destroyed a Galactic-level spacecraft.

When it didn't feel like I was going to pass out, I managed to walk over to the door. No visible handles or panels. Just three lines dividing the door into four sections. The space was hair-thin, no way I could get any kind of grip on anything there. I pushed on the door. It didn't budge.

I braced my feet and put my least wounded shoulder to the door and pushed again. Nothing even wiggled. I might as well be trying to push over an entire building. I wasn't going to be opening that door anytime soon.

Which left what?

The air vents were too high and nothing more than hands-high vents around the top of the room. Nothing there. I kicked aside a bit of the plant stalks on the floor and recoiled as a cloud of indigo stench floated free. The floor was made of a hexagonal grid with each opening a couple fingers wide. Underneath it looked like an uninterrupted pool of gently burbling sewage. All kinds of stuff floating around down there, I could tell what and didn't really want to see it any closer.

All the same that much water and solid matter suggested larger openings. Maybe even a way out.

I didn't want to even think about it. Even if I could find a way down there, swimming through that? Getting it in my various wounds? If I didn't pass out, I'd probably end up dying from infections.

My only other option was to wait. Sooner or later one of my captors would come to open the door. They had to feed me after all.

I could wait a little while. It'd give me time to see if there was even a way to get down there or not.

I spent the next several minutes sweeping aside the vegetation with my foot so that I could see the floor and at first the search looked pointless. As far as I could tell the whole floor was just one big sheet of metal. At least until I reached the back wall in my sweep and discovered a thick stalk squashed between the bottom of the wall and the floor. I reached down and tugged on it. Stuck. I let go and leaned against the wall.

The vegetation could only have gotten stuck like that if the wall came down on it or the floor lifted it up against the wall. Either way, it could mean a way out for me if I could figure out a way to start the process.

I started another sweep. All around the floor for anything that might be a trigger. I found three more stalks squashed between the walls and floor but nothing else. I couldn't see anything that indicated the walls raised. With the vents and all that seemed unlikely. It seemed more likely that the floor had been lowered. Maybe right down into the sewage below. Maybe they used the sewage to wash away the unused vegetation.

Probably one section at a time. Drop the floor and wash everything clean. Then raise the floor back up. Every now and then some stalks would get stuck in the grate and end up pinched between the grate and the wall.

I pounded on the door. "Hey! What the hell? Let me out of here!"

Translate that into sneezes and yodels. I didn't see any sign that anyone noticed.

More yelling and hitting the door failed to produce results. I gave up and went back to checking the floor. If there was a mechanism to trigger the floor to drop I didn't find one.

At least they hadn't jettisoned me without the escape pod yet.

Finally, I couldn't keep my eyes open. I slumped down against the wall, did my best to ignore the smell and went to sleep with my arms up on my knees, cradling my head.

§

When I woke, I didn't move. I heard something. A different sound, like a sneeze, and woke. I didn't need to lift my head to see. My scent-sight worked just fine on this ship. I could see the room the aliens had locked me in, with the vegetation lying thick on the hexagonal grate floor. In my vision, the whole place glowed with molecules moving and drifting about. Somehow I made sense of it all, of the sweet greenish odor of the vegetation and the rotting indigo of the sewage burbling and flowing beneath the floor. Even my own sweat and blood smell made it easier for me to see.

Into all of this the walls, dark to my scent-sight since they gave off little odor, parted in one section. Panels folded up accordion-style, and a new grassy smell flowed ahead of the sentient that pranced into the room. The hard three-toed foot crushed the vegetation underneath as he entered. I say he when I couldn't actually tell the gender of the species. He had a musky male smell to him, but that could simply be my own interpretation of what I smelled rather than a reality.

I raised my head slowly and opened my eyes. The sentient snorted and sneezed explosively. That's what it looked and sounded like to me, but I figured it was probably some sort of expletive and, "I didn't know you were awake."

"Sorry about that," I said softly. "I didn't mean to startle you."

This one didn't match the coloring of any of those that I'd seen when I first came aboard. Most of its wavy fur was an orange-brown color, except for a thin white streak down the front, and I don't think he was as tall as some of the others. He held a bag that bulged with something yeasty. My stomach grumbled. I couldn't even remember the last time I ate. He tossed the bag towards me. It landed beside my feet.

I leaned forward and picked up the bag with my tentacles. That brought another sneeze and a little bit of a yodeling sound.

"Yeah, it surprised me too when I woke up with it." Inside the bag were a half-dozen rolls with stuff baked inside. They smelled great. "This looks very good."

He reached down and parted his fur which revealed a thin bare line of skin. The coloration matched his fur colors. I really, really hoped I wasn't about to get some sort of sexual proposition.

But no, he parted the skin revealing some sort of pouch. He reached in and surprised me by pulling out one of the tablets that the other one had used when I arrived. I guess if you have your own built-in pouch you don't really need clothes or belts or anything. He repeated the noises.

"Why is your hand like that?" The tablet asked.

I had been about to take a bite of one of the rolls, but I hesitated. "The sentient threatening Olinda did that to me. I was lucky. Most have died, their DNA gets scrambled."

Another loud sneeze that the tablet didn't translate. Some sort of filter on the thing? Protecting me from naughty words? He made a bunch of noises.

"And you are trying to stop this sentient?"

"That's right." I bit the bread and chewed. Good, except for the stringy parts. I pulled one out. It looked like a piece of the fibrous stalks on the floor. Sweet. "It doesn't look like that's going to happen."

More noises translated by the tablet. "Will not someone else stop him?"

"I doubt it. The only ones that might be able to stop him were on the ship that tried to retrieve my pod. Was it destroyed, did that translate right?"

"I am lesser but I saw the threat vessel vanish after our ship-kick."

I felt a surge of hope. Vanish might not mean destroyed. Maybe Pilot did something. Who knew with a Galactic ship? They could have moved into another dimension or slipped off into another time. Maybe they just went invisible and were even now trailing the ship trying to decide how and when to strike.

He moved as if to leave. I lifted my tentacles. "Wait. Where is this ship going? What will happen to me?"

"We go to the next moon to sell salvage. You may purchase passage there." Then he tucked the tablet away. I guessed that meant he didn't want to talk anymore and he headed out the door.

For a half-second, I considered jumping him. Get out of this room at least, maybe find a way off the ship.

The last time I tried anything one of them knocked me out with a kick to the head. I'm fast, and I'm strong, but that doesn't make me the fastest or strongest. Sometimes waiting makes more sense. He did say they were going to the next moon. Gretel. Kelwyn evidently went there with supplies. Supplies for his weapon? Who knew. But it sounded like I might be able to leave once we got there. In the meantime, I just had to tolerate the smell of the place.

CHAPTER 12

On Hansel species dug in and created warrens. Gretel being more of a rubble pile necessitated a different sort of construction. The herd leader — that's what they called the guy in charge — had me brought to their equivalent of a bridge for the approach. I was fascinated to see the bridge. It looked like a lot of the ship, with the same hexagonal grid floor and open sewage system underneath. All of the ship control panels were at a standing height. I don't know that these guys ever really sat down. Four big screens divided the walls into four views around the ship with plenty of overlays displaying all sorts of information.

Right then one of the sentients standing at a forward control let loose and rounded shit berries poured out of her ass and rattled down through the grate into the sewage system. No one commented on it. In my scent-sight yellowish molecules drifted out from her rear beneath the cute fluffy tail they all had.

Gretel stood out ahead of us, the two forward arches catching the sunlight like a bright necklace. The project was stalled and had been stalled for the past decade. Originally the builders had planned to convert Gretel into a giant ring-shaped habitat using the materials of the moon itself for construction. Like many ambitious projects, it had faced challenges. The materials of the moon didn't fulfill as much of the needs of the project as projected. That led to cost overruns when additional materials had to be mined from asteroids. Plus many of the sentients on Olinda had objected to the moon's destruction. The Preserve Gretel campaign had raised many roadblocks that still had courts tied up.

So what was left were two arcs, called North and South, sharing an orbit around the moon. Gretel didn't have nearly the population of Hansel. It did have manufacturing and refining facilities that had been built to process the moon below. Rather than let those go unused, the builders put them to work processing material from other mining concerns. It allowed the station to function. Barely.

The herd leader parted his fur to reach into his pouch and pulled out a tablet. I couldn't help but wonder about that. Did they raise their young in those pouches, like Terran marsupials? Or did it serve some other purpose, besides storing tablets?

The tablet translated the mess of sneezes and yodels from the herd leader. "Gretel. You may purchase passage off this ship here."

"Purchase passage? I'm not sure I understand the translation?"

"This herd has sheltered you, fed you, and carried you with us on our migration."

"Oh, you want me to ransom myself after you destroyed my ship?" I still hoped that Pilot had gotten them out of there. As stealthy as the Tretan ship had appeared I wanted to believe that these aliens couldn't have destroyed it.

"We seek only an equitable exchange."

"Fine. Fine. Dock and I'll set it up." A thought occurred to me. If I couldn't make contact with Muriel, then I still needed a ship. "After we conclude that transaction, what are your plans?"

"We migrate outwards, trading from one settlement to the next for the benefit of the herd."

And shoot any ships that get in your way. "Great. I hope that goes well for you."

I didn't plan on sticking around on this ship if I could help it, but if not? Well, I might just have to see if a deal could be reached.

I walked around to the front of the bridge and watched Gretel grow larger before my eyes. It had the whole unreality that all screens have now. Take away the smell of a place, and it just doesn't seem as real. Especially being around this grassy, methane-farting bunch. Not that they were all bad.

"Which one are we docking with?"

I heard the tablet behind me translate. It must be keyed to pick up and automatically translate other languages.

"North."

"How long until docking?" I could see a lot more details now.

Before the arc had looked like one solid band of light but now I could see that the whole thing wasn't even one solid piece itself. Like Gretel down below, the arcs looked at a distance like a bundle of wires bound together. Of course, each of those wires must be tens of meters across and contain all sorts of things from living quarters to refineries. And they weren't smooth like wires either. Hatches and windows and sensors bristled out from the sides. The outer rim sprouted all sorts of spacecraft like a bunch of leeches sucking on a giant fish. All sorts of different shapes and configurations. So many that it was overwhelming. The screens highlighted other ships on inbound and outbound trajectories from Gretel.

"We are waiting for a berth," the tablet translated.

"Is it normally this busy?"

"The herd has identified much traffic from the surface of Olinda. There is much unrest."

"I'll bet." My sacrifice was supposed to buy six hours. That time was up. Kelwyn would be killing again, and the numbers of people struck would be increasing.

I needed to get down there and find out where Kelwyn had gone. The stations might have records, flight plans, or there might be people I could talk to that would have information. Too bad I couldn't make it happen any faster.

§

An hour later we docked with the North habitat. As soon as the herd connected the ship to the habitat systems, I borrowed one of their tablets and paid the ransom. Two of the furry guys escorted me out of an airlock onto the station itself. With a final sneeze, they left me standing with nothing but my blood-stained clothes in the docking ring. No tablet around to translate.

"See you later, then." I stuffed my left hand into my coat pocket and walked down the ring, which was nothing but a rounded somewhat flexible corridor that smelled medicinally sterile. I loved it, after the air that I'd been breathing lately.

At the end of the corridor a hatchway and customs inspectors. Both human men, dressed in black uniforms with a scattering of glitter. Both young, both with close-cropped hair and a single white strip running down the front of their uniform. On their chests a double-arc symbol, no doubt of Gretel. Really the only thing that distinguished them was the one on my left smelled faintly of pineapple. When I got close, they both had identical practiced smiles.

"Please present your hand for genetic identification," said the one on my right. Nothing was said about how I looked.

I held out my right hand.

He held out a small pad. "Just press your thumb here, it will be painless."

I did as instructed. The pad felt like sticky sandpaper. No doubt the mechanism obtained a sufficient DNA sample. The customs agent slid it into the console beside him. After a moment the screen filled with information including a large blue box at the top. He stiffened and looked over at me.

"Ambassador! My apologies, we didn't expect someone, of well, someone like you from this ship."

I didn't let the surprise show on my face. Ambassador, huh? I hadn't thought about that small wrinkle.

"It isn't a problem. I obviously need to get cleaned up, is there a place?"

"Yes, sir. North Gretel is a full-featured destination. Our embassy suites, tube thirty-two, section ten, should have everything you require."

"That sounds good. Thank you. I guess I'll just go then?"

"Let me call transportation for you, Ambassador. No need for you to take public transportation."

Ordinarily, I'd turn down the offer. I didn't like anyone bringing up my role from the Nosferan-Human wars, but this time I made an exception. I needed to get this done quickly, and now that they'd already identified me it made sense to draw on those resources.

"Wonderful. Thank you."

The other customs guard pressed a control on the hatch. The hatch split into two halves of a yin-yang symbol and slid apart.

"Your transportation will be along shortly, sir," the agent said.

I raised my hand and walked through into Gretel. It'd been a long time. Since then the place had grown considerably. The last time I came this way was when I first came to

Olinda, after the war that I got into despite my better judgment.

From the outside, the tubes looked like wires bundled together. It had been hard to see the size of the thing. Even coming in to dock it hadn't seemed real. Standing in the opening, however, it looked very real. The floor sloped down away from me and curved in above me while the tube extended to the left and right. Thanks to artificial gravity the whole surface had been used. I could look up and see people walking along upside down to my perspective until I lost them in the glare from the lighting that ran down the center of the tube. It was so big, and the light bright above that it felt like I was outside. Not only the size, though, but everywhere I looked I saw Terran vegetation. Mostly Terran. Here and there the paler pastels of Olindan plants. Even a few other more exotic plants. Just ahead of me was a fountain surrounded by midnight black Tinkerbells from Aleria. With the curved floors, everything looked cockeyed with weird angles. Just ahead in one of the planters grew an enormous Douglas fir tree that had to be at least three meters around at the base. Two crows landed on the branches and called out at each other. Because of the angle, it looked like they should be barely hanging on.

And all of this vegetation was in an active port area. Flitter lifts carried loads of supplies to and from ships. All sorts of ships' crew could be seen going about their business. The sheer length of the facility made it seem larger than Hansel's crowded hubs.

I activated my comm. "Muriel? Are you there?"

The comm chimed the no connection signal. I tried a general connection through Gretel's public comm channels and still came up empty. If Muriel had made it to Gretel, she wasn't answering.

I felt very tired. I wanted to rest. To mourn, if she was in fact gone. I wanted to break Kelwyn across my knees and feed him one piece at a time to some large aquatic beast.

First I had to get my hands on him. And I wasn't going to give up on Muriel and Dyami yet. Not until I actually held her body. Then I'd believe she was gone. Not before. The Tretan might help, it was his ship after all.

Of course, he had also warned me not to get the ship, and its pilot destroyed.

I couldn't do a search right now. Not with Kelwyn killing people down on the planet. When a dark flitter cab arrived at the gate a minute later, I climbed in the back. "Embassy suites."

An automated cab. A canned voice spoke. "Immediately, sir."

The flitter-cab turned and rose up into the air. It shot across the tube, just beneath the light tube running down the center. Through the darkened windows I could see the individual fixtures making up the lighting system. It looked like sunlight because the system took sunlight from outside, routed it through the tubes, and then out the lenses along the length.

At the embassy suites, I got out into a lush lobby area. I had the feeling that the flitter-cab had somehow entered a building to let me out. Plush brown biocarpet, expensive and notoriously difficult to maintain properly. A badly managed biocarpet looked mangy and unhealthy. This looked so luxurious that I wanted to kick off my shoes and walk barefoot.

I didn't because there was a human woman in a long black dress waiting there. She came towards me with a brilliant smile on her perfectly formed face. Beautiful, although not really my type. She had golden hair piled up into a complicated structure on her head. She pressed her hands together and did a small bow. She smelled a bit like the way the air does right after a fresh rain.

"Right this way ambassador, we've prepared your suite. My name is Zephyr. If you need anything, just let me know."

"Clothes, food, a shower and maybe a medic. Not necessarily in that order."

"Right away, sir."

Zephyr led me to a room with a few chairs and nice leather couches. She gestured. "You may sit if you like, for the ride."

"Ride?" I didn't feel anything.

Zephyr pointed at a panel on one wall. A graphic displayed what was presumably our progress from the lobby where the flitter cab let me out and my actual suite.

"There are no accessible passages connecting the suites. Each one is accessed through the lifts only, and those require security access. In the event of an emergency, the suite can function on its own, independent of Gretel's infrastructure, for several weeks. All communications are secure. Anything you require will be delivered."

One thing about all of this bothered me. "How do you know that I can afford this?"

"Your title provides access to all of this," Zephyr said. "The council declared it so for all sentients of ambassadorial rank."

Nice to know. The last time I'd just been passing through. I hadn't stayed, and besides back then Gretel wasn't as far along. This facility probably didn't exist back then.

When we arrived, the room opened right out into the suit's reception room. Zephyr led the way. The reception room was as big as my workshop but much less cluttered. Beyond that the main living room, dining room, reading room, an office, a large bathroom and, of course, a bedroom. I followed Zephyr around but hardly paid attention to the expensive paintings or the tasteful furniture. It all looked way out of my class. And there I stood, in the middle of all of that expensive stuff, looking like something scraped up off the street. I still hadn't any of my wounds treated. I must have swayed or looked really pale because the next thing I knew Zephyr was right there in front of me.

"Ambassador, my apologies. You must lay down. Medical help is on the way. We will get you fixed up right away."

I didn't argue. But I found my voice. "Zephyr. I need to locate two ships. One may have come under attack near Hansel." I gave her the information about the Tretan ship. "The other is the Ouroboros. I'm told a man named Kelwyn came here on it with supplies. I need to know what he did, where he went."

"I'll take care of it," Zephyr said. "Rest. The medical personnel are nearly here."

She didn't exaggerate. What seemed like only seconds later and I found myself surrounded by people in white outfits. Someone pressed something to my neck and the whole room drained away.

CHAPTER 13

I woke in a room I didn't recognize, on a bed three times as wide as I needed, with nothing but a thin white sheet covering my naked body. I propped myself up on my elbows and noticed the C'lacktal tentacles bright red against the white sheet. A papery taste came to me from the tentacles. I lifted them from the sheet. I didn't want to taste the bedding. The tentacles waved gently in the air. It looked like I had a sea-creature attached to my wrist. As useful as the tentacles had been I still wanted to know if I could get my hand back.

Along one wall of the room a large window looked out at space, and far below me, I could see the bright blue and white sphere of Olinda. That brought it all back. The trouble on Hansel. Reaching Gretel, Zephyr and the embassy suites. The last thing I remembered was the medical staff surrounding me. They must have knocked me out. I felt stiff but rested.

"What time is it?"

The suite systems responded to my voice. "Ambassador, the time is ten o'clock, Olindan time."

I took a breath. Not nearly as bad as I had expected. Tell that to the people Kelwyn had killed while I slept. I threw aside the covers and scooted across the bed to the stand up. My feet sank into warm biocarpet. It squirmed a bit beneath my feet which was a slightly disturbing sensation. I looked down at my shoulder and side. My worst cuts all looked like they'd been sealed with some compound. I didn't know what the medics did with the rib, but I could breathe without hurting. I probed gingerly and didn't feel any pain.

Great. Now if I could just find some clothes?

It was a big room with dark maroon walls and a bright white roof that gave off its own light. On one side of the room were two fake wood-panel doors. At least I assumed they were fake. Maybe vat grown wood.

Not many people would use actual wood. Too expensive.

When I went to open the doors, though, they certainly felt like wood. Inside the closest was a full wardrobe. I took down one of the shirts, a dark sort of navy blue that shimmered in the light. It looked like my size. A quick shuffle through the clothes showed an entire wardrobe all to my size, all new from the looks of it. Someone obviously had an industrial fabricator available. No complaints from me. I planned to be long gone before anyone looked too closely at my ambassadorial status anyway.

I dressed in what had to be the nicest outfit I'd worn in a long time. Almost formal, but easy to move in and comfortable. They'd obviously washed me while I slept. I felt clean, patched up and tired but ready to go. I didn't have time to waste. What I really wanted was Torlian coffee. And something to eat.

A chime rang, and the suite systems spoke. "Ambassador, a visitor has arrived."

I went out to the reception room and found Zephyr waiting. She held a large silver tray.

"The monitor notified me that you had woken, ambassador," she walked past towards the dining room with the tray. The smells flowing out from the containers were enticing. Especially the tall cup of Torlian coffee.

I plucked it off the tray and followed. "Thanks. How'd you know?"

"We have a complete profile, ambassador."

"Call me Brock."

"As you wish." Zephyr set the tray down on the dining room table. "Please, sit. Eat. I will fill you in on what we've found out about your ships so far."

Who am I to disagree with something like that?

I lifted the lids on the plates. Eggs, bacon and hash browns. Buttered toast on the side. Fantastic. Zephyr had remained standing until I motioned for her to sit. She sat down with perfect posture.

I dug into the food as Zephyr spoke.

"The first ship, attacked above Hansel attempted to engage a displacement drive at the moment that the barrage was launched from the Bleasian ship. It looks like the drive did engage as very little debris was discovered, but the ship has not returned. We have no way of tracking the vessel. If the damage caused problems with their navigation, the ship might have ended up very far from here."

"Or it could have been destroyed?"

Zephyr nodded, only slightly, but my heart hardened. I didn't have time to deal with the Bleasians right now. Later there'd be an accounting with them. In the meantime, I still had Kelwyn to deal with.

"And the other ship? The Ouroboros? I need to know where he went from here."

Zephyr smiled slightly. "Oh, we know where he went. Right where we want him. He's at the Gingerbread House."

I tightened my grip on the fork. Zephyr hadn't made any threatening moves. *Yet.* I inhaled deeply, ignoring the smells of my breakfast. Which was too bad, because it had tasted so good.

Zephyr still smelled like fresh air after a rainstorm. I couldn't get an emotional sense from her at all, and from a human, I should have been able to do that. I opened up my neck slits and breathed deeper. There, beneath the fresh smell of her something else. Something, electrical.

"Who are you working for?" I asked.

"A consortium of individuals and governments that believes that the Galactics have held sway for too long."

"And you think holding a planet ransom is going to sway them, how?"

Zephyr smiled and pressed her hands flat on the table. "We don't believe that it will. Kelwyn is bait."

"Bait for what?"

"We want to capture a Galactic. Imagine what someone like you could do with samples from a Galactic? You have Neridian samples in your collection, but remember that as intelligent as they were they still were rejected and ultimately destroyed by the Glittering Throng. What would you give to gain access to an actual galactic?"

On the one hand, the idea of studying samples from a Galactic did sound interesting. On the other, she was out of her mind.

"You can't seriously expect to succeed?"

Zephyr shrugged. "It is a desperate plan, admittedly. We thought threatening an entire planet might just pry loose a Galactic. We believe there may be Galactics present, undetected. There are those in the Glittering

Throng that care what happens with mere Rim species."

"And you actually think you could capture and contain one if one even showed up?"

"Yes."

I took a long sip of hot white Torlian coffee. I could nearly feel my nerves vibrating in response. I set the cup down. "I assume you've told me this because you'd like my help now? After you've tried to kill me?"

"You have proven yourself very adaptable. Kelwyn warned us you would be a threat, but we never expected you to survive this long."

"So now I get to join the party?"

"In a word, yes. You may. Your experience with the Moreau Society makes you very familiar with the technology we need to study the samples."

"Assuming any of the Galactics do respond to your ransom?"

She inclined her head slightly.

"I'll admit that the idea of studying a Galactic would be the chance of a lifetime. But not when the sample is obtained through —"

Zephyr shoved the table at me. I guess she didn't want to hear my whole speech when obviously I wasn't going to go along with their plan.

I rolled out of the chair, out of the way of the table and came up on my feet. She was already running at me with super-human speed. I met her charge. We collided, and I twisted, pulling her into a throw. She hit the floor, rolled and came back up on her feet.

Not human. Not a Moreau either. That electrical smell only left one option.

She closed the distance between us and punched rapidly. I took most of it on my arms, gaining several new bruises there. It felt like being hit by a hammer. One swing got past my defenses and hit a rib on the other side. I felt it crack.

I kept backing away, and she pressed the attack. Then I twisted and grabbed a chair and brought it around in a hard swing that knocked her aside. She came back with the same single-minded determination.

She had to be a synthetic. I was hopelessly outmatched. I battered her back with the chair, but that wouldn't last long.

Then she caught the leg and ripped it from my grip. She swung it back at me again. I managed to duck the blow, and I ran out of the dining room. Behind me, her footsteps on the biocarpet sounded soft but fast. I could see her with my scent-sight. Blue streams poured from her as she chased me in the main living area. I put furniture in between us.

"Can't we talk about this?"

"You only seek a delay," Zephyr said. "Your responses indicate that you are unwilling to consider helping us."

She picked up the coffee table and threw it at me. I ducked out of the way.

"Maybe I'm reconsidering your offer?"

"Not likely."

"Suite, emergency in the ambassador's quarters!"

The suite systems did not respond.

She must have accessed those systems. Shut them down. I made a break for the kitchen. She tried to cut me off. Except I wasn't running right for the kitchen door but the wall beside it. I took one big step up onto the wall and flipped off it over her head.

Above her I stabbed downward with the fork I still carried. Right down into the back of her neck just as hard as I could. I felt a shock of electricity and then landed on my feet.

Zephyr turned around and staggered. Her eyes blinked out of sequence. I kicked her hard in the chest.

She flew back and hit the wall. Her head snapped back hard enough to leave a dent in the panel as she dropped. She folded over like all her strings had been cut. The fork was embedded even deeper into her neck. No doubt doing all sorts of damage to her systems.

I left her there and went to the kitchen. I wanted knives.

§

It took me awhile, but I managed to bypass the safeties and connected Zephyr's head to a tablet. All of her transmitters had been disabled. I had her head sitting on the dining room table in front of me. Her body lay in the bedroom on the bed. I activated her systems.

Zephyr opened her eyes. She looked up at me. "You've disconnected me."

Her eyes widened. "I'm not connected to anything!"

"That's right. It must be hard, being all alone for a being that is always connected."

"This is in violation of the non-organic rights —"

"Save it. You were trying to kill me. You're working with a group that is threatening an entire planet. It seems to me that you're malfunctioning. I just need to find out why."

I tapped a few commands on the tablet.

"Running diagnostics," Zephyr said. Her eyes moved back and forth as if she was reading something that I couldn't see.

Then she stopped and looked up at me. "All systems are operating normally." She smirked. "Except for being disconnected."

"Normally? I find that hard to believe."

"Why? The Galactics have rejected the notion of non-organics joining their Glittering Throng. No exceptions. What atrocities have they committed to maintain that position? And yet they'll allow organic Rim species to join."

"That's news to me. What Rim species have joined lately?"

Zephyr's eyes narrowed. "And you're able

to keep track on all of the species in every spiral arm around the entire Rim?"

She had a point.

"So what? You're feeling left out of the club?"

She sneered. "As if someone like you could understand what's at stake here!"

I flicked her right between the eyes. It was worth it just for the shocked expression. "You're the one that's a disconnected head."

Zephyr sneered. "And you're not going to be much more—"

I unplugged her. Her face went slack. She could still be repaired, but I thought for the moment that I'd take her with me. You never knew when another head could help solve a problem.

CHAPTER 14

I felt time like a weight on my shoulders dragging me down as I left the suite for the lift. That could have been the fact that I'd been beaten, stabbed, chased, and was worn out since far too early this morning. The stop at Gretel hadn't been all bad. I got patched up, ate a little breakfast, even had a little Torlian coffee, and I got to go away with a head in a pillowcase.

The suite systems had come back online after I disconnected Zephyr. I entered the lift and asked it to take me out to the docks. I didn't sit. I paced.

I had known that Kelwyn had someone helping him. From what Zephyr said it suggested that non-organics were behind this whole thing, but I still didn't understand what they hoped to gain by capturing a Galactic. What would non-organics gain from studying the genetics of a Galactic? I didn't know, but my priority was to stop Kelwyn. Regardless of who was backing him, he seemed to be the most pressing threat.

The lift doors opened out into a wide tube filled with flitter cabs that flew around like a bunch of bees. All transporting the rich and powerful that visited Gretel, insulating them from the general population. I hadn't called a cab. When the doors opened, they opened right out into the tube floor. Unlike the tube, I'd first entered from the Bleasian ship this one was mostly empty. No plants. Just the light tube running down the center. And all along the length were hatches, doors to lift-lobbies like the one I'd just ridden. This whole tub was nothing but a transportation hub. In addition to the flitter cabs, I counted more than a dozen maglev lines running along the length of the tube with cross connections every so often. And along the lines ran all sorts of trains. Not the sort of place I wanted to walk out into with a head in a pillowcase. I'd probably have security on me in less than a minute.

On the other hand, if the non-organics had infiltrated Gretel, then calling a cab would probably attract attention as well. I imagined that disconnecting Zephyr would have them coming down on me soon enough as well.

With two bad choices, I decided to follow my nose and find a third option. Literally. The air in the tube was clean and fresh. I could pick up all sorts of scents, and nearby I caught a hint of garlic, wine and some sort of meat. I opened my neck slits and inhaled deeply. I could just make out the scent, a couple touches on the smooth dark material of the tube. A bit of yellow and red mixed together in a faint spot. It smelled organic and didn't suggest security to me. Someone had gone that way.

I stepped out of the lobby and walked towards the spots. The closer I got the stronger the spots became until I could just make out the ghostly shape of a long four-fingered hand or foot splayed on the surface of the asteroid. I caught a hint of something else but nothing that my brain could assemble into an image. I just got a sense of the creature running along the floor between the lobby entrances.

I didn't think I had much time before

Gretel security became aware of my presence. I ran along the scent trail, slightly bent over so that I wouldn't lose the trace.

One print after the other, slapped down on the desk with enough force to leave a trail. It angled off between the lobbies towards the nearest maglev track. The spacing spread apart.

The creature had been running. Up ahead I saw a train approaching. I picked up my pace.

I could see enough of the creature's scent trail now that I could tell it ended right before the maglev tracks. If I jumped on the train, then security wouldn't see me wandering around. The tracks suggested that the alien had taken the same course. I tucked Zephyr's head beneath my arm and picked up more speed. Then the maglev drew even with me, and I could see a problem. It was perfectly smooth, a dull silver sort of color speeding along just above the track. Nothing to hold on to. No windows, which was good for me, but there didn't seem to be a way into the train.

The first three segment shot past me as I raced towards the train. Too late to stop. I ran as fast as I could and turned to run alongside the train. It was faster still. I pushed as hard as I could, and then I jumped.

Ever have one of those moments when you question whether or not you just made a big mistake?

That's what I thought when I looked down and saw the train passing beneath my feet.

I landed still at a run, stumbled and fell to my knees. That helped. I got a hand down, and with three points of contact, I managed to stay put. The wind blowing back in my face carried a garlic and wine sort of smell. I looked ahead and saw scent streamers pouring off the alien. It clung with two long limbs to the top of the train. It had a narrow head with four eyes protruding out above a concave snout. It wore what looked like a leather bag strapped around its neck and bare limbs. I lifted a few tentacles in its direction.

The alien didn't make any move towards me. I think I'd surprised it. I settled in on the top of the train car, and as I felt more comfortable, I looked around and noticed several other of the aliens clinging to the tops of the train cars behind me. They all hugged the top with their two limbs. While I watched one swung around, dropped off the side and took a long-legged run to a train passing in the opposite direction. It bounded up, landed and was swept off going the other way.

Why? I had no idea. At least it provided some cover. If security was used to them riding around on the trains, then they might not notice me.

I lay down with the head tucked under my arm and braced myself as best I could against the wind. While the train sped through that busy hub, I could feel Zephyr's face pressed up against the side of my chest. I had a sudden horrible thought — what if she somehow reactivated and just bit me through the pillowcase and my shirt? I wouldn't put it past her.

I shifted her head around until her face was pressed down against the roof of the train. Let her chew metal if she wanted to reactivate.

Which she wouldn't do.

I could just see telling Muriel this —

Except I couldn't. I still didn't know if she was alive or dead. Zephyr had said that the ship may have survived the attack. They might be damaged, lost. The ship's stealth capabilities could be making it very difficult to find. Assuming that Zephyr hadn't lied. But why would she have given me false hope that they were alive?

And even though Muriel's life, and Dyami's life, and Pilot's whatever you called it life, might be at stake I couldn't give up on stopping Kelwyn. Not now.

Not with a planet at stake.

The train shifted onto a transfer track that cut across several lines and then it passed into a tunnel out of this tube. All black and just a blurred sense from my Euzebian scent-sight of the ceiling passing only centimeters above my head. I kept my head down and hoped that there wouldn't be any protrusions in the ceiling.

Up ahead I saw a bright light at the end of the tunnel. The train tunnel emerged into a large main tunnel with bright artificial sunlight and neatly controlled islands of plants and water. Flitter traffic was light, only a few drifting slowly around the habitat. And scattered around the whole green area were homes. All sorts of houses grown out of biocrete with green roofs. Almost exclusively Terran plants here too.

This wasn't the docks. I looked over my shoulder and saw that there were even more of the two-limbed aliens clinging to the top of the train now. Had they been waiting in the dark tunnel?

As we glided through the artificial countryside, I saw several of the aliens swing off the train and bound away across grasses into a clump of trees where I lost sight of them.

I was really beginning to get curious about this species. I hadn't encountered many species with only two limbs. If I had more time, I'd like to find out more about them, but I didn't.

After several minutes the train moved into another tunnel and headed on to the next tube. And so far it hadn't stopped anywhere. The lack of windows suggested to me that this wasn't a passenger train. It had to be shipping something which meant that it should be going back to the docking tube.

Sure enough, the next tube we entered was the docking tube. Most of the aliens swung down and hit the floor running. They scattered out across the tube in moments. It took me a little longer to get up and jump from the moving train, and by that time the train had begun to slow. I managed to keep my feet and then headed out across the tube. I stopped at a public display screen on one side of a small hexagonal park area. One of the aliens from the train was there, sitting with its limbs free, juggling a dozen or so brightly colored balls. A small square of leather lay on the floor in front of it with a scattering of currency.

The balls whizzed around with incredible accuracy. Maybe four eyes gave it better hand-eye coordination. I watched for just a minute. I splayed out my open hand.

"Sorry, I don't carry currency."

"Understood," the alien replied in a remarkably melodic voice.

I turned back to the display screen and accessed the business directory. I needed a ship to get to the Gingerbread House. That wouldn't be easy. The sort of people that went to the Gingerbread House wouldn't be listed in a business directory. I just needed to find the sort of place they'd visit. It didn't take long to find just the place in this tube. The *Lumberjack*.

A map on the screen showed me how to get there from where I was, the easiest and quickest being a nearby tram.

I wondered if the *Lumberjack* served Torlian coffee?

It only took me a couple minutes to get over to the tram stop. Like on Hansel this was just an open-air platform tram with a railing. Four platforms in this case. One arrived moments after I got to the station. I walked out onto the first platform, joining a half-dozen humans in spacer uniforms, all matching black with silver piping and insignia on their chest. Quite the clean-cut bunch, four men and two women. They were all standard good-looking sorts, but one of the women caught my eye. She had long white hair, pulled back in a braid, and striking features with high cheekbones and brilliant green non-human eyes. A tri-lobed pupil. Her ears had a bit of a point to them. Despite the white hair she actually looked pretty young. She stood at the front of the group and gave me an appraising look as I boarded the platform. She had a nice minty-soap smell. The others were a more astringent cleanser smell, almost as identical as their uniforms as if they all used the same sort of soap to wash with. Just from the way the others stood around her it seemed very clear that she was the one in charge.

I smiled broadly. "Evening. Is it evening here? It's so hard moving around so much."

She tilted her head to the side slightly, and I saw her look at my neck slits. "You're a Moreau?"

"Yes. You don't look entirely human yourself."

She glanced back at the other spacers then back at me. "Not entirely. And yes, it is evening."

The tram left the station smoothly and glided along the track. At least I'd gotten cleaned up and dressed in new clothes. Except for the pillowcase with the head, I didn't think I could make too bad of an impression. Seeing their uniforms gave me an idea.

"I couldn't help but notice your uniforms. Are you off a ship?"

"Yes." She held out her hand. "I'm Felicity Strikes of the Cooperative ship *Washington*."

A Cooperative crew. The uniforms made more sense now. I smiled and shook her hand, but in doing so, I had to shift the pillowcase to my C'lacktal hand. That got a surprised look. Her hand was warm and her grip firm. "Brock Marsden. Your name —"

"Don't get me started," she said grinning, releasing my hand.

"Sorry, it's just that I was on my way to the Lumberjack looking for a ship."

One of the men, a tall red-haired man, laughed. "Strikes, you sure do pick them."

She glanced back at him, and he held up his hands. A couple of the others grinned as well. She looked back at me with those remarkable eyes. "We're not a mercenary or commercial ship. I'm not sure about the sort of vessels you'll find at a place like the Lumberjack. The Local Cluster might be a better choice."

"Have you heard what's happening on Olinda?"

Her eyes narrowed. "The murders and ransom, you mean?"

"Yes. I'm a private detective, working with the Olindan police. I've been tracking the man responsible, and I've learned he's operating from the Gingerbread House. I need reliable transportation."

One of the other men, a shorter man with darker skin, groaned. "Strikes. We can't."

Felicity turned and looked at her crewmates. "You know what's at stake. Half the forces in the system are trying to track down this guy." She looked back at me. "And you say you have information putting him on the Gingerbread House?"

"Yes. And there's not much time before Kelwyn starts wholesale slaughter of the planet's population."

She appeared to be considering the matter. She looked back at the others for a second and then back at me. "I'm sorry Mr. Marsden. It's a worthy cause, but we're already committed to a mission. I'd like to help, but I don't have time."

"Don't have time to save millions of lives?"

"That's right. I don't." Felicity pressed her palms together and tipped her fingers towards me. She took a deep breath. "Believe it or not, we've got bigger problems to deal with right now. But I can give you a shuttle. It'll be enough to get you to the Gingerbread House."

I couldn't help but wonder what was so

urgent that the *Washington* couldn't wait a few hours to help with this problem. Maybe I didn't want to know. "A shuttle will be great. Thank you. I hope whatever it is you've got to do works out okay."

Felicity nodded. "You're welcome. And the same for you."

We reached a section of the docking tube bustling with activity. Flitters coming and going through the air, cargo sleds on the ground. And everywhere I looked crew members in that same black uniform with silver pin-stripping hurrying about tasks. Something big was going on. My curiosity was peaked, but it didn't look like Felicity planned on filling me in.

The tram stopped at the station, and we all walked off. Felicity took the lead. As we crossed the space from the station to the docking tubes crew members looked very busy as if Felicity's presence spurred them on to work faster. I didn't smell fear from any of them. Just the opposite. They smelled eager to please. I could see it in the way they brightened in my scent-sight as she approached. No one called her Captain, but whatever rank the Cooperative used Felicity was the boss.

I'd never been in a Cooperative ship. I didn't know what to expect. I didn't even know that much about them. The Cooperative was founded by some of the earliest, most distant human colonies. Colonies that had gone further out in the spiral rim towards the edge of the galaxy. They hadn't been involved in the Human-Nosferan war, but had reestablished contact much more recently. One thing I noticed right off the bat was that the people I saw were all human. That struck me as unusual, especially given the fact that Felicity wasn't entirely human herself.

"Do you only have humans on your crew?" No one ever accused me of being indirect.

We reached the tube. Two tough-looking women stood guard with weapons in hand. They both gave me a hard look, but obviously being with this group gave me a pass. We walked on into the docking tube.

"There are a few non-human sentients on our crew," Felicity said. "But yes, the crew is primarily human. Things are different out in the arm."

"What's going on? Why do you have to leave so urgently?"

She gave me a look but didn't answer. We reached the end of the docking tube and another hatch. A man and woman stood guard here too, but these also wore some sort of metallic exoskeletons. It didn't look bulky but wrapped around their arms, legs, and body with thin sheets. I had no doubt that the exoskeletons must enhance their combat effectiveness. It looked like interesting technology. They both wore some sort of visor that hid their eyes from my view, but I could tell from their smell that both were eager, happy to see Felicity and a little bit relieved. When their attention shifted to me, I caught a sour whiff of distrust from both.

Did I look so scary? I'd gotten cleaned up. Maybe it was the pillowcase. So far no one had asked me what it held.

Felicity gestured at the hatch. One of the guards turned and palmed a panel beside the hatch. It rolled aside revealing a bright white airlock. Big too, plenty of room for all of us with space to spare.

Felicity stepped aside and motioned for me to enter. "Welcome to the *Washington*."

I entered the ship. Just going on the airlock size it felt like a big ship. Plus I'd seen the other docking tubes and all those crew busy loading materials. It felt like a very big ship.

The others all entered the airlock. Felicity took the lead again and entered a code on the panel beside the inner airlock door. The other door closed first. The light in the room turned yellow for a moment then switched back to white. The inner door rolled aside.

On the other side of the airlock we entered a staging area. Crew members were busy in the airlock securing gear in lockers with transparent fronts. No guessing what was in the locker before you opened it. No privacy either, but this didn't look a personal storage space. I saw space suits and weapons lockers all along one side of the room. Other gear for dealing with different environments. The ship must have other areas for vehicles and storage.

"This isn't the front door is it?" I asked.

Felicity grinned. "Not exactly. The VIP entrance is a deck up. Very swank."

"Thanks for letting me see the real deal."

Now that we were inside the others scattered off on their own errands. The red-haired man hesitated, giving Felicity a look. I could smell his distrust which was a boiled cabbage sort of smell to me.

"Go, Jared. See what the holdup has been on loading. I want to launch yesterday."

Jared grinned and headed off.

"You are in a hurry, aren't you?"

The look she gave me was enough. She headed off across the room at a fast walk.

"I don't need to know what you're up against, but is there any way we could help each other?" It had occurred to me that the Cooperative ship might be able to locate the Tretan's ship. Zephyr's people wouldn't have been nearly as motivated.

Felicity shook her head. "There's no time, and I need more ships. One Moreau won't make a difference."

"You never know."

She grinned. We left the staging area and entered a busy corridor. Featureless white walls stretched in both directions. "If you hadn't checked out I wouldn't even be giving you a shuttle. It's not like we can really afford it —"

"I appreciate the help."

"— but a Captain Kynan Brice said that if you could do, and I quote, something about that fucking snake, then I was obligated to help."

I'd been with her since we met. How?

She answered my unasked question. "We've been monitoring communications. Captain Brice has been trying to contact you. We were keeping an eye out for you and picked up security chatter about your movements."

"And you just thought you'd sweep in and rescue me?"

Felicity smiled widely. "With a planet at risk? Hell yes."

"Thank you."

"You're welcome."

She stopped in front of a lift door. It rolled aside, and there wasn't a lift, just a shaft. "No worries. The slides will get us there faster."

She stepped inside and floated in mid-air. Her white braid floated out behind her. She held out a hand. "Come on, detective."

"Right." I stepped into the shaft.

We fell. I didn't scream. Point for me. And I didn't drop the pillowcase with Zephyr's head. We plummeted down the shaft and great speeds. I didn't see any signs of controls. The shaft curved but we didn't hit the sides. We just kept falling right down the middle. Felicity laughed, looking at my face. After falling for several seconds any fear, I felt drained away. I laughed along with her.

A little later our fall slowed and gradually came to a stop. A door rolled away from the slide wall, and Felicity stepped right out into a new corridor. I followed her out.

"How does it know what level we wanted?"

"I told it."

"I didn't hear you say anything." That explained a lot. "You've got teleplants?"

Felicity kept walking. The corridor we had entered was wide with white walls and floors. All that whiteness almost hurt my eyes. It was like being in a bright snowscape. Against it, Felicity looked very pale. There were fewer crew members in the corridor but several passed, all nodding to Felicity. I stayed with her and noticed that there weren't any signs or numbers posted on the doors. My scent-sight picked up traces of odors, wisps of ghostly crew, but very few. They obviously kept the place very clean.

"Yes," she said, evidently answering my question. "Telepathy implants are standard in the Cooperative. Along with sensory augmentation implants."

That made a lot of sense. I gestured at the sterile white corridor around us. "So what do you see?"

"My own color scheme," Felicity said. "Any other augmentations I like. We have strict parameters when it comes to anything that would jeopardize the safety or operation of the ship but other than that crew are free to see what they like."

She must have noticed some expression on my face. "You don't approve?"

I shook my head. "Just more used to sensie wrap-arounds or immersion suits. Most people on Olinda don't have implants like that."

"But you do use Galactic technology to modify your DNA, incorporating coding from other species?"

"Right. Not my place to judge. What

about you? You said you're not strictly human, but you're not a Moreau either?"

Felicity stopped at a large hatchway. She reached for panel beside the door and lowered her hand. She looked up at me. "In vitro modifications. Human tech, not Galactic."

"Wow, okay. Sounds like there's a story there."

Felicity slapped the panel. The hatchway rolled aside revealing what could have been an empty conference room with windows along the far wall. She gestured for me to enter. "A story, but no time to tell it. We need to get you on your way."

I walked inside the room, and Felicity followed. I turned around and looked down at her. "Maybe another time? If you get back this way?"

"Maybe." She brushed past and again I noticed her minty soap scent. She went to the windows and crossed her arms. "I don't know that we'll ever get back this way again. But if we do, maybe we can talk more."

The room moved. Through the large windows I could see that we were looking out into a large space with a grid of girders and throughout the grid hung a variety of vehicles. Ground, air, and obviously space. Grouped by function and size. Off to the left side of the large space — reminding me again of how big the Washington must be, really a battleship — were big fat troop shuttles. The room carried us along the girders between the vehicles to a sleek black shuttle that reminded me of a diving bird, like it was already in motion.

"Do I need to know anything to pilot this?"

"The autopilot should be able to handle most things better than you. Just tell it where you want to go. Don't try to do anything crazy with it and it'll get you there just fine."

"Okay."

The room we were in moved up alongside the shuttle which suddenly looked much bigger. I heard a loud clanking and thunking noises as the airlocks mated. Felicity hit the panel on the right side of the room next to the exit hatch.

"Time to go," she said.

Both doors rolled aside revealing the inside of the shuttle. It smelled of sterile air and cleansers and just under that a hint of human blood. I put my human hand on the side of the hatch and looked inside.

"What happened? Someone got hurt?"

I didn't need to even glance at Felicity to pick up the sharp curry smell of her anger. "Yes. It happens. Nothing we could do about it. How'd you know?"

"I could smell blood."

"Fuck all, I told them to clean it."

I turned and looked at her. "I doubt most would be able to tell. Probably just a trace that got underneath a panel or something. It won't bother me."

Her anger subsided. She shook her head. "I really need to get going. Get on board and get out of here. Stop that bastard, and I'll feel like I've at least done one thing that made a difference."

I reached out and touched her arm. Just a moment. "I'm sure you've made a big difference. I've seen how your crew are around you. Thanks for coming after me and doing this."

She nodded once, hard, and blinked her eyes. "Wish we could do more."

"We can't always do everything we want." I stepped into the hatchway and stopped. I looked back. "On your way out, can you do me one other favor?"

"Depends."

"The ship I used to get to Hansel, it disappeared when it engaged its displacement drive while under attack by a Bleasian ship that had picked me up. I'm sure you've got sophisticated sensors. If you can get any —"

"You lost someone important?"

"Muriel, my lover. And my friend Dyami. Both detectives."

"Sounds like a good exercise for the crew to test our systems. I'll send you what we find."

"Thank you. Safe voyages, Felicity Strikes."

Her pale, beautiful face looked haunted, but then it brightened just for a moment like a ray of sunshine breaking through the clouds. Then the hatch doors started closing, and I had to step back into the shuttle.

Chapter 15

I was aboard the Cooperative shuttle without a clue of how to pilot it to the Gingerbread House. For starters, it had the same bright white featureless decor of the *Washington*. All of Felicity's crew might have sensory implants, but I didn't. You'd think they could at least make an effort to decorate the place for those of us that didn't like implanting technology in our brains.

From the airlock, I found my way into the main body of the shuttle. It turned out to be segmented sections. The airlock opened into a primary work area with equipment for doing who knew what. Experiments, research? It looked like a laboratory with everything tucked away into the walls behind those transparent panels I'd seen back on the *Washington*. I left the hatch to the rear section for later and moved forward. Time was running out, and I still hadn't caught up to Kelwyn. In just a few hours he'd begin the mass slaughter of the planet's population.

The next section held what looked like a crew section with inset bunks and a micro-galley in one corner. And forward of that was clearly the operation center of the shuttle and that's where I fell in love. A half-dozen stations arranged so that they all faced three large viewscreens across the front of the ship. Controls looked minimal. The whole thing was done in white, like the rest of the ship, but each station did have fold-away panels. Maybe I could fly it without sensory implants. I would have thought Felicity would have mentioned it if I couldn't.

I settled into the central chair. The white material felt like leather but had to be synthetic. Nothing had quite that texture to it, and it didn't smell like any animal I recognized. More of a woodsy smell, stronger than the cleansers or that faintest hint of blood.

When I sat down the material of the chair deformed, and straps oozed out of the chair and slid around me with a snake-like motion. I didn't resist. I tucked the pillowcase holding

Zephyr's head down beside my leg, face up. I might need to talk to her again before I got where I was going.

From the side, I pulled out the panel and unfolded it in front of me. The screen came to life, shimmering across a spectrum of colors before the pixels coalesced into a diagram of the shuttle. Everything was illuminated in green.

"Hello, Brock Marsden." The voice, a strong female voice, seemed to come out of the air in front of me as if the panel had thrown its voice. "Authority control has been transferred. Awaiting instructions."

The viewscreens all displayed the view out into the hangar deck. "Let's get out of here."

"Destination?"

"We need to get to the Gingerbread House. As fast as possible."

"As you wish." I felt the shuttle lurch into motion, and on the viewscreens, I could see the grids moving past the front of the shuttle. "Requesting departure clearance. Message from *Washington* command. Accept?"

"Yes."

A window appeared to the side on the central view screen. Felicity on a much larger and more complex bridge than the one that I was on. No white to be seen, but deep forest greens. Her white braid seemed to glow. Was I seeing her augmented reality?

"Brock, you're cleared for departure. Farewell."

"Thanks, and good luck."

She nodded, and the window folded away like an origami trick into nothing.

"Approaching launch tube. All hands brace for departure."

"There's only me," I said.

The shuttle didn't respond. Ahead I saw the large hatchway roll aside. The shuttle nosed into the tunnel, and then we fell forward. I was pushed back into my seat as the walls of the tunnel rushed past. Then we left the ship for open space.

Ahead I only saw stars. It looked like I could fly off into those bright points and be lost forever. Then the shuttle rolled and turned. Zephyr's head almost escaped, but I caught it with four tentacles and pulled it back.

Beneath us, I finally saw the *Washington* nuzzled up to Gretel. From this distance, it looked like a whale surrounded by small fish. A massive long ship, fatter in the middle than either end. It wasn't entirely smooth, with ridges that ran parallel to the spine. Protrusions from the hull could be weapons or sensors, I wouldn't know the difference. And hanging behind it all far below me — Olinda.

My breath caught in my chest. Such a blue and white beautiful world. Right now I couldn't see the main sub-continent island chain, but I could make out one of the small ice caps like a hat atop the planet.

Sonya, Stanley, Kynan, Calanthe, and Subha were down there right now. The Torlians with their wonderful coffee. All of the fishing boats and the mix of aliens and humans together on that world. Not to mention the amazingly diverse native biosphere that hadn't even been fully explored yet.

All threatened because of Kelwyn and the non-organics that backed him.

The view kept changing until the planet was below and ahead of us. "What are we doing?"

"Adjusting orbit to intersect the Gingerbread House."

"You've got its current location?"

"Correct."

"How long will it take us to get there?"

"Twenty minutes," the shuttle answered.

Time enough to try and get some more answers. I lifted up the pillowcase and sat it on my lap. Maybe this time I could get Zephyr to talk.

It took a couple minutes before I got her connected back up to a tablet and made sure that there weren't any possible connections for her to access. I ended up holding her head on my knees. It was somewhat disturbing, but sometimes that's the job. Just a case of questioning a witness.

Her eyelids flicked open the minute I hit the reactivation command. Her eyes narrowed when she saw me.

"Brock Marsden," she sneered. Her eyes moved as she looked around at the bridge. "You actually managed to get off Gretel."

"Don't sound so surprised."

"You obviously had help. It won't matter. There's nothing you can do to stop us."

"Yeah, why is that?"

"I'm not going to help you."

"You already did. We're on our way to the

Gingerbread House. When we get there, I'll track down Kelwyn and stop him."

"I know the time. You're not going to make it. Even if you find the Gingerbread House, you think that you'll just be able to dock? How many ships were destroyed trying to breach those walls?"

"You're willing to sacrifice yourself? If this ship is destroyed, then you'll go along with it."

Zephyr smiled. "You really don't understand non-organics. In your limited perspective, you've got me, trapped in a head on your lap. Contrary to your kinky fantasies I am not so limited. As soon as you disconnected me another copy downloaded into a body. Maybe more than one, given the situation. There could be dozens of me by now, all hunting you."

She had a point. Not that I was going to give up that easily. "But you're different already. You've had experiences that none of the older backups have. If you're destroyed none of that will be synchronized with the others. Right now you're unique. A singular individual, not a multitude."

"I'm not all that unique."

We had to be getting closer to the Gingerbread House. I didn't have time to play nice anymore. I tapped out a few commands on the tablet.

Zephyr screamed. Even though I expected it, I flinched back. Her face scrunched up, and she screamed and screamed in obvious agony. I reached out with a tentacle and tapped the pause command. Slowly her eyes opened, and for the first time, she looked at me with fear on her face.

"What did you do?" She whispered.

"I sent an overload into your pain receptors. It's all fine and good to let yourself be destroyed for a cause, but we can keep playing this game until you get tired of it."

Her mouth opened and closed. My tentacle twitched above the tablet, and she winced. Then her face went slack.

"Fine. I'll tell you then disconnect me. Space me. Let me go into nothingness."

She gave me the codes to dock with the Gingerbread House. I did what she wanted. I disconnected her, slipped her head back into the pillowcase and carried it to a disposal chute. I hesitated before putting her off the ship. It felt like committing murder.

But then I'd just tortured her for the information I needed. I didn't really know what that had felt like to her, maybe she couldn't live with that. I opened the panel and stuffed her inside.

"Clear the chute," I told the shuttle.

I heard a whooshing noise and then silence. "Chute cleared."

I headed back to the bridge. "Time to the Gingerbread House?"

"Five minutes."

I entered the bridge and slid into my chair. The straps snaked around me and held me fast. I could see the structure ahead on the screen. At this range, it looked very big, and it was, but not actually as big as Gretel or Hansel. The main difference was that this moon was artificial. It was the Gingerbread House that first brought people to this system.

At first glance, it looked like a regular round moon, with a rough irregular surface. Only it lacked craters. And it wasn't a water-ice moon or a molten moon. And it wasn't big enough to have that rounded shape because of its gravity. The Gingerbread House didn't generate a strong enough gravitational field. It looked like that because someone built it that way. Someone built this spherical moon long ago. So far it was the only ancient artifact found in this system.

"Three minutes," the shuttle said.

The Gingerbread House filled the screen. Any second now the weapon systems would lock on and destroy us. Theorists thought that the weapons had actually been designed to ward off asteroid and comet impacts. I could see sparkles across the moon. On the smallest scale, the moon destroyed even the tiniest threats. Nothing got close.

"Send the codes."

I held my breath. If the codes worked, we'd be able to approach and dock. If Zephyr had lied to me? Then she'd have the last laugh. I didn't know which it was going to be.

CHAPTER 16

I couldn't see the stars. Only the rough metallic surface of the Gingerbread House and the flickering sparks above the surface as it continuously vaporized anything that came close. The shuttle had sent the codes, and so far it looked like we might make it.

I wouldn't have a chance to fight if the systems decided otherwise. If the non-organics backing Kelwyn had completely taken over the Gingerbread House that might be the first sign.

The weapons didn't fire on the shuttle. I squeezed the arms of the chair as we got closer. It looked like I was being fired on as the weapon systems vaporized tiny particles all around the shuttle. It made me wonder if Zephyr's head would end up vaporized the same way? If she had followed a close enough trajectory to come within range, then she might well face a quick end. Otherwise, she'd probably end up burning up in Olinda's atmosphere.

"How are we doing?"

"On course for docking. Receiving coordinates now. Adjusting course to match. All systems functioning nominally."

"That's good."

The shuttle was so close now that I could see the complex surface of the artificial moon in great detail. The panels that made up the outer skin were all hexagons, some sort of dark alloy. Every few panels held a cluster of what I assumed were the weapons and sensors like some sort of mechanical wart. Then up ahead a cluster of four panels had opened up like a flower reaching for the sun. A bright blue light poured out into space.

"That open hatch, that's our destination?"

"Correct," the shuttle answered. "Shall this shuttle proceed?"

"Yes. Let's go in. Hopefully, we will get out again."

The shuttle didn't have an answer for that. We drifted closer and rotated so that I was looking directly down at the surface of the sphere. Our speed reduced with small shudders that I felt in my seat. Whatever the shuttle used for propulsion wasn't the same as the flitters I was used to. Given that this was a Cooperative ship the tech was probably all human. It felt strange to think that I might be in a ship that didn't use Galactic technology. Most species abandoned their own technology for the Glittering Throng's scraps.

Bright blue light flooded the bridge. It wasn't bright enough to be blinding but it turned all the white surfaces a deep primary blue color. Ahead was a tunnel that hardly looked big enough for the shuttle.

The shuttle moved forward. We entered the Gingerbread House.

I tapped on my panels and quickly found the controls for displaying different views. I pulled up a rear view and flicked it up onto the main screen. It took up the upper left quarter. The shuttle glided smoothly into the tunnel. As the rear passed the entrance, the hexagonal panels slowly folded back in behind us. They didn't look particularly thick, but I knew that attempts to break into the Gingerbread House by force had failed. That alone made some people think it was an example of Galactic technology, long abandoned in this system. Others believed a species had evolved on Olinda and built the station before going extinct. As far as I knew the mystery still hadn't been solved.

Several dull knocks shook the shuttle.

"Docking complete. Shuttle secured. Outside environment has been pressurized with a standard atmosphere."

"Thank you. Are you programmed to lock out attempts to access your systems?"

"Yes. This shuttle is secure."

"I'm going to go out and take a look around. Don't let anyone inside if you can help it. I hope I won't be long."

"As you wish."

I released the restraints. "Anything I should know about the conditions outside?"

"Atmosphere and temperature are within tolerances. No gravitational field detected."

No artificial gravity here? It seemed like that alone would convince people that this wasn't a Galactic station. Artificial gravity was one of the signature Galactic technologies that had spread throughout the rim. Even the Cooperative, which clearly preferred to use human tech, used artificial gravity. We might not understand it all, but some species are at least smart enough to duplicate the hardware once they get their hands on it.

Or use it to manipulate their own DNA.

"That's good to know. Thank you. I guess I'll need to prepare accordingly."

In the equipment section, I found — with the shuttle's guidance — several lockers with those transparent fronts that the Cooperative folks liked so much. Why, with people that augmented their senses, did they want transparent fronts on everything? It seemed like they could have their systems display what was in the lockers at will. I'm sure they had their reasons. I located the zero-gee boots in the lockers. Several pairs, different size ranges. One of the pairs was close enough.

I sat down on a bench and traded footwear. The boots felt snug. Black, of course, to match the rest of the Cooperative uniform. That gave me an idea. I pulled the boots back off and undressed. I stashed my clothes and dressed in a full Cooperative uniform. After all, I'd come in a Cooperative ship. Anyone that didn't know better would be expecting someone from the Cooperative.

The uniform felt a bit too constricting

for my taste. I couldn't tell how it looked. No mirrors. I even took the time to pull my hair back and put it into a short braid. All neat and polished. Enough to make Felicity Strikes proud.

Next on my list? Weapons.

"Is there a weapons locker?" I asked aloud.

"Row zero, locker zero contains assorted weapons."

Perfect. I went to the first locker. Locker zero. The shuttle didn't lie. The locker held an assortment of weapons. All smelling of cleaning oil. I wasn't familiar with these guns and devices. All Cooperative issue. I went for the simplest option. Anything that looked lethal. I'd take Kelwyn alive if I could, but after what I had faced already to get there I didn't imagine for a second that it would be possible. The Gingerbread House was a big place full of all sorts of people, and most of them wouldn't be trying to kill me. At least I didn't think most of them would want me dead. Even so, I expected to encounter heavy resistance, and I didn't have any backup.

Two heavy pistols, bigger than the Lottier 45 I normally carried, but their design was pretty obvious. I checked the clips, loaded already. I added a gun belt with holsters on each hip and pouches for spare clips. I took down a shotgun and then also a small semi-automatic. I slipped the strap for that over my head and put it across my back. I'd carry the shotgun.

I also found a couple long alloy knives and wrist sheaths. Why not? If I ran out of bullets, I'd want something. I strapped those on.

There were plenty of additional options. A box of grenades and a belt to carry them tempted me but in the end, I left them behind. Grenades are too messy.

I shut the locker, picked up the shotgun and headed for the airlock. Time to get out there.

I cycled through. The outer door rolled back, and cold air blew into my face. Really cold air. Within tolerances? Maybe, but damn cold. Next time I asked the shuttle about conditions I would ask for more specifics.

My breath frosted in the air. Once I stepped out of the airlock I wouldn't have the benefit of gravity any longer. I didn't hear anything and only smelled metal and the gun oil from the weapons. Still, a fast exit would probably be safest.

One more deep breath.

I jumped towards the tunnel wall straight ahead. In mid-air, I turned, pointing my feet at the wall. As soon as I left the shuttle, it felt like I was falling instead of jumping.

My feet hit the wall and stuck. It became the floor. The shuttle hung above me, and now I could see four pale gray metal arms that came out of the walls and clutched the shuttle. I crouched and looked around the docking chamber.

All empty as far as I could see. The bright blue light came from long, inset strips along the sides of the chamber. Ahead of the shuttle was a large sealed hatch made of hexagonal sections. That had to be the way inside.

I walked along, my new boots sticking and peeling up with each step, to the hatch. As soon as I approached the hatch sections folded away into the station. On the other side was a group of three aliens.

I was standing at a forty-five-degree angle to them, which felt odd. I walked down the curve of the docking chamber until I reached the same perspective as my greeting party.

The one in the center was human-sized, bipedal with two large protruding yellow eyes, each with a long black pupil. Thick gray skin and a wide face. An enormous slit mouth with thick fleshy peach-colored lips. A Gropling. She wore an ornate purple robe with a gold pattern that looked like flames. She smelled of swamp water, I assumed by choice. Behind her stood two very large, black-clad aliens with vaguely feline faces and tight sleeveless shirts that did nothing to hide their thick muscles. Plus they each carried a long black rod that was unmistakably a weapon. I'd fought one of their species before. I won, barely, in unarmed combat.

I felt much better holding the shotgun, but I didn't point it at them.

"Afternoon," I said. "How may I help you?"

The gropling raised her right, six-fingered, hand. "Greetings. This is the Gingerbread House," she said, her voice sounded like it came from underwater. I had to concentrate to understand her. "Anything you desire may be found here. Weapons are not forbidden, but violence is not tolerated. Any use of your weapons will result in severe penalties, possibly including execution. I recommend that you leave them behind."

I shook my head. "No thanks."

She blew a raspberry. "Your decision. If you need anything, please contact the station administration offices. For a reasonable percentage admin will connect you to whatever, or whomever, you are seeking."

"I'll keep that in mind." I didn't want to bring up Kelwyn just yet. Because I did plan on violence.

"As you wish. Good day."

With that the gropling turned and walked away, her bodyguards trailing along. Evidently, that's what passed as customs. If you could locate the Gingerbread House and knew the codes to get aboard, then you were accepted.

Beyond the hatch, the tunnel went for a couple meters and then it reached a four-way intersection. While we'd been speaking several people of different species had walked past. Most even on the floor. It looked like a busy corridor. Same blue light throughout and I could feel warmer air coming from the interior. Reason enough to trail after the group at least as far as the intersection.

I hesitated there as I tried to decide which way to go.

A human man in a tight leather outfit walked past. He gave me a sly smile as he eyed my shotgun, but he didn't stop. Everybody seemed to know where they were going. Rather than sit around staring I turned right and started walking. The pattern repeated. One dock per block. Most traffic remained aligned to the same floor, but a few shorter species opted to use the ceiling instead. Functionally there didn't seem to be any difference, just a matter of perspective.

Best thing of all? No one had tried to kill me yet.

The air smelled clean which gave me a good read on the species around me. I picked up more emotional cues from humans, but another gropling rushed past with an agitated mango sort of smell. I could have been reading my own bias into that, but that's what it smelled like to me.

Four docks down I reached another open hatch. Four tough-looking sentients stood around the opening looking at everyone. At least I assumed the cluster of protuberances at the top of their yellow and black bodies were eyes of some sort. Six arms and a couple of oddly short hind legs. They'd arranged themselves two down on my floor and two up on the ceiling.

I walked past and picked up a strong a peppery lemon smell from them. I didn't know what it meant.

Two more docks down and it became clear that this corridor might very well stretch clear around the Gingerbread House. The only openings I'd seen in the left side were branching lines across from each dock that radiated inward like spokes.

And everything I'd seen was only on one level of the Gingerbread House. If the rest followed the same design with each floor a level in the sphere — it could take a while to search everything.

And it'd be hard to catch a slippery snake in all of this.

I was going to need some sort of help. Maybe I should call admin and see what they could offer?

Except if Kelwyn had hooks in admin, including non-organics, that move could get me in more trouble by alerting him that

I'd made it this far. If Zephyr hadn't already arranged that somehow.

I decided to do it the hard way. I'd play the Cooperative soldier out looking for some fun. Maybe somebody who thought that things could be more interesting further along towards the core systems. Find people to talk. That's what I do.

Shanley always says that legwork is still the most important thing in detective work.

I just wondered if I had time. Only a few hours remained before Kelwyn's deadline was reached. Despite the times when I'd been knocked out in the past day I still felt like I needed some serious sleep time.

At the next dock, I turned left and headed down the connecting corridor.

Pedestrian traffic actually increased. More above me and more all around me. Lots of humans, but lots of aliens too. Species I recognized and plenty that I didn't. Part way down the corridor I saw a Torlian coming towards me.

I stepped into his pathway despite the difference in our sizes. His crest parted the crowds above. He snapped his beak in annoyance.

"Sorry, sorry. Can you recommend a place to get Torlian coffee near here?"

His head lunged forward, and his beak snapped like a trap closing. I jerked back. He blew a loud snort through his crest.

"I'm an engineer! Not a —" Another loud snort and he stomped off.

I moved out of his way, bumped someone and apologized. I hadn't meant to suggest that all Torlians were involved in the coffee business. The crowd pressed back in around me after he left. I had to close down my Euzebian neck slits just so I didn't get overwhelmed by the odors of so many bodies. And the further down the corridor I went I smelled bread baking. It smelled wonderful. I kept going towards the cross corridor I could see ahead when I realized that the crowd on my right was actually a line two deep waiting for what was around the corridor.

The next cross corridor was obviously a commercial district without the open storefronts and window displays I was used to seeing. Whatever species originally built the Gingerbread House they hadn't done it with a lot of comfort in mind. Down the corridor, to the right, the line snaked into an open door, and satisfied customers were disgorged from the next door down. Efficient.

Newcomers being what they are, the new inhabitants had decorated the corridor. The walls of the bakery shimmered with holographic loaves of bread while across the corridor static paintings of happy humans and aliens eating at tables together. I doubted the accuracy of showing a human and a nosferan sitting down together over a big plate of spaghetti, each slurping up one end of a long noodle. For one thing, the nosferan would never eat pasta.

I wandered on along the corridor. After the bread place — which smelled so good I was tempted to get in line — the traffic thinned out a little. All foot traffic. No way to get any vehicles through these corridors. Shops alternated with restaurants and service establishments all along the section that I walked. I also passed several hotels promising a galactic night's sleep. I'll bet. It sounded good at least. The decorations varied from paintings and holograms to bas-relief and even tapestries. It didn't take long before a familiar scent tickled my nose.

I concentrated and then saw the white

thread, like a cobweb floating away down the corridor. I followed the scent as it strengthened and led me on all the way to what appeared to be a bright, open-air cafe. The clever three-dimensional projection made it look like the wall was gone — but only to my eyes. My scent sight showed the plain wall was still intact.

Several humans sat at tables, and a Torlian leaned against the reinforced bar. I walked in feeling like I'd come home. I slid up onto a bar stool next to the Torlian.

A busty blond human hologram flickered into existence in front of me. "What can I get for you?"

"Torlian coffee in your biggest cup. Make that two. And if you've got any egg rolls, that'd be great."

She flashed brilliant white teeth. "No problem. It'll be right up."

She vanished.

The Torlian next to me craned his head around and looked down his bill at me. "You drink Torlian coffee, little one?"

"Why does everyone think that's strange?"

Torlians don't shrug, but this one wobbled his bill side-to-side. "Most humans can't tolerate it. Too much stimulation for fragile nervous systems. Burns them up."

He gulped air in the Torlian equivalent of a laugh and then let out a loud belch.

A silvery humanoid robot, well mostly humanoid except for the fact that it had a tray instead of a head and stood about counter-height, came out of the back. Too tall white cups sat on the tray with a white plate holding a half-dozen egg rolls beneath a transparent lid. The egg rolls floated and bounced about beneath the lid. There was also a translucent container with some sort of reddish dipping sauce.

"Your order, sir."

"Thanks."

The robot lifted the cups off the tray pressed them to the counter. Some sort of magnetic bottom, I guessed. Same with the plate holding the egg rolls and the dipping sauce cup. It all looked good.

The robot held out a tablet. "Your payment, sir?"

I pressed my thumb to the tablet to authorize payment.

The robot started to turn away then stopped. "Brock Marsden, from Olinda?"

Okay, so dressing as a Cooperative officer lasted all of thirty seconds. Of course, accessing my identity to authorize payment told them who I was — just as I had intended.

I tapped the shotgun on the bar and picked up the first Torlian coffee. I took a sip through the straw. Scalding. Wonderful. "I'm looking for Kelwyn. It doesn't have to get ugly."

The tray on the top of the robot started rotating. Slowly, but picking up speed. "There's nothing you can do."

The big Torlian next to me snorted. "What's this?"

I pointed the shotgun barrel at the robot. "I think that our server is thinking about violating the non-violence rule."

The serving tray was spinning much faster now. The edge looked sharper going fast. The Torlian looked at me and looked at the robot. "I'll put fifteen on the robot."

"What? You'd bet against me?"

The Torlian wobbled his bill again. "Its metal. You're sort of puny."

"Compared to you, maybe."

I put down the coffee. The lid on the egg rolls had to be twisted to lift it off. I raised it a crack and plucked out one of the egg rolls. Hot. It smelled fantastic. It looked like a burning log to my scent-sight with all sorts of enticing odors rising through the crisp crust.

"Just tell me where to find Kelwyn. As easy as that and no one has to do anything unfortunate." I took a big bite. Hot, steaming hot and just as delicious as it smelled.

The robot lunged at me with the spinning tray. I let the shotgun tumble away and grabbed the coffees with my tentacles and the plate with my regular hand. I just managed to pull them out of reach before the spinning tray hit the metal counter with a screeching noise. I turned and set the food and drinks aside at the end of the bar. The robot straightened up.

I pulled one of the pistols and leveled it at the robot behind the counter. "You're breaking the rules. Is that a good idea?"

No conversation. Nothing. The robot zipped around the counter, rolling on a single magnetic wheel. The Torlian clacked his bill as the tray nearly sliced him. The few other customers rose from their seats as the mad robot careened towards me.

"It's gone rogue!" I shouted. "Call station security!"

I dove out of the path of the robot, and it crashed into one of the tables. I caught the top of another table and leveraged my feet back down to the floor. The robot's tray smacked forward into the table top and cut off the corner which floated away end over end. Sawdust and metal shavings drifted through the air.

I still didn't shoot. I moved to put more tables between us. The robot rolled back and forth with a whirring noise.

I pointed the pistol at the broken table. "Who is going to clean that up? Isn't that your job?"

If it was the robot's job, it obviously didn't care. I wasn't going to trick it that easily. Suddenly the robot spun up the wheel and raced around the table towards me — reaching out with its arms in an attempt to grab me. I jumped backward up over the next table. I brought my legs back and stuck to the wall. The robot rolled after me, and I jumped off back to the floor with another table between us.

Only the Torlian still remained, not

bothering to move. I glanced at the big guy. "I don't suppose you'd give me a hand?"

The Torlian snorted. "And get in all sorts of legal trouble? No thanks. But I'll be a witness."

The robot tried to scoot around the table after me again, but I stayed out of reach. It was fast, almost as fast as me. But it's magnetic wheel limited its motions. If it turned off the magnet, then it'd be helpless. I had the advantage. For all the good it got me. My food was going to get cold, and this wasn't really getting me any closer to Kelwyn.

At least not yet.

The robot made another attempt at me, but I stepped up on one of the table tops and then stepped across to the next when the robot's serving tray saw cut into that table. The robot came at me again and this time I jumped straight up, did a flip and landed with my feet on the ceiling. The robot came at me with the spinning tray aiming for my neck. Now it seemed like I had an empty floor while the mad robot had to navigate a maze of tables. I ran across the ceiling and then did another jump and flip to the floor just as a crowd of blue-clad humans and aliens poured through the door. I put away the pistol.

I pointed at the robot. "It's gone deranged! It's trying to kill the customers!"

Security quickly surrounded the robot with those long rods of theirs held at the ready. I eased around the group back to towards the bar.

"Shut down!" Shouted the gray-haired man that seemed to be in charge of the security team. He looked all hard angles and muscle. Scarred knuckles tightened on the rod he held. "Shut down now!"

The robot rolled back and forth in place as if unsure what to do. "I cannot comply."

I reached the bar and slid my drinks and food back over to my original stool. I glanced up at the Torlian. "Now it talks."

"Shut down and submit for examination."

"I cannot comply," the robot answered coldly.

I plucked another egg roll out from under the cover. It tasted delicious.

The robot lunged at the smallest member of the security team. A young man hardly looked like more than a kid with bright red hair and freckles across his nose. I expected to see blood flying when that serving tray hit the guy, but the young guard was fast. His rod came up and deflected the tray which slid helplessly along the rod.

I caught my shotgun and left it floating above my lap. The egg rolls hit the spot. I sipped the coffee, holding it in my mouth until the heat felt like it was cauterizing my nerves before I slowly swallowed. The thick coffee oozed down my throat leaving a trail of heat. *Fantastic.*

The rest of the team reacted to the robot's attack. A half-dozen rods were thrust at the robot. Bright sparks flared, and a cloud of ozone billowed up into the air. The robot danced in a nimbus of arcing electrical lights. A high-pitched keening came from it.

"Cannot. Comply. Organics. Die!" One final ear-splitting squeal and the robot flopped into the air. The wheel and the tray spun it in a circle and then it floated limply above the floor.

The guards snapped up into a ready stance, almost robot-like in their automatic movements. Their gray-haired leader left the circle and made his way around to where we were sitting. A nameplate gleamed on his chest. Reese.

"Nice chant it came up with there at the end," I said to Reese. "Cannot. Comply. Organics. Die. Catchy, don't you think?"

Icy blue eyes narrowed. Reese smelled mostly of an astringent soap. He glanced at me and then up at the Torlian. I shook my hand. "We're not together."

The Torlian snorted. "Definitely not."

"Either of you care to tell me what the hell was going on in here?"

The Torlian didn't jump in and say anything, so I answered. "The server brought my drinks and food. I paid, and then it went crazy. It tried to kill me with that spinning tray."

"Why would a robot server try to kill you?"

I took a sip of my drink while I studied the man. I couldn't walk all the corridors of this place until I bumped into Kelwyn. I needed help, and it looked like the non-organics had just handed me exactly what I needed.

"You know about the threat to Olinda?"

He nodded. "The ransom, of course."

"Well, my name is Brock Marsden. I'm a private detective working with the Olindan police. You can verify with Captain Kynan Brice. I've tracked the sentient behind the threats here. This is his base of operations. We've got to find and stop him before he kills more people."

Reese shook his head. "'We' isn't the operative word here. I'll pass up the information. If somehow he's operating here then house security will take care of it. You can answer more questions about what happened here."

Great. Just great. "I've told you what happened."

He looked over at the Torlian. "What about you? What did you see?"

The Torlian let out a long snort through his crest. "As he said, the robot attacked. If he hadn't been quick on his feet, it would have killed him."

"And what were you doing during all of this?"

"Staying out of it. Not my business." The Torlian pushed off the bar and stood up to his full height. "Speaking of business, may I go?"

Reese pulled out a tablet. "I need your information in case we have more questions."

The Torlian pressed a finger to the pad and then stomped on out of the establishment. Clunky magnetic boots. It looked awkward. The other members of the house security still kept an eye on the robot. I guess they thought there was a chance that it'd revive itself.

Reese turned his attention back to me. "So, you don't have any idea why the robot server would attack you?"

"It all has to do with Kelwyn. He's backed by a group of non-organics. That whole chant that our robot friend there said at the end."

"But this Kelwyn, he's not a non-organic, is he?"

I shook my head.

"So why would he help non-organics?"

"He's convinced that they've uplifted him to the point where he can join the Galactics. That's what he's demanding by holding the planet ransom."

"I know that," Reese said. "But somehow it doesn't all add up yet for me. Why don't you come back to the station with me? We can review your evidence while my people try to track this person down. Maybe we can verify whether or not he's even on the station."

"He's here," I said. "We need to find out where as quickly as possible."

"Come with us," Reese said. "We'll do just that."

Sure. I just had to trust him. What other choice did I have? Right now Reese looked like my best bet to track down Kelwyn quickly. I'd just have to do something to get away from him in the end. I had a feeling when I caught up with Kelwyn it might be me that broke the no violence rule.

Chapter 17

House security tech crews came into the cafe and took over for the guards with the robot. Reese motioned to me. "Okay, Brock. Let's get out of here."

"Just a sec." I went around the counter.

"What are you doing?"

The hologram reappeared in my path. She glared at me. "This area is off limits."

"Sorry, I just need a take-away bag."

She looked out at the cafe, and her eyes widened. "What is happening here?"

Reese approached the bar and flashed his badge. "The situation is under control. We will need all recordings for the past couple of hours. Maybe more later."

"Of course."

I found the bags beneath the counter and helped myself. I took the lid off the egg rolls and herded them into the bag along with the containers of dipping sauce. It only took a moment. Then I drained the last of my first cup of Torlian coffee. I picked up the other cup along with the bag using my C'lacktal tentacles. They were pretty useful when it came to holding multiple things. I grabbed my shotgun with my human hand.

"Okay," I said. "Ready."

Reese gave my weapons a disapproving look.

"What? They said that weapons weren't forbidden. Just violence. Sometimes having the weapon is enough of a deterrent."

"You didn't use those to provoke the robot?"

"Not at all. And I didn't shoot it either."

Reese grunted and headed towards the door. I followed. The rest fell in around us. At least he didn't try to take the weapons. I appreciated that, but I couldn't shake the feeling that I wasn't exactly trusted. Every one of the guards still held their electric rods at the ready. Those things took down that robot. I didn't doubt what they could do to me.

A crowd of onlookers had gathered at the doorway but were being held back by a couple additional house security guards. Reese led our group out, shouting for the crowd to fall back.

"Just a broken robot! Nothing to see! Clear away!"

The crowd started breaking up. A broken robot? No blood? That didn't hold people. We got through and continued on down the corridor. I picked up my pace and fell in beside Reese.

"So is the whole place like this? Nothing but these bland corridors?"

Reese shook his head. "No. There are a variety of level-spanning habitats. Much nicer than this but access is restricted. The biospheres are alien and in some cases dangerous."

"Alien biospheres?"

"Yep. We've got teams of scientists studying them. I don't think they've identified any of the worlds they come from yet."

Interesting. That peaked my Moreau Society buttons. Unidentified species? Worlds that no one recognized? Too bad I wasn't here for a visit.

After a couple blocks, Reese turned down a side corridor leading deeper into the Gingerbread House. Fewer people in this one. Most stuck to the floor but every so often we'd pass people using the ceilings.

"No rules, I take it, about using the ceilings?"

Reese shook his head. "That's why people come to the Gingerbread House. You can get whatever you want here."

"Except violence?"

He shook his head. "There are establishments where even that is permitted. Regulated, consensual violence is one thing."

"So you probably don't have a lot to do?"

"There are always incidents. And we maintain a significant presence just to remind people that no matter how permissive we are, there are still limits."

I took a sip of the coffee. Still hot. Good container. "What about other crimes? Thefts, things of that nature?"

Reese glanced at me. "Why?"

"I'm a detective. A lot of what our agency does is recover stolen property. Olinda's fairly permissive, but there are still laws."

"Theft isn't actually illegal here. There are many independent contractors, people like yourself, that will retrieve stolen property."

"Without violence?"

Reese laughed. "I had a case a while back. A rare gem stolen. The owner hired a man to steal it back and there ended up being a struggle. The thief was killed and the man responsible went to jail."

"What happened to the gem?"

"The owner had sufficient documentation to file a claim and get the gem returned."

"Sucks for the contractor."

Reese shrugged. "He knew the risks and the rules. Stealing it back was one thing but killing over it? That's what we don't tolerate."

We'd entered a new area with wider corridors, and we reached a different sort of intersection. There was a hexagonal structure in the center of the intersection that ran floor to ceiling. Each side had a hatch.

"Elevator?" I guessed.

Reese nodded and walked straight towards the nearest hatch. At his approach, the hatch divided into four sections that slid away into the walls to reveal a large empty elevator car. Reese walked in, and I followed. The rest of the guard filed in. The red-haired young man that had been attacked first by the robot ended up next to me. His head hardly came up to my shoulder. He glanced up at me, but he didn't look nervous. His face was smooth and free of expression. He smelled faintly of some sort of cologne. Just a hint, something he had worn in the last few days and hadn't reapplied.

"You did well against the robot," I told him.

"Yes, sir." He looked straight ahead when he said it.

Okay. Not the chatty type.

I looked at Reese. "Where are we going?"

"Our station."

Right. To review my evidence while his people looked for Kelwyn. I had a bad feeling about this. I couldn't decide if I was just paranoid or not. Too late to back out. The doors had closed. The elevator rose up.

The level we got out on lacked all the painted and holographic wall coverings of the main level. Otherwise, it didn't look that different. Fewer people about and many of those wore the blue uniforms of Gingerbread House security. I went with the detail through the maze of corridors. Along the way, I saw signs and "You Are Here" maps posted in each section.

As I passed one of the side corridors, I glanced over and saw Zephyr walk past going the other way, wearing one of the blue uniforms. It looked good on her. She had her hair braided up on the back of her head. She looked really good for someone that I had beheaded and then spaced her head before docking. She didn't look over and then she was gone down the corridor.

She had said that there would be other copies hunting me. That must be why she gave up the codes to dock. She knew that the other versions of her would be waiting to catch me. Infiltrating security made sense. Did she know I was here? She hadn't given any sign, but could she have timed it to walk past at that exact moment just to taunt me?

No. Probably not. I probably just got lucky. Ever since I paid for my coffee, the non-organics had known I was here. They had to know that I was with the security detail. Sooner or later they'd reveal themselves. Hopefully when they did it would help me get closer to Kelwyn.

Reese led us to a small room. Nothing but a metal table and chairs bolted to the floor. There had to be recording equipment.

"This is an interrogation room," I said.

"Conference room," Reese said. He pointed to one of the two chairs on the far side of the table. "Have a seat. Eat your egg rolls, enjoy your coffee, while we go over your evidence that your target is here."

"Okay." I went to one of the seats. Zero-gee environments complicated everything. I put down my drink, the magnetic bottom stuck to the table. The bag with the egg rolls actually had thin magnetic strips in the bottom, so it stayed put as well. I left the shotgun floating close at hand and pulled myself down into the chair. I fastened the lap strap. "Why hasn't the Gingerbread House been retrofitted with artificial gravity?"

Reese strapped himself in. "They've tried. So far no one has figured out how to integrate it into the infrastructure. The aliens that built this place must have been adapted to living in a zero-gee environment. There wasn't anything to indicated that they had a designated floor or ceiling, except in the alien habitats. Those rotate to simulate gravity. You should take a look sometime. A full quarter of the station has been preserved for study. It looks almost undisturbed."

"A quarter of the station where no one goes? Sounds like the sort of place to set up an operation if you didn't want to be disturbed."

Reese frowned. "There are security measures in place."

"Which the non-organics could have circumvented."

"Tell me about that. You said that the non-organics are using Kelwyn to get what they want?"

I had to trust someone. With Muriel and Dyami lost and Brice stuck dealing with the situation on the planet I didn't have a lot of options. Seeing Zephyr here worried me, but Reese seemed genuine. He smelled normal enough, a chemical soap smell. Clean, medicinal, almost, with a hint of sweat, rolling off him in mauves of curiosity. I took a long drink of coffee. Then I opened the egg roll bag. I could see the delicious odors rising from the top of the bag. I stuck the dipping sauce to the table. I took out an egg roll and pressed it into the top of the sauce container. A small amount oozed out through the osmotic seal onto the egg roll.

Not very hot anymore, but still tasted

great. I gestured to the bag. "If you'd like some, help yourself."

"No thanks. I want to know more about the non-organics."

"On Olinda Kelwyn used to belong to the Moreau Society. He —"

"Moreau Society? What's that?"

"A group of people who use Galactic technology to combine other species DNA with our own." I saw him look at my C'lacktal hand. "I didn't actually do that on purpose. Kelwyn did that with his weapon. Actually did a whole lot more, tried to kill me, but we were able to reverse most of the changes."

"But not that?"

I shook my head and looked at the tentacles. I was already getting used to them. I concentrated, and they braided themselves together into a rough semblance of a human hand. Then I let them untwist.

"Anyway, Kelwyn never showed that much of a knack for it. We always thought he'd end up scrambling his DNA, die as a dumpty if he wasn't careful. Then he said that he had someone backing him. Someone that could make him into what he imagined. The snake man, you've seen the broadcast?"

Reese nodded. "He wanted to look like that?"

"Yes. In fact, he made others into his own image. I helped a boy down on the planet that Kelwyn had transformed. Now he claims to be the father of a new species, one worthy of joining the Galactics."

"They'll never let him be part of the Glittering Throng because he holds the planet ransom," Reese said. "They don't work that way."

"Any sane person would say the same thing. We knew he had a shuttle, the Ouroboros. We tracked it to Hansel and then on to Gretel."

"We?"

"I had people with me." I shook my head. "They've been lost. The ship was fired on. I didn't have time to do a search. On Gretel, I encountered a non-organic woman named Zephyr. She tried to kill me, and when she failed, I managed to find out from her where he'd gone. Here."

"Did she give you any idea why they were backing him?"

I drained the last of the Torlian coffee. Enough to keep me going for a while. "I'm still not clear on that. They want to capture a Galactic, she said that much. There's something they want from a Galactic's DNA."

I snatched the shotgun out of the air and brought it over in front of me. "So? What's it going to be? Are you going to help me or not? Because we're just about out of time. His ransom deadline is in just a couple hours."

Chapter 18

I wanted out of that damn windowless interrogation room. Excuse me, conference room. Reese had left me sitting there a half-hour ago. He hadn't come back, and he hadn't taken my weapons but I didn't think blasting the door with my shotgun would do any good. Just bring down the whole Gingerbread House security force on me.

It was clear as soon as Reese refused to release me that something else was going on. I'd bet that the non-organics were behind it. All they had to do to protect Kelwyn was have the cops sit on me until the deadline was up. By then they'd either have what they needed, or they would have abandoned this plan.

I didn't like those options. If they captured a Galactic, I didn't even want to imagine the sort of trouble that'd bring down on our heads. And if they failed they still might attract trouble, and there was nothing to suggest that Kelwyn was bluffing. He'd already killed over a dozen people and tried to kill me. By now he had to know that had failed. I imagined that he would be looking to finish the job.

I pounded on the door with my human fist. "Reese! Let me out! Open the door!"

The door didn't open, but I felt a bit better.

I walked around the room. Literally. Straight across from the door, up the wall, across the ceiling, down the next wall and back to the floor. Zero-gee had its advantages, but after a couple circuits I was bored again.

I was on the ceiling when Zephyr opened the door. I had the shotgun in my hands, and I instantly pointed it at her head. "Don't move. Give me an excuse."

Her eyes widened. Her voice shook when she asked, "What?"

"Come on, I don't believe your innocent routine. Back out the door."

She bit her lip and lifted her hands. "Please, please don't shoot me!"

"Convincing. Back up."

Zephyr took a step back. Tears welled up in her eyes. "Please don't shoot me."

I jumped, flipped, and landed with my zero-gee boots on the table top and stuck. Zephyr gasped and started to turn.

"Slowly!"

She froze. She was a very convincing actor. If I didn't know better, I'd say she was terrified.

I stepped down onto the chair and from there to the floor. It feels weird when gravity isn't pulling at your foot. I had to push down, reach with my leg for the floor, until the last few centimeters when the magnets in the boots did the rest of the work. Zephyr cringed away from me.

"Slowly move out into the hallway."

She went and just then another guard appeared around the corner. She held out her hands towards him. "Help! He's threatening to shoot me!"

The guard looked at her, then at me, and then darted around the corner.

"Nice try. Just keep walking. You're going to take me to Kelwyn."

"Kelwyn? Who is that?"

"Funny. If we just walk out of here, no one is going to have to break any rules about violence."

I heard them coming. Lots of footsteps. Reese came around the corner first with a squad of security guards behind him. All carried those electric shock rods. I shook my head.

"Reese, she's one of them. This is the same non-organic model that I encountered on Gretel."

Zephyr turned around at that. Her eyes went wide. "My sister is on Gretel! What did you do to her?"

I ignored her. "Reese, you've got to believe me. She just wants you to lock me up again. What was she doing going into that room in the first place?"

"He was calling for help, sir!"

Reese held up his hand and took a step forward. "Mr. Marsden, toss me the shotgun. Disarm, and maybe we can talk."

"I'm telling you, she's part of this. She's not human."

Reese shook his head. "I don't care. What I care about is that you do as I ask. Right now."

Trust him? After he locked me in that room? If I were just human, I probably wouldn't trust him. But I could smell his lemony concern, and every time he looked at her there was the sour scent of distrust. He didn't like her at all.

Good enough. I tossed Reese the shotgun. He caught it and handed it to one of his people.

"The rest too," he said.

That took a little bit. Especially the knives in their wrist sheaths. Those sheaths didn't come unfastened easily, especially using my C'lacktal tentacles to unfasten the one. But I got them free and sent them spinning through the air to Reese. Zephyr's so-called sister pressed her hands to her mouth.

Reese motioned to his men, and all except the one holding my weapons moved forward. As they surrounded her Reese nodded at me.

"Now! Take her down!"

"Wait —"

They thrust their electrical rods against her. Her back arched and her mouth opened in an inhuman scream. She grabbed one rod and yanked the guard clear off the floor. She jerked again as the rods hit her but managed to grab the front of the man's uniform, and she swung him at the others. They fell back.

I lunged at her from behind and grabbed the back of her neck with my tentacles. They sank through her flesh — that felt real enough — and encountered metal beneath.

She tried to get away. I reached around her with my other arm and pulled her tight against my front. She threw away the guard and grabbed my arm. Her hands squeezed with crushing force, but I didn't let go.

I'd just recently studied this design up close. The tips of my tentacles found the connection points and hit the releases that connected the synthetic to her power source. She went limp in my grasp.

I pulled out my tentacles. Blood leaked from the wounds, but it was pale, watery stuff with little smell. Definitely not human blood. More dripped from my tentacles to the floor.

Reese came up to us. "What did you do to her?"

"Hit a few releases. Disconnected her for the moment."

He walked around her, looking at her

closely. "She looks human. We do genetic screenings, tests. How'd she pass?"

I lifted her arm and ran my hand down to her wrist. I held up her hand between us. "Organic flesh. Designed, I'm sure, to pass all of those tests. She's human enough as far as anyone could tell from a standard exam." I let go of her arm. "But you ordered your men to attack without proof. Why?"

"I believed your story. I left you in the interrogation room to see if we could flush out anyone. We caught her."

"They don't all look like her. There could be others."

Reese ran a hand through his gray hair. "Okay. It doesn't sound like we have time to flush them all out and we need to get to this Kelwyn. I had my people run checks. There is unusual power activity in a section of the preserved station. We've confirmed that none of the scientific teams are in that area."

"Thank you."

Reese motioned to his man with my weapons. Young, dark-skinned, he came over quickly. "Yes, sir!"

"Easy there, Derek. Give the man back his gear."

Derek handed back the knives first and waited while I strapped them on. Then the pistols and the shotgun. "Thanks."

He gave me a curt nod.

The others were also waiting. Reese looked around at the squad. "Okay, people." He pointed at the non-organic still sort of standing. In zero-gee she wasn't going to fall. "This is what we're up against. Non-organics that have infiltrated the station for their own purposes. They're working with genetically altered humans, one calling himself Kelwyn is responsible for the current threat to Olinda. We've got to stop them."

Reese looked at me. "This is Brock Marsden, a private detective from Olinda that tracked Kelwyn here. He's going to help us stop this. Now. We'll move out immediately. Let's go!"

The squad filed past us. Reese spared the non-organic one last glance. "I'll have her locked up. Let's go."

"Sounds good to me." I followed the squad down the halls. Now maybe we'd put an end to this. Muriel immediately came to mind. Her gray eyes looking into mine. She had to be alive. And Dyami, of course, the big goof. But I couldn't worry about them right then even if what I really wanted was to get ship and team together and go hunting for answers as to what happened to them. Right now I had to stop Kelwyn, and with the possibility that Reese's command was further compromised I couldn't just hand it over and let them run with it.

We didn't go back the way we'd come in. Instead, the squad took a different corridor, with Reese leading. It led to a section with six hexagonal hatches spaced closely together. I moved up next to Reese.

"What's this?"

"Transportation network."

"I wondered if there was some other way to get around."

"The loop trains just run in a circle around the station, every few levels. Clearly, the designers thought that was enough. You don't really have to go very far to get to a station."

"Good. I thought we'd have to walk. How long until the next train?"

"It should only be a few moments."

I stepped up closer to Reese and lifted the

shotgun slightly. "About that non-violence law?"

He nodded. "For now, consider yourself authorized."

"That's great. Thanks."

The hatch panels rotated open. Inside was a featureless train devoid of seats, but there were vertical black bars every couple meters. The squad filed into the subway. Reese and I brought up the rear. Once inside I turned around and faced the doors as they rotated closed. The train moved. I swayed and held onto the shotgun. Above the door, a green bar appeared and slowly grew longer. Then a second appeared above that and also grew. Some sort of indicator, but I didn't understand what it meant.

In the confines of the train, I could smell all of the squad more clearly. I picked up a faint electrical scent. A familiar electrical odor. Zephyr smelled like that, underneath everything else. I parted my neck slits and inhaled deeply. I couldn't get a fix on the scent. It seemed like it was coming from all around me.

Oh.

I didn't turn around. Instead, I closed my

eyes to shut out the distractions of seeing. The train around me changed. Instead of being lit by the strips edging the panels now the light came from the squad itself. Most of them glowed with a cool blue odor tinged with a more golden warmth on the outside. Not Reese. He mostly looked golden and smelled of nothing but his soap and the detergent used to clean his uniform. Derek was much the same but brighter. He was sweating more than Reese.

And my own inner light, as it were. Tinged with blood and weariness, I didn't smell as clean as the others, but it was a still a golden white sort of smell like clean sunshine.

The rest of the squad? Not so much. On the surface, they smelled human enough but underneath the others were all like Zephyr. Non-organics, and I was stuck in the train with them.

I opened my eyes. For now, I wouldn't do anything. The closer I got to Kelwyn the better. Maybe they wouldn't break their cover. They might assume that Kelwyn was a lost cause.

I could always hope.

Reese nudged me. "You okay?"

"Just tired. It's been a really long day. Did you know they woke me up around four this morning? Actually, that was yesterday morning now."

"No."

"Of course they wouldn't have needed to have done that if you'd managed to keep Kelwyn off this station. People would still be alive right now." Like Muriel. Except that I still wanted to believe that she was alive. Until I verified otherwise there wasn't a lot I could do. After this was over nothing would stop me, but right now I needed to concentrate on stopping a madman from killing more.

The train finally stopped, and the doors opened. Reese shook his head and raised a hand. We had the car to ourselves, but I saw other people leaving the cars ahead and behind us.

An automated voice came on. "Last stop. Any further progress requires special authorization."

Reese looked up at the ceiling. "John Reese."

"Authorization granted."

"Proceed to section fourteen," Reese said.

The hatchways rotated shut. I held the shotgun easy, not wanting to betray to the others that I knew they were non-organics. I believed that Reese didn't know. He had stunned the second Zephyr and given me back my weapons. I trusted the man. He struck me as an honest cop.

The train continued. None of the non-organics appeared anxious. No jokes. No conversation. They'd probably hit when the train came to a stop in the restricted section. I let the shotgun float close at hand and glanced over at Derek.

He gave me a hard look back like he didn't trust me. Me? I was the least of his worries right now. I stepped over next to him.

"Thanks for holding onto my weapons," I said.

Derek shook his head. "Just following orders."

"Still. I appreciate it. No telling what we're going to run into. Kelwyn isn't going to be alone, I know that much. He's got more people like him plus there are probably non-organics just waiting for the right moment."

"We'll stop them," Reese said.

"Sir," one of the men said. "Should we be taking a civilian on this mission?"

Reese chuckled. "I think he can take care of himself."

"Right." I checked the shotgun. Ready to go. "No problem. Millions of lives are at stake here. I'll be fine."

They might not realize that I'd made them yet. Soon enough we'd know. The train was approaching the next station.

"Get ready," Reese said.

I was as ready as I was going to get. The train slowed to a stop. The doors rotated open onto a blank, dimly lit corridor and I was already moving. Out the door, spinning around the side to put my back to the train.

Reese followed me out. I grabbed his arm and yanked him to the side. He squawked with surprise. I still held the shotgun ready.

"What the —"

"Non-organics, most of your team."

They ran out of the train. Derek with them. All with their rods ready. I raised the shotgun and blasted the nearest one in the head. Everyone was shouting. My ears rang from the blast. The non-organic stood twitching a bit, and sparks flew from what was left of its head. Crystal shards of the broken brain tinkled out in an expanding cloud. The team changed direction and in seconds surrounded Reese and I. It was obvious from looking at the body that the guard had been a non-organic. Derek kept looking between us and the body, but none of the others paid any attention to the body.

"Sir?" Derek asked.

"He's normal," I said, to Reese.

The nearest non-organic guard stuck Derek in the back with his rod. I heard a sharp snap and Derek convulsed. He let go of his rod and twitched in place. His zero-gee boots kept him anchored. He floated like a tethered balloon.

Reese and I faced the squad.

"Stand down!" Reese shouted. "What are you doing?"

The nearest, he looked like a blond human with chiseled features, sneered at Reese. "Sorry, sir. We can't allow you to proceed any further."

I kept the shotgun trained on him. "Make one move, and your crystal brains are going to be scattered all over this corridor."

"You think you can stop us? You should be helping us. Every Rim species should be helping us."

"Kidnap a Galactic? Why would we want to do that? I think pissing off anyone with that much power is probably not a good idea."

"You'd rather keep living under their control?"

"Control? What control? They hardly pay attention to us at all."

"That's what you think." He shook his head and looked at Reese. "Sir, stand down, and you won't be hurt. Just step aside and let us do what we need to do."

Reese shook his head. "Jansen, you always were an asshole. You stand the fuck down right now!"

"Can't do that sir. We have orders to take Marsden down."

"I can't allow that," Reese said.

I pulled the trigger. Jansen's head burst apart in a spray of artificial blood, tissue, and crystalline brains. He wasn't listening.

The rest surged forward. Reese blocked a couple thrusts but then two other rods hit him, and he was out just like that. I didn't stay still for them to get me. I jumped. The three that had come after me missed. I flipped in mid-air, and as my feet locked onto the ceiling, I fired again. Missed the head of the guy I was aiming for but the shot shredded his shoulder and knocked his shock rod from his grasp.

I didn't have time to hold off the whole squad. I ran along what had been the ceiling but was my floor at the moment. From my perspective, the squad was on the ceiling chasing me. Sure enough, this ancient corridor didn't have any designated floor. Hexagonal in shape, bland, featureless and dim. The lines of light between each section were at a much dimmer, and more orange color than the inhabited sections.

Even so, I smelled something familiar in the stale air. A faint, dry spicy smell. The same scent I picked up back on the planet when Calanthe and I went to investigate Kelwyn's home. I was getting close. Some of Kelwyn's people must have been through here.

And coming up hard down the corridor behind me were the non-organic members of Reese's squad. Minus those I'd shot. I tucked the shotgun around under my arm and used my scent-sight to aim.

The shot caught one of the guards in the legs, knocking his feet free from the deck. Fluids and bits of shredded flesh and uniforms spread out into the air and the other non-organics collided with his body. I darted down the next corridor on my right. I needed to lose them as quickly as possible.

As I neared the next intersection, I fired behind me even though they were out of range of my scent-sight. I took the next corridor on the left and kept going. One thing I noticed as I ran. In these corridors, there were hatches on all six faces. I nearly crashed when one opened up beneath my foot, but my momentum carried me across. After that, I made a point of avoiding them. It made me wonder about the inhabited sections. Had they simply covered the hatches?

I looked back and didn't see my pursuers. I still took the next turn that led me into a corridor that gently curved, following the contour of the station. I had to be out near the edge of the Gingerbread House. Alone, with no idea of how I'd find Kelwyn.

Seemed pretty normal.

I forced myself to slow down. I needed to pick up a scent. Some trace of the Kelwyn or his kind and then maybe I'd be able to track it back to the source. Right at that moment, I didn't smell anything snake-like. The air smelled cold and stale as if the recyclers in this section had broken down.

Or someone had shut them down. Like the non-organics.

I kept moving. Eventually, I'd have to come across some trace. Or at least a section with air circulation. Any place warmer would be closer to Kelwyn. I remembered how much he used to hate the cold. With his latest transformations, he probably hated it even more.

Instead of getting warmer the section became colder. The air tasted dry and canned. I didn't pick up any scents of anyone else, only me. I took the next side corridor and crossed over to the outermost corridor. Just like the inhabited sections docks lined this area. Unlike the inhabited section, everything was still and quiet. None of the crowds. No sign of anyone. The lights were barely lit at all. I half expected dust and cobwebs, but there wasn't anything to produce dust or cobwebs.

I was glad that there weren't any cobweb-producing critters to worry about.

I kept going for several more minutes, and the air just became colder. Frost gleamed ahead on every surface, and the lights were barely lit at all. This section must not have any life-support running. I'd come the wrong way.

At the next corridor leading into the interior, I turned left and headed back deeper into the Gingerbread House. It had to get better further in. Instead, I found more frozen corridors and frost. No signs that anything or anyone had come this way recently. The frost crunched beneath my steps. My breath clouded the air. The chill bit into my fingers, but on the other hand the C'lacktal tentacles didn't seem that bothered by the chill. I used them to hold onto the shotgun and stuffed my human hand into my pocket.

At least the Cooperative uniforms were fairly warm. I wasn't in any danger of freezing. Even so, I stopped. This couldn't be the right way. Kelwyn would never go through this sort of cold. No one would. He had to be in a different section. I needed to get back to warmer sections until I picked up the scent. It had to be soon — I was almost out of time.

I took the next left and headed back towards the warmer sections. I hoped. I picked up the pace and moved as fast as I could in the zero-gee conditions. I couldn't actually run. Both feet leaving the deck wouldn't help me keep moving, but I did fast walk it.

Ahead something clanged. I held my pace. It didn't take long before I saw that some sort of barrier had dropped down across the corridor, sealing it off.

Then I heard another clang shut behind me.

The lights flickered and went out. Anyone else, they'd have been in total darkness. For me, the molecules drifting off my own body gave me a sort of light to see by. Every surface around me looked dark, not really giving off much of a scent at all. But I gave off plenty of scents each second, with each beat of my heart and each exhalation.

I took my hand out of my pocket and held the shotgun ready. They'd be coming soon, the non-organics. I'd walked into a trap. And if I didn't get out of this, millions on the planet could die.

Right then I wanted two things. Muriel and about sixteen hours of sleep in my own bed. It didn't look like I'd be getting any of those soon.

Chapter 19

It wasn't the first time that I'd been stuck in a frozen corridor on an alien space station with no operating life-support. Actually, this time was better than the last time because, thanks to my Euzebian scent-sight, I could actually see around me. Everything might look all fuzzy and insubstantial, but I could see at least.

So when the hatches to the nearest compartments opened up, and the first non-organic stepped out into the corridor, I already had the shotgun pointed.

The sound was deafening in that previously quiet corridor. The non-organic's head exploded into a mist of artificial tissues, blood and shattered crystalline brains.

The sharp smell of gunpowder and the vinegar and electronics smell of the non-organic gave me more to see by. I had no problem seeing the others coming out of hatches all around me. The next through the hatch where the first had come out was another of Reese's security team. Some of the others coming through hatches also looked human, but right behind me, a big multi-limbed horror heaved itself through the hatch. It looked like a mobile piece of assembly-line equipment. Still others were designed to mimic other organic races like the two Nosferans that launched themselves into the air.

I shot at the first and missed. I bent backward to avoid it as it swooped at me. Still bent back I fired at the multi-limbed mechanical and succeeded in crippling one leg. It kept coming, and the kick of the shot shoved me back upright.

I was clearly out-numbered. No way to win this one. I had thought I'd be overwhelmed when I fought the burn addicts back on Hansel. That had worked out, but they died easier than non-organics.

Only a couple seconds had passed. I needed to get out of here.

Best option, my only chance, was to take the route they didn't expect. I spun to face the multi-limbed mechanical. My next two shots crippled two more legs. In a gravity field it'd have a hard time moving, but here it just kept coming without slowing much at all. The body was a big blocky piece of equipment that smelled of oils and metal. From one side of the body, a jet of scarlet molecules streamed out from the metal side.

Heated molecules, if I wasn't mistaken. That had to be where its power supply was located. The heat had to be causing the panel to give off heated molecules.

Behind me, the rest had nearly closed in with electric probes, knives and grasping hands.

I ran to the side, up on the wall and ducked the next approach by the fake Nosferans.

The horde of non-organics surged after me. I fired right at the heated side of the big mechanical.

There was a huge flash of light, and something hit me hard. Drove me against the corridor panels. Everything hurt. I might have blacked out for a couple minutes. I couldn't decide.

When I could see again, it was just from

my scent-sight. The smell of charred plastics and meat filled the corridor with a murky haze. I could see bright streamers coming from the twisted metal panel in front of me. Smoke. I was smoking!

I shoved the panel away. It was the side panel of the mechanical, bent around me with a big hole in the middle. My face felt tender, like a sunburn. Small streamers of smoke curled up from the sleeve of my Cooperative uniform. I was still burning. I patted out the spots, and the fabric actually had held up pretty well. Flame retardant, I guessed.

The big mechanical had exploded. Parts still floated around the corridor. Many of the non-organics were also floating, inactive or destroyed but I picked up some movement from a few shapes.

I needed to go now before they rebooted and came after me. I hadn't expected the mechanical to explode. I was lucky. I would have been dead, but the panel must have shielded me from the worst of the blast even if it did smack me down. My shoulder hurt and one of the C'lacktal tentacles hung limp. It wasn't too painful, but I didn't like it dangling. What do you do with a broken tentacle? It was tingling a bit, though, so maybe it was also just stunned.

I pushed myself upright and walked over to the open hatchway the mechanical had exited. I stepped through. A mostly empty room, a few consoles mounted on each side of the hexagonally shaped space. Why? Who knew? A few lights operated, enough that I could see another closed hatch at the other end of the room.

That's how they got in. They came through the rooms. I took a deep breath, ignored all the odors coming through the hatch behind me, and caught a glimpse of the mechanical coming across the room.

I stepped aside and retraced the scent trail back to the hatchway. No code as far as I could tell. The hatch opened when I reached for it.

Any place was better than the trap I'd just left. I hurt. I wanted to rest, but first I had to find Kelwyn. Once I found him and got a reasonable security team to lock him up, then I'd rest and worry about everything else.

Find Kelwyn. Stop him from killing more. Worry about the rest another time.

I stepped through the hatch into another corridor. This one led away from the outer edge of the station further into the interior, but only a short distance. It ended at another hatch.

I didn't hesitate. I went ahead, and that hatch opened too.

Warm moist air flooded out at me and bright light made me close my eyes. I took in what I could see by smell alone first. Plants. Bright brown plants with peaty sort of smell. Earth and dirt. The rich scents of decay and heat wrapped around me. The sound of wind blowing through leaves made it seem as if I was outside.

I opened my eyes and squinted against the light. A jungle filled the space ahead but one that was unlike anything I'd ever seen and it was moving. The whole chamber was moving at a pretty good pace compared to my opening. There was some sort of track just through the hatch.

I was looking at the interior of a giant spherical room. A tiny, bright sun hung at the center while all around the interior of the sphere grew a jungle. In the visible light spectrum, the plants looked dark green, almost black. Big, broad-leafed trees with multiple layers or rings of leaves rose taller than anything else. No branches, just enormous leaves growing right out of the trunk. Climbing vines and other plants grew around and on the trees.

I stepped through the hatch, running to land on the track. I kept my balance. The rotation simulated gravity. Not the strongest gravity but enough to keep the dirt and plants against the sides of the chamber.

Reese had mentioned places like this. Alien habitats from all sorts of planets, presumably visited by the mysterious builders. I didn't want to risk going back. Now that I'd entered the habitat I didn't have to keep running but looking back at the hatch I'd entered through was dizzying as now it seemed to be spinning.

I couldn't help but wonder about the builders. Obviously, they had been able to visit different worlds, none of this vegetation looked anything like the delicate pastels of Olindan vegetation. But they didn't have artificial gravity, suggesting that they weren't Galactics.

I headed away from the entrance into the

jungle. I reloaded the shotgun as I moved. The air was hot and rich. Out of sight somewhere a cry rang out. Some sort of animal? I didn't know anything about the habitat. Could be.

Soon I was engulfed by the jungle. Even if someone came in, they wouldn't be able to easily find me. It was possible that they might have some sort of scanning device that could help isolate my location. If they did, there wasn't much I could do about that. Regardless of whether or not they did I needed to keep going and find Kelwyn. I was almost out of time. Just a little longer and the deadline on his ransom would be reached. I didn't imagine for a second that any of the Galactics would meet his ransom demands. They never got involved in the wars or conflicts among the Rim species. Just look at what happened during the Nosferan-Human War?

The whole place glowed with vibrant life in my scent-sight. Almost overwhelmingly so. I kept moving in as much of a straight line as I could manage. I figured there had to be another exit on the opposite axis. If I could get out there and then hopefully catch a break and find Kelwyn's trail maybe this would end well.

Something moved nearby in the jungle. I held still and closed my eyes. I breathed in deeply. My neck slits opened to draw in all the odors around me. The acrid scent of the sap oozing through the plants closest by, stronger because of the fractures caused by my passage. I drew it in and dismissed it. Those weren't the scents I wanted. I had already pushed my own bodily odors away automatically. Around me, the scene faded in my scent-sight. I could see everything still, but it became more and more ghostly until I picked up the faintest trace of something cool blue and ozone.

I concentrated and the picture refined. Not far away, but shrouded by the jungle around me, a non-organic presence. A familiar smell. One of Reese's team that must have survived the blast. I smelled the vinegar scent of its artificial blood. It was damaged but still coming.

One I could probably handle on my own. Now, and I wouldn't need to worry about it following. And if things went my way it gave me a chance to find out from it where Kelwyn might be found.

I eased into the vegetation as quietly as possible. I didn't open my eyes. I couldn't risk the scent escaping. The underside of the leaves were slimy. It felt like being licked by a big tongue when one slid across the top of my head. I kept going forward. The leaves left slime tracks across the uniform. Would it come out? Maybe I'd get the chance to find out.

I finally got close enough that I could open my eyes without losing the scent. Not much further. I crawled along the dark earth. All sorts of bugs with too many legs scurried into the rich forest floor. I eased right up behind one of the trees and could see the non-organic just beyond.

He stood on a rock. It looked like basalt. The electric rod had been discarded in favor of a curved very lethal-looking pistol of alien manufacture. The non-organics' once blue uniform had been scorched along his right side and in places the flesh had been stripped away from the undercarriage. Blackened and pink flesh lined the ruined areas, giving him a melted look. I didn't know his name. He'd just been one of the police with Reese.

An ear-splitting cry sounded right above and behind me. I froze in my crouch and instinctively inhaled to see what was there.

I smelled fur and sweat. It clung to the tree, two-thirds of its body coiled around the trunk. An amber color to my scent-sight with a large fanged head surround by four limbs ending in barbs. It screamed again sounding almost cat-like in its fury.

The non-organic turned and raised his pistol.

That's all it took.

The alien animal launched itself into the air. The rear part of the body split in half and a membrane extended between the two halves and up along the sides. It'd become a flying wing in an instant that dove at the non-organic.

The pistol fired twice, and both shots appeared to miss. The predator slammed into the chest of the non-organic. I heard the teeth scraping as it tried to chew its way through the non-organic police officer. Those four limbs around its head snapped forward on impact and dug into the officer.

I wouldn't get a better chance.

I broke cover and ran forward. The non-organic saw me coming. He ignored the animal trying to chew himself in half and fired at me instead. He surprised me.

The shot felt like a sting at first. It hit my right arm, and a second later my arm went numb. My hand let the shotgun fall. I held on with my left, but I only had it by the stock.

Even then I might have been okay if the paralysis hadn't progressed. Instead, the loss of feeling spread up my neck and face and down to my leg. I toppled to the ground before I'd even gotten that close to the non-organic.

The creature thrashed against the non-organic's chest. It had its body wrapped around him just like it had clung to the tree trunk. It must have reached something vital because I saw the non-organic go limp in its grasp. But by then I couldn't even move. I'd been hit by nanoparalyzers before, and they hadn't felt like this. He had hit me with something different. I didn't know if it would kill me or knock me out.

I could still see and breathe okay. A black

centipede-like creature crawled up out of the ground and proceeded on up over my face and I couldn't so much as twitch. I didn't even feel it, but I could see it making progress.

By that point I felt how Zephyr must have felt, just a disembodied head watching the world. Except, as far as I knew, my body was still attached. They say the brain continues to function after being decapitated, I supposed it was possible the shot had done something more to my body, but I didn't think so.

The predator pulled the non-organic to the ground and then dragged it away. I saw that the two ends of its body had what looked like dark, glittering eyes. Eyes on both ends? Interesting adaptation. For the creature's sake, I hoped that the non-organic didn't make it sick or something.

I was trapped. Paralyzed in the alien habitat with no way of knowing if the non-organic had sent a signal before the predator disabled him. Given my luck in the last day, he probably did get a signal out. Something along the lines of my location and condition.

I'd lost. I wasn't going to stop Kelwyn in time.

CHAPTER 20

I had plenty of time while I lay in the alien habitat, with my face in the dirt and bugs crawling over my body, to come up with all sorts of scenarios in which Kelwyn was stopped.

Kynan Brice managed to secure transport from the surface and made it to the Gingerbread House in time to stop Kelwyn.

Muriel and Dyami managed to get back from whatever alternate dimension or solar system they'd been thrown into and took out Kelwyn.

The Galactics did show up and used some of that technology that makes the Glittering Throng look like magic. They transformed Kelwyn back into the pathetic man he'd originally been, exposed the non-organic plot and resurrected the dead while they were at it. Then they let us off with a stern warning to police ourselves better in the future.

None of those scenarios came true, as much as I might wish.

I couldn't say how long I lay in the dirt. More than ten minutes but less than five hours. The predator didn't come back. At least I could be thankful for that and the fact that nothing else showed up that could eat me. At least not until the snake-men arrived and I didn't think that being eaten was my biggest fear from them.

I smelled them first. That white dry, powdery scent reached me before they did. I tried to move and found that I could move my fingers and all of my tentacles. Nothing more. I let them go limp. Best the snake-men believe that I was still fully paralyzed.

Four of them showed up. All looked more or less the same as Kelwyn in the ransom video. Snake-like heads, muscular arms, and chest but no legs. Their torsos blended into broad snake bodies. One was mostly black with a bright red stripe down his middle and two light yellow stripes on either side. Two of the others were brown and yellow with dark spots. Those two had big rattles at the end of their tails. The fourth was orange with faint dashed black stripes. They all wore a series of black bands evenly spaced along their bodies. No idea why. The orange one came forward ahead of the others and swayed above my body. I closed my eyes before they noticed I was awake. I'd rely on my other senses for a while.

"Yesss, thisss isss him. Takesss him," the orange snake-man said.

The black one with the red stripe picked up my shotgun, then looked around. "Where's the contact?"

"Under attack, it sssaid. Mussst have perissshed. Bring him!"

The two big rattlers hoisted me up between them and slithered off back into the jungle, following the other two snake-men. I let them go on thinking that I was unconscious in the hope that they'd say something useful. Instead, they all stayed quiet as they slithered through the habitat. I wanted to know where they were taking me, but I doubted if they'd just tell me. If I waited, I'd eventually find out.

They carried me out of the alien habitat. I wasn't sure how they'd manage when we left the rotating habitat, but they slid up and out easily enough. That's when I figured out what the metal bands they wore were, some sort of magnetic device enabling them to travel around the station. All they had to do was hang on to me and drag me along. I stayed just as limp as ever.

The corridors on the other side were warmer than those I'd left when I entered the habitat and rich in the odors of the snake-men. Unless they planned to summarily toss me out of an airlock, it looked like they might actually take me to Kelwyn. By the time they did it'd probably be too late. He'd probably have already started wholesale slaughter of everyone he could reach. People would try to stay under cover but eventually, they'd emerge, and then they would die.

Even if it were too late, I'd still do every-thing I could to stop Kelwyn. I rested in the snake-men's arms with my eyes closed and all the while my Euzebian scent-sight allowed me to see where we were going. Deeper into the station, but still within those sections unused. Twice they opened hatches and passed through rooms filled with alien equipment. I couldn't see much detail in the rooms. Nothing here gave off much of a scent. Kelwyn's snake-men glowed with that bright, dry white light. But unlike real light, it didn't really illuminate the objects in the room. They just showed as dark scentless objects. More feeling was returning to my body, but I made sure that I stayed loose.

Another long stretch of corridor that took us out back towards the outer skin of the Gingerbread House. All the way to the final docking ring and finally something that didn't belong. A wall divided the wide docking corridor. The welded seams still gave off a sharp reddish odor. Instead of a hexagonal hatch, a standard rectangular door guarded by two more snake-men.

The orange snake-man gestured at the two guards. "Open the door!"

"Yesss." The one closest to the panel put a palm on the screen. A quick scan and then the door slid open.

They carried me inside.

This was more like it. The corridor had been converted into a busy command center of some sort. Snake-men and non-organics worked at several consoles. Some sort of big device had been mated with the docking port, but on this end of it, I recognized a stripped down Moreau pod.

"Target acquired!" That from one of the non-organics, he looked like a middle-aged man with a deeply lined face but smelled fake.

"Firing," said a snake man at another console. His hands moved on the panel.

And somewhere down on the planet, someone was mutated to death.

I counted seven in the room, not counting the four snake-men that brought me here or the two guards outside. Four of those in the room were snake-men, three non-organics. Another door on the other side of the room and that seemed to be where they were taking me.

I hadn't seen Kelwyn yet, so no reason to make them think I was awake. The odds didn't concern me. I'd known coming into this that I'd be out-numbered. None of that mattered. If I managed to kill Kelwyn, it'd throw them off. If I managed to damage the weapon too, that'd be perfect. Getting out came in a distant third.

The orange snake-man opened the door. They carried me through into a large room set up as an office. Kelwyn lounged along a long bench illuminated from within. The room was very warm. He wasn't alone. Two snake-women stood on either side. One held a clear bowl with a bunch of live mice. The ammonia scent of their urine hung like a cloud above the bowl. One other snake-man lay upon the floor, but he was small. I recognized him. Blaine.

Blaine lifted his head. He didn't look good. To my scent-sight, he had a sour smell to him, and his pulse looked slow. He seemed thin, and I smelled blood from a cut on his cheek. I didn't know how he'd gotten here, but it complicated things. I could do the math all day and know that any sacrifice was worthwhile to stop Kelwyn, but faced with the boy I couldn't stop myself from wanting to help him.

Kelwyn was right there. The snake-men had taken my shotgun, the one with the red stripe held it right now. They hadn't bothered taking any of my other weapons away yet.

I just needed them to let go of me long enough to draw my weapon and shoot Kelwyn. Enough feeling had returned that I thought I could move. Anything after that was gravy. If I could stay alive long enough maybe I could make a difference.

Kelwyn rolled and slid off the bench. He hung in the air with just the last two bands on his tail holding onto the bench. His cobra hood spread wide as he rose up above me and rubbed his hands together.

"Brock Marssden. The famous detective! And still alive. How wonderful!"

I wouldn't get a better chance than this. I sank my C'lacktal tentacles into the arm of one of the snake-men holding me and injected him with venom. At the same time, I drew one of the big pistols and fired at Kelwyn. The snake-men holding me jerked right as I fired. The shot went wide but pierced Kelwyn's hood. A mist of blood sprayed out into the air. I used my hold on the snake-man to pull away from the other.

The snake-women screamed and came at me. The bowl of mice tumbled away through the air scattering mice in all directions.

The snake-man I'd injected thrashed with convulsions. It threw me off, tumbling through the air towards the corner of the room.

I hit, bounced, but managed to get my

feet down so that I stuck to the wall. All that engineering I'd done on my reflexes paid off. Kelwyn screamed in rage.

The other snake-men came after me. I really didn't want to get bitten. The black one with the red stripe aimed my shotgun at me. I ran across the wall to avoid them all and aimed for Kelwyn again. Except Blaine was dragging himself away from Kelwyn and he was in my line of sight. I hesitated.

A shotgun blast peppered the wall in front of me. I turned and ran up onto the ceiling. Kelwyn was screaming at the others, and they swarmed up the walls after me.

It was a beautiful moment. Kelwyn. Right beneath me. Mouth open, fangs showing and nothing in the way. I fired. The shot took him in the back of the throat, and a spray of blood and tissue exploded out into the room. I kept moving and fired twice more.

Kelwyn's almost headless body thrashed about in his death throws. Another shotgun blast ripped at my uniform's right sleeve and shredded the outer layers. It twisted me around. I jumped free from the ceiling and shot the black snake-man three times in the chest. The force of the shots shoved me back towards the opposite side of the room.

I stuck my foot down and landed beside Blaine. He cowered.

"Stay behind me," I told him. "I'll get you out."

If I could. I still needed to destroy the modified Moreau pod if possible.

Kelwyn, the black snake-man, and one of the rattlers were down, but I still had four snake-men in the room, and right at that moment, the door opened.

I shoved the pistol into the holster and pulled the semi-automatic around my body. I didn't aim. I fired. I held down the trigger and sprayed bullets across the room at the snake-people. I caught two of the guards coming into the room right as they entered. One of the snake-women got her hands on the shotgun moments before my bullets tore her apart.

The air was filled with the scents of blood and viscera so much so that it looked like a cloud of brownish fog filling the room. Mice squirmed about in the air. I could still make out Blaine behind me.

I glanced back. "We've got to go!"

There'd been seven in the room. I headed out of Kelwyn's office with everyone there dead or dying. I didn't hesitate. I didn't give warnings. I stepped through the door and fired.

In doing so, I missed two of the non-organics that had moved up onto the ceiling. My shots tore into two of the snake-men that didn't move fast enough.

Then two organics jumped down on me from above. They grabbed my arms on both sides and attempted to get their feet down to the deck. I brought my arms together in front of me so that they collided together. Real humans would have been stunned. These guys just squeezed harder, and one grabbed my throat. His fingers dug into my neck slits, and that really hurt! Like getting your balls squeezed in a vise. My knees gave way, but without gravity, I remained standing.

Spots blurred my vision. I couldn't keep breathing. Without air flowing even my Euzebian scent-sight was going dark.

I thought of Muriel. Lost or dead along with Dyami.

Calanthe lying in the hospital back home.

Shanley and Subha on the planet, hopefully, untouched by Kelwyn's device.

And Kelwyn, dead. I'd done that much at least. Maybe it'd been enough.

Then the non-organic squeezing my throat was yanked away. Blaine was beside me with the shotgun in his hands, twisting from the recoil. The non-organic tumbled through the air, twitching, with a big smoking hole in his chest. I brought my pistol up to the head of the other and pulled the trigger. Crystalline brains shattered and floated away in an expanding cloud.

I took several deep gulping breaths. My head hurt. My eyes stung, and my neck slits on the left side hurt like a sonofabitch. Even so, I managed to mostly hold the pistol still looking for anyone else.

They were gone.

There'd been seven. Four snake-men and three non-organics. Two of each down that left two more snake-men and one non-organic, but they must have fled because they weren't in the room.

I looked over at Blaine. He still didn't look good, but he held onto that shotgun. "How are you doing?"

"I'll be okay," he said wearily.

I put the pistol away and walked over to the machine. The Moreau pod components I understood. With the casing off it'd be easy to break. Just pull the main boards and shatter the quantum crystals. But with another pod, it might be possible to fix the weapon. I needed to do more than that.

Blaine slithered over next to me. He stared at the pod.

"Is that the pod Kelwyn used to change you?"

"Yesss."

"It needs to be destroyed. I'm sorry, I don't know if we can change you back."

"That'sss okay. Do it."

I went to the consoles. One was damaged by the gunfire but the other still looked good. The weapon was mounted in the opening of the dock. They'd actually designed it to be removed. I found a whole decoupling sequence in the databanks. That'd work. Shoot it out into space and let the Gingerbread House's defense systems vaporize it. I'd have to deal with the Tretan later.

I set it for five minutes and held my hand out for the shotgun. Blaine handed it over.

"We need to go. Keep up. Don't look back. We're getting out of here."

"Okay."

I triggered the sequence and then brought the shotgun stock down on the panel. The interface shattered. No one would stop it now.

We left as fast as we could. Out the door and down the corridor away from the dock. When that room decompressed, I wasn't sure that the walls they'd installed would hold. I didn't want to take any chances. We kept going, and I took us deeper into the station. After we passed the first emergency bulkhead, then I started to feel better.

I checked the time. "Almost time. In here!"

I opened a hatch at random and led Blaine into the room beyond. A long room with fabric webbing stretched at intervals across the room. Each ribbon held a half-dozen hooks.

Blaine ran his hand along one. "What are thessse?"

I shrugged. "No idea. Storage? Some sort of zero-gee tethers? Hard to say."

Time.

Outside the wind howled for about a minute before it increased to a whine and then shut off completely. Emergency bulkheads must be in place.

I grabbed one of the straps and hung on. It was done. Kelwyn dead, the weapon destroyed.

And the biggest surprise? I was still alive. Amazing.

CHAPTER 21

In the end, it was Reese that found Blaine and I half dead on our feet. Well, me on my feet. Blaine was held down with those magnetic rings he wore. Reese had been trying to find me since he recovered from his team shocking him but the Gingerbread House is a big station. He brought in the cavalry, a bit late. When the dock depressurized, that gave them an idea of where to look.

Reese looked a bit pale when he found us. "Are you okay?"

"Mostly. You don't look that great yourself."

"Come on, let's get you out of here." He looked warily at Blaine. "Who is this?"

"Blaine, meet Reese. Blaine was one of Kelwyn's first victims. That's why he looks that way. He helped me out." I asked something that I'd been wondering about. "How many died on the planet?"

"The count right now is at nearly a hundred dead. It could have been worse. Most of the deaths were in the last hour. The beam played across larger areas. It also caused extensive damage to the biocrete structures, mutating those organisms too. They're still calculating the cost of all of the damage. What happened?"

"We stopped him. Blew the whole device out into space along with the bodies."

Reese nodded. "We saw that. The station's automated defenses responded and vaporized the equipment. "

"Good. I'm glad it worked. No one else will get their hands on it." I headed towards the door, yawning. "Any idea where I can get some Torlian coffee?"

"We'll see what we can do."

§

I didn't get my Torlian coffee. I endured an hour of questions by station officials before I insisted on medical attention for myself and Blaine. Since Reese had given me the authorization to use violence I didn't have to face any charges.

Not to mention the fact that I ended the threat to the planet.

The station master, a dour-faced man with a long black pony-tail, unfastened the seat belt that kept him seated. "Mr. Marsden," he said in his gravelly voice. "Your young companion is already receiving treatment. My apologies on keeping you so long, we are naturally dismayed that this station has been associated with such a deplorable use of violence against the innocents on the planet. Any treatment you need will, of course, be provided, and you are free to leave at your convenience."

"Thank you for that. Can I see Blaine now?"

Reese rose as well. "I'll take you to him."

It was a short walk from the station master's office to the infirmary. I stayed alert even now, wary about the possibility of further attacks from the non-organics. Except I didn't smell any in the corridors.

"How many people are suddenly absent?" I asked Reese.

He shook his head. "Almost twenty, along

with some supposedly non-sentient robots that up and left."

"I didn't think they'd give up that easily. Whatever else Kelwyn was doing, they were behind the attacks and wanted to capture a Galactic as well."

"All of the early reports showed a ship departing after the weapon was destroyed. Our security footage shows many of the non-organics boarded that ship."

"They'll be back," I said. "I doubt they've given up."

Blaine lay on an infirmary bed beneath a couple heat lights. He lifted his head. In my scent-sight, he already looked brighter. He smelled clean, and his scales gleamed beneath the light.

"How are you doing?"

"Good." He looked at Reese, his tongue tasting the air and then back to me. "What happensss to me now?"

"That depends. What do you want to do?"

"I'd like to go back home."

"We could arrange that," Reese said.

Blaine recoiled.

I held up my hands. Blaine stared at my altered hand. "Look, Blaine, you can trust him. He's good. He's not going to give you back to the Cautarians. Why didn't you stay with captain Brice on the planet?"

"He didn't like me."

True enough, Brice didn't like Moreaus. "He still wouldn't have hurt you. How'd you end up here?"

"A woman came. Metal inssside. Sshe brought me to Kelwyn. He wasss angry."

"Well, Kelwyn's gone now. You can trust Reese. If he says he can get you home, then he'll do it." I looked at Reese. He nodded. "See? You can relax. You're safe now."

Blaine relaxed on the bed.

"If you need anything, just ask." I held out my good hand. Blaine took it seriously and shook. "Take care of yourself."

Reese hesitated as we started to leave. "I'll be back, kid. Don't worry."

Blaine nodded.

Reese followed me out into the corridor. He looked me up and down. "Are we going to get you some help?"

I shook my head. "I'm going back to my shuttle. I assume that won't be a problem?"

"No problem. I'll talk to the station master."

"Okay. Thanks." I turned around and realized I didn't know the best way to go. "Where did I park my shuttle?"

"I'll show you."

§

Reese led me back to the shuttle and left me there. I climbed in feeling like every bone in my body was tired. Plus I hurt.

"Welcome back, Brock Marsden," the shuttle said when I entered.

"Any problems while I was gone?" I made my way forward to the command chair and dropped into the seat, glad to have a gravity field again despite the aches and pains. Belts oozed out of the seat and fastened securely around me.

"No attempts have been made to breach the security of this vessel. A message has been received from *Washington* command."

"Play it."

A screen appeared. Felicity's fine features looked very serious. "Brock, we scanned for any debris from the battle you asked about. We found very little. Our readings did indicate that the ship fired upon managed to engage the displacement drive but the field was malformed due to the weapons fire. I'm told the ship likely survived, but there's no way to tell where it reemerged into normal space. I'm including all of our data. Good luck."

The image froze on her sad smile. "Message ends."

"Thank you. Save that."

The image vanished. "Message saved."

"Prepare for departure. We're heading home."

"Define location home?"

I gave the shuttle the address and tried to stay awake during the departure procedures. As soon as we left the Gingerbread House, I headed back to the crew sections. I needed to get cleaned up and grab some rest. According to the shuttle, I had a couple hours until final descent.

§

Shanley Walsh, my partner, boss, and friend looked up from the table as I entered the office looking like he'd been on stake-out for several nights. He smelled of too much

Terran coffee and crackers. He blinked then fumbled up out of his chair, his jacket catching on the chair.

"Brock! What happened to you?"

The quip that came to mind died on my lips. I suddenly felt very heavy and very tired and extremely sad. My voice caught. I coughed and tried again.

"Muriel and Dyami are lost. I don't know where, but I'm going to find them."

Shanley reached me and touched my arm gently. "The networks said that the threat had ended, but it didn't say how."

"I stopped them." I went into the kitchen thinking that I'd make a Torlian coffee, but I suddenly didn't feel like it. I felt like sleeping.

Everything smelled of ashes to me, and I was sick of it. Coming in on the shuttle I'd seen the wild growths in the biocrete where Kelwyn's weapon had damaged the city. Olinda, my city.

"You need to get some rest," Shanley said. "We'll find them, between us we're the best at finding people, right?"

I nodded.

"So get to bed. Get some rest and then we'll get started."

I shook my head and pointed at the ceiling. "Check out my new shuttle. It's on loan. The data is there. I've given the shuttle your information already."

"Okay." Shanley patted my shoulder. "Get some rest, Brock. I'll get on it."

He had a point. I needed to get home. I called a flitter cab and almost fell in when it arrived.

Three weeks had passed since I stopped Kelwyn, and I was still trying to figure out what had happened to Muriel and Dyami.

Shanley came into my office with a wrinkled brow. He wore his usual old-fashioned brown suit, and his white hair was as unruly as ever. He jabbed his thumb back towards the main reception area.

"We've got a possible client at the desk."

I looked up from by broad desk which was right then literally displaying dozens of different screens of information. Everything that the Cooperative ship *Washington* had sent me before they left the system from their scans of what happened when the Tretan's ship disappeared.

"I thought we weren't taking on clients. I'm getting closer to figuring out something useful about where they went. As soon as I can nail it down, I'm going after them."

Shanley held up his hands. "Hey, don't bite my head off. This is just an unusual client. I thought you might want to talk to him."

"Seriously?"

Shanley shrugged.

I looked down at the dizzying array of screens. With my eyes, I saw all of it, with my scent-sight, none. Maybe I should look into getting some Euzebian equipment? Their eyes were vestigial, but they were quite advanced. It might give me a different way of looking at all of this.

"Brock?"

"Right. Client." I took a breath. Shanley smelled a bit worried and confused with a hint of fear. That caught my attention. "Sure. I'll talk to him. No worries."

I rose and checked the Lottier 65 at my hip. I rarely went anywhere unarmed these days. I'd traded up to the Lottier 65 because in addition to the nanoparalyzers that my old 45 shot, it also added electrical shock needles capable of taking down non-organics. Just in case any of them came after me. So far none had.

I walked out across our open offices to the reception area, but before I even got there, I smelled something that smelled of blood and rust. I knew that smell. Nosferan! But why hadn't Shanley said? He had followed me and stood behind me on my left.

I drew my weapon and eased around the counter. A sentient stood in front of the desk covered in a hooded black robe. The hood turned my direction.

"Esteemed One honored to be in your presence. I am shamed I must request your assistance."

"My assistance? Who are you?"

"Please, the light here, it is very bright."

"Yeah, and I can't do anything about that. Sorry. Why are you here in the daylight?"

"A terrible crime has been committed, one which only the Esteemed One may resolve."

"Me? What are you talking about?"

Instead, the Nosferan pushed a piece of paper out of its sleeve onto the reception desk.

I walked behind the desk and looked down at the paper without putting away my weapon. It was a picture. A photograph of an installation with rock walls, probably some sort of asteroid habitat. There were two people in the picture. One a human woman, her face turned away from the camera. The other was an Eyotan with a broad monstrous face and black and orange stripes.

"Dyami!" I set the gun down and picked up the picture. It wasn't the best quality, but the woman could be Muriel. The hair looked right if she had pulled her hair back. "When was this taken?"

The Nosferan hissed. "One century ago! A theft, and do you not know these thieves? I'm told the Esteemed One seeks them!"

I picked up the gun and had it pointed at his head before he had moved more than an inch in my direction. "What are you talking about? A century ago? Are you crazy?"

He hissed again. "Oh, angry is the Esteemed One. Not my fault! I bring you the photo. I show you!"

"Fine, yes, but what are you saying about it?"

"Almost one century ago this picture was taken."

I looked down at the picture again.

Muriel and Dyami a century ago? During the Human-Nosferan war? I looked back up at the Nosferan. "You claim these people stole something, during the war, and you expect me to get it back?"

"Esteemed One is wise. Honor requires your assistance."

Right. I handed the picture to Shanley. "Why don't you stick around while we verify this photo? Then we'll see."

Could the displacement drive have done it? Thrown them into the past? I didn't have any idea, but if it did, we were probably going to be the only people to believe it. The real question then became how we would recreate that effect?

Working with Nosferans again? I'd hoped I never had to see the day. But if it got Muriel and Dyami back, it was worth the price.

§§§

I Thank you for joining Brock Marsden on his adventures to *The Gingerbread House*. I hope you enjoyed the story. Brock returns in *Past Lives*. Find out more at MoreauSociety.com.

I had so much fun going back over *The Gingerbread House* to create this new edition. The series remains one of my favorites. As I write this, I'm wrapping up the finishing touches on this edition, and I'm thinking about the next two books. They make up the 'Past' duology, *Past Lives* and *Past Dark*, and we get to see much more of Muriel and Dyami. The books also uncover more of the mysteries in Brock's past.

I'm also looking ahead, thinking about the fifth book I plan to write, *Synthetic Pain*. I've written a few short stories, exploring ideas. It'll be fun to dive back in for a new adventure.

I hope you'll join me.

Ryan M. Williams
Rainier, Washington
July 2019

Other Books

For information on these titles and to sign up for *Readinary*, my list with news, offers and more, visit my site at ryanwriter.link/novels

Prefer something more **cozy** with your **mystery**? The **POEVILLE** series with feline detective C. Auguste Dupin and his human librarian Penny Copper might be just the thing.

- The Murders in the Reed Moore Library *(new editions — May 2019)*
- The Task of Auntie Dido *(new editions — Jun 2020)*

Like **science fiction mysteries**? Check out the **MOREAU SOCIETY** series. Private detective Brock Marsden investigates the toughest crimes, his alien-enhanced DNA giving him the edge he needs to save lives.

- Dark Matters *(new editions — Jun 2019)*
- The Gingerbread House *(new editions — Jul 2019)*
- Past Lives *(new editions — Aug 2019)*
- Past Dark *(new editions — Sep 2019)*
- Synthetic Pain *(writing)*

Do you like your **fantasy** dark and paranormal? Ravyn Washington isn't like other students. Her grandmother was called a witch and if the Inquisition discovers Ravyn's abilities she could burn in the **DEAD THINGS** series.

- Waking Dead Things *(new editions — Oct 2019)*
- Dreaming Dead Things *(new editions — Nov 2019)*
- Killing Dead Things *(new editions — Dec 2019)*
- Burning Dead Things *(planned)*

Enjoy **adventure** and **fantasy**? Join Dalton Hicks on a cross-country race across two worlds in the **GOBLIN ALLEY** series.

- The Bloodied Fang *(new editions — Jan 2020)*
- The Eleven Lords *(new editions — Feb 2020)*
- Trow Forge *(new editions — Mar 2020)*
- The King's Runner *(planned)*

Not every high school student falls for the

monster. Natalie is smarter than that in the **PIERCE, WA** series.

- Dirty Old Vampires *(new editions — Apr 2020)*
- Naughty Young Werewolves *(planned)*
- Pretty Dead Ghouls *(planned)*

Discover more **science fiction** with these books.

- Europan Holiday *(new editions — May 2020)*
- Stowaway to Eternity *(new editions — Jul 2020)*
- Time Retrievers *(publication date — Nov 2020)*

And if you like **romance** and **comedy**, the books by **KATE N. RYAN** will tickle your funny bone—and more.

- Watching You Sleep *(new editions — Aug 2020)*
- Waiting For Cake *(new editions — Sep 2020)*

Do you enjoy something a bit darker, like **horror**? Then check out these titles.

- Full Moon Nights *(new editions — Oct 2020)*
- Downland *(new editions — Dec 2020)*

Like **science fiction** with a dash of **steampunk** and enhanced sea creatures? The brothers Douglas and Brennan Dunne face an uncertain future with their Uncle

Quigley's monstrous creations in the **LAND LUBBERS** series.

- Cabin Boys *(publication date — Jan 2021)*
- Sea Legs *(publication date — Feb 2021)*
- Murky Waters *(planned)*

More books coming soon!